crashing america

"It's like if Janis Joplin wrote a novel and didn't die on us but sang the whole damn thing. I love this writer. She's animal royalty. Her brain has teeth. In this book she makes the people talk, the bus driver, even. It's old human stuff, Chaucer, even; François Villon, that's right. But always, as never before, the writer is a brave dirty girl. The earth is her place, yet she loves the stars. It's to live, this book."
—Eileen Myles, author of *Cool for You*

"If you've ever gotten lost and then found your way, and gotten lost and then found your way and gotten lost (and then maybe found your way?), *Crashing America* gives you the road map. It's about trying to die without growing old, or trying to grow up without dying."
—Mattilda, a.k.a. Matt Bernstein Sycamore, editor of *That's Revolting! Queer Strategies for Resisting Assimilation*

"Katia Noyes does an impeccable job of delineating an age in which gender, family, and country have failed us and we must invent mythologies and heroes for a new era."
—Daphne Gottlieb, author of *Final Girl*

"Katia Noyes writes with compelling authority. Her eye for detail and landscape extend to her 17-year-old heroine's interior, a vividly rendered region of unexpected exile and vulnerability. It's a rare, daring, and poignant novel, fueled by intelligence and skill, hungry for illumination, and written in the unmistakable dialect of blood. This isn't a snapshot from the edge, but a sophisticated dissection of our country at the millennium."
—Kate Braverman, author of *Frantic Transmissions to and from Los Angeles: An Accidental Memoir*

"In this impressive debut, Noyes tackles the road novel with finesse and originality. An outsider leaves the frontier to get inside—her history, her country, her self—and finds a heart-land of sublime desolation and quiet grandeur. In our times of rigid red or blue identities, Noyes's mashup of bohemian and rural offers refreshingly complex shades."

—D. Travers Scott, author of
One of These Things Is Not Like the Other

"*Crashing America* gives us a misfit's view of the American land-scape, a gorgeous and lonely place populated by christian punks, lonesome housewives, tweaking teenagers, and corn farmers. Best of all, it stars a tough-talking vagabonding starry-eyed thieving innocent named Girl. Noyes takes us on a fearless queer adventure, using a dashing slangy language all her own."

—Michelle Tea, author of *Rent Girl*

CRASHING AMERICA

CRASHING AMERICA

a novel

by Katia Noyes

alyson books
los angeles

Celebrating Twenty-Five Years

MANUFACTURED IN THE UNITED STATES OF AMERICA.

THIS TRADE PAPERBACK ORIGINAL IS PUBLISHED BY ALYSON BOOKS,
P.O. BOX 4371, LOS ANGELES, CALIFORNIA 90078-4371.
DISTRIBUTION IN THE UNITED KINGDOM BY TURNAROUND PUBLISHER SERVICES LTD.,
UNIT 3, OLYMPIA TRADING ESTATE, COBURG ROAD, WOOD GREEN,
LONDON N22 6TZ ENGLAND.

FIRST EDITION: SEPTEMBER 2005

05 06 07 08 09 **a** 10 9 8 7 6 5 4 3 2 1

ISBN 1-55583-911-8
ISBN-13 978-1-55583-911-6

COVER ILLUSTRATION AND DESIGN BY AMY MARTIN.

DEDICATED TO MY MOTHER

Look up.
Look up and fall down
—Apostle Rods

EVER SINCE I CAN REMEMBER I've figured my life would end with a big bang on my eighteenth birthday. Like my mom's.

Sometimes at night her ghost comes to settle in the middle of my chest. With a jolt, I remember what I've tried to forget. Feels crazeee, like death will bring me everything and nothing at the same time.

I push away the truth. Then reach for it. No matter; I can't stop what will come.

san francisco

CARA AND I WENT to my granddad's and tried to get Mrs. Jam, his landlady, to let us into his apartment. It was afternoon, June 1999. A ghostly bit of warmth managed to find its way through the early summer fog.

We stood just on the inside of the smell zone. Mrs. Jam's couch had the remains of her shwilly life stuffed inside the crevices, and the place reeked like a rotting pier. I kept my arm around Cara.

"Can't do it." Mrs. Jam shook a little. Wore a blue nightgown and a big plaid jacket.

Last month I had watched *Jeopardy!* with Mrs. Jam, curled up on her couch. Helped her fix her antenna. And now she was squeezing me out.

I tried to get through to her. "We aren't gonna bite. You want something from the store?"

"Your grandfather said he's not letting you stay with him anymore." Mrs. Jam's bird-claw hands crumpled a Kleenex from her big plaid pocket. She turned around and looked through a pile on her table. Her hands shook back and forth, grasping at an envelope with my name.

I stepped over and reached for it. "So what now?" I grabbed the note and stuffed it in my jacket pocket. My granddad was probably going to meetings and getting clean again.

Mrs. Jam didn't answer. She looked outside. "Is your friend sick?"

Cara had wandered away and was bent over on the stairs, spitting on one of her knees and rubbing it. She had this thing where she rubbed her legs over and over.

"You girls shouldn't even be on my property."

I walked down the stairs to my granddad's in-law apartment and tried to get the window open, which was stupid because there were bars on it. So I went to his front door and kicked it hard. *Bam!*

"Let's go. I'm hungry." Cara squinted down at me from the stairs, her long brown hair falling over her face. Behind her I could see the fog-smeared hill. A little smile curled on her mouth as if she heard a good song playing. "Come on, Gir-r-rl."

I crumpled the envelope with my granddad's handwriting and threw it on the sidewalk. Mrs. Jam poked her head out the door.

"I need to get my stuff sometime," I yelled. "I'll be back. You'll have to let me in." I had some clothes in there and Flopsy, my old raggedy sleeping companion.

Cara took my hand and blinked like a cat. We walked down the hill. She always knew how to chill. Cara never believed in giving in when bad things happened. She just scrawled another mark on one of her legs. The wavering star on her ankle, the Taurus sign on her calf, the snaking branches wrapped around her thigh. Every time something bad happened, she made a tattoo. "They make me safe again," Cara would say. She rubbed them all the time.

After my first arrest for being Beyond Parental Control, it was Cara who came all the way back to Redding to hang with me. By then, I was crashing in the semicarpeted chicken coop outside the big house, way outside from my dad's latest girlfriend, Marianne, and her kids, and the kitchen, and the big happy family my dad was trying to make. (My Clorox-smelling dad. Mistah White Socks, Cara called him.) Enough of that. Enough of trying to be some funkabilly punk corpse, with my eyes locked up, in a town on the way-too-far edge of the Trinity Mountains. Easygoing Cara came to rescue me, helped me open my eyes and see again. Got a ride in the back of a pickup—over the Golden Gate Bridge at midnight, heads up out of the blankets. Be-you-tee-full, as my granddad would say.

As we walked down the hill, Cara rambled on. "You smell her breath?" She blinked at me again and held my hand tight. "You kookamonga. Shwilly old Bird Beak told you this was going to happen. So did your granddad. Remember, Girl. Gir-r-rl. You don't listen to what people say. You get so mad. Way too ma-a-ad."

"Yeah, sure."

"Here's my theory about our new home. Do you want to hear it?" Cara sucked on a long brown strand of hair. She always had theories. "Everything in the city is connected to our underground place, all the pipes and Muni stations. It's a labyrinth. We need to explore it further."

I waited as Cara bent over her sandal in the middle of the street. Her eyes went far away, in one of those exotic mute looks that guys liked.

"Really?" I said. "Tell me more." She liked to talk about our special place in the Castro Street Station, a nook we'd found down in the tunnel. Cara found it cozy, but I hated hearing the trains running.

We meandered down to the corner store on Mission, and Cara

chattered on about her dreamy labyrinths. I couldn't listen. All I could think about was how much I was going to miss my granddad's hot shower and soft blankets.

With the last of my spare change, I bought us a bag of trail mix at the corner store. We were both sleepy from partying all night with Angus and his new guy.

We climbed back up Coso Street to sneak under the crawl space of the Winfield house. With driftwood-colored shingles and wide dirty windows, the house perched on cement-pillar stilts and looked ready to collapse. Rocks and weeds gathered under its hollow foundation, a crawl space where we had slept a couple of times in the dark. Now it was light and people might see us sneak underneath and call the skunkers, but I didn't care. We wouldn't get arrested— they'd just tell us to move on.

Cara and I snuggled up by the stilts and we talked serious. What were we going to do?

I suggested we head right to Nebraska.

"All we need is some money." I looked at the weeds around us. "I want to see the cornfields."

Cara twisted her hair around a finger. "You and your cornfields!"

"Yeah." I tapped Cara's ankle star a couple of times for luck. "Let's leave soon. Anywhere."

After losing my granddad's place for good, I knew it was time to get on the road and leave San Francisco for real, or I would implode.

I let Cara hold me tight, as if she could keep me close forever. "Gir-r-rl. Gir-r-rl," she chanted.

I REMEMBERED LAST YEAR when I showed Cara the Winfield house the first time. We stood arm in arm, and I told her all about it.

"My mom had me the all-organic method, right on the couch,

right there in the living room." I pointed over the high deck to the big dirty windows. Never showed anyone my birthplace before. I usually even avoided walking by. "My first look at the world."

I didn't tell Cara how I cringed when I saw the house, how I wanted to go up to the door, break it down with a battering ram, kick out the people who lived there. I didn't tell her because she'd make fun of me, make fun of how much my eyes locked up when I got mad.

I described the view from inside, how great it was to look down from the deck at the color and flurry of Mission Street, over at the pearly skyscraping buildings of downtown, and way over to the westward mounds of Twin Peaks. The truth was that I only wished I could remember being inside.

"So...yeah." Cara sucked on her pretty brown hair and blinked. "You really lived there?"

"It's kinda nice knowing you came from some place."

"Gir-r-rl...look." Just then more sunlight broke through the morning fog.

The beyouteefull mockery of light touched everything—our faces, the hill, the chrome on the cars. Fresh. Oh, yeah. So Sa-a-an Fra-a-ancisco. You could call it a god tease, a sea-smelling drift of visible gold. Up above us the house had looked almost wet from the sun. Even the weeds glistened underneath its high deck. The big dirty windows faced us, making glint, glint, glint. And we drank in the smell of the Pacific, a salty whiff, flying all the way across town.

Yes. The sunlight was holy, even when I wasn't up to being part of it.

KNOWING YOU DON'T HAVE much time left to live makes you truly freaky-brained. Like you are taunting something. Come on, come on, already!

How was I going to get out of California? All I knew was that if

I stuck around longer, I'd probably get exterminated. I'd be one of the kids that the city had to identify, and none of my famileee would believe I was really gone. Till they made the phone call. And then I would be another flash bulletin on the street, a sad joke, a skanky tale. I wanted it to happen far away from everyone I knew. Somewhere they could never find me.

"RANDA?"

It was the third time I tried and I couldn't believe she had answered. My sweaty hand held the slip of paper with her phone number.

"Speaking."

"It's me, Girl."

"Flower Girl!"

I could see her eyes gleam, feel the warmth of her voice all the way through the wire. "I can almost see your face," I said. "All the way out there. Are you really in Nebraska? Did you get to the farm and all?"

"Are you coming? I'm waiting." She said it so matter-of-fact.

"Did you really mean it?" My voice broke like I was about eight years old.

"Waiting for you, Flower Girl."

I could see her tanned, callused hands gripping the phone, and her feet planted in the ground as she spoke.

"Really?" I asked.

"*Hmm—mmm—uh—hauh—hau-u-uh, yeah!*"

The laugh. The one that made Cara and me think Randa was a maniac when we first met her in Redding.

"Randa, what are you doing out there?"

"Get on out here. I'm doing plenty."

"You can still get me work?"

"You betcha. Things look pretty good this year. You never know about the weather, but the wheat looks good anyway."

She sounded like a real farmer.

I'M TRYING TO REMEMBER how everything came down. It was our last night in SF, but we didn't know it then. Cara and I must have left Bernal Hill and gone all the way across town to the Haight at sundown. She needed some smoke and said she wanted to go to the Page Street house, but I told her no way. I was feeling restless from knocking around the Winfield house, and my granddad's apartment, and knowing I wasn't wanted anymore at *all*. I had always told people that I had a place to crash in town. *I was once from here*, unlike all these other wanderers. And now, nothing. No purple futon in the corner behind the screen, no peppermint soap showers, no more towers of my granddad's books. I was itchy, itchy mad, and afraid I'd never find a way to Nebraska.

So Cara left without me, ambling down Masonic, rocking slightly from side to side. Soft on her feet as always. It gave me the creeps, made me want to grab on and shake her. Or protect her.

Angus was nowhere to be found. Probably off again with his new fun-daddy, the guy with the big head, Jim. After all, Angus had needed a new place, too. When he brought too many friends home, he had lost his welcome with the guy couple who served Manhattans and let him stay in a room off the garage in their Pacific Heights Victorian. They had given him a big bed, which he covered with long scarves and funny hats and old velvet robes. I'd slept over a few times, inside his big nest of clothes, and then sneaked upstairs to nibble on turkey slices and maraschino cherries in the middle of the night.

For tonight, I wasn't sure where to sleep. Cara had always relied on the Page Street house as her fallback, but I hated it—too many fights, too many druggy, slugged-out eyes. The men who came by the house had a certain smell, like compost, as if their insides were going backwards day by day. I despised those lurkers and their festering crotch smell. My dream was to get a pistol like Randa's and blast them all. Bang. At least hold the gun to their twisted brainboxes and get them down on their knees.

Instead I leaned against the neon-blue pillar of the Absolutely Psychedelic store—a hippie-memorial that takes MasterCard. Looked around for somebody to hang with, asking for loose change, avoiding the men who leered (it's only the women who give you money anyway).

As usual, the high school kids were working on getting damaged. I remember the nervous pretty girl who smoked on the sidewalk and watched me. Her heavy jeans closed at the insides of her thighs like curtains.

I winked at her, and she stepped forward to give me a cigarette. Then a Nazi wannabe came over and was talking about the world coming to an end. He ranted about Jews and blacks, about all the devils. I couldn't take it anymore and took off.

Why did I head into the park?

It wasn't just to look for a place to sleep. Maybe something in me had wanted to test myself. Get it over. Let my mom's ghost take me. *Bring it on,* I'd thought, bring on that something called *the end.*

THE DIZZY WET GREENS of the trees started to blur. Soon it would be too dark to see their color. I sat on my favorite bench in Golden Gate Park, looking into the grassy stretch that leads all the way from the Haight to the ocean. A few joggers and dog walkers passed by, some workerbees swarmed to their cars after long days. By the hood of night, the drooling bums would be crawling out from their hidden nests in the groves.

I sat for a while, daring anybody to come get me. When I got too cold, I tried the passenger side of cars, the older ones without alarms. One door of a Mercury Cougar was left open. I jumped inside, punched the lock, and nestled on the backseat. It was warm and smelled of people and fast food. I calmed down as I heard the car sounds rolling by, slow as street sweepers—*shoosh-sh-sh*.

Above the front seat, I saw the top floor of an apartment building on Lincoln. Most of the windows were dark, but one room on the top floor taunted me with three bright yellow windows. What about breaking in? Run up there, pound on the doors, and take the place over. Kidnapping an apartment! Kick some poor soul and his big pet TV out on the street and make the whole place mine.

Then some woman had to come and disturb me. She opened the driver's door.

"Excuse me," I said. I got out, taking my time because I had been pretty comfortable. She honked really loud as she drove away.

I took off my cap to feel the cool touch of air on my head when a sports car slowed down. The window lowered. Couldn't see anything but gaping nostrils. Nostrils big as black eggs.

"Hi." He had small teeth. His voice squeaked. One more personal devil.

"You ain't sucking my dick, mister." I put my cap back on and walked farther into the park. I sat down at the top of a grassy amphitheater place, feeling itchy like I should go, but also knowing that staying was a test.

There was no wind. The mowed fields reeked with a full-tilt, summer's-near smell.

A skunk car drove by, and I ducked. The headlights were dim in the spread of night, like passing lanterns. I walked lower into the safety of the bowl of grass. I crouched, then lay flat. The smudged orange and indigo evening sky had long since drained away. Five stars from the Big Dipper became visible.

Then I heard the sound. Light pad feet. Way too light, as if they had thin soles on their shoes, slipper-clad steps. A pervert in slippers.

"Hey, sweetheart. You know what time it is?"

"This park is mine. You get outta here." I waved Nostril Man away.

He stood above me on the path. Small and twitchy, he held something behind his back.

"What you got there?"

He snorted. From behind his back I saw him move the tail end of a piece of rope.

Whoa! Giddyup. My feet charged, flapping against the dirt. Dodging trees, leaping over roots, searching for the path. I looked behind, and Nostril Man was running, too. I fled to where I knew there would be people. Spread my arms. Shooting into total darkness.

When I landed at the grove, some scraggly old bums sat around a small fire. A couple of them stood and held their arms to block me. They gestured in a panic, long beards shaking, as if I was charging the wrong way on a one-way street. Still too scared to stay alone in the dark, I fled right into the fireside scene. A skinny white man was getting his ass branded by a young pig-faced guy. I jumped on his pile of clothes. When somebody touched me, I grabbed a rock. *Don't mess with me.* I kicked the ground and neighed like a horse. Backed away and kept running.

I guess I still wanted to live.

FIVE REASONS TO HEAD FOR NEBRASKA

Why not do something with my last summer? My eighteenth birthday fell at August's end and I'd be lucky to make it that far.

My long-gone ghost of a mother had people from out there somewhere. The simple, clean, sweet rural life. My own blood wa-a-ay back. Why not take it easy? Lounge in the pastures, watch the clouds, find a little shack on the prairie.

If we had to, we could get jobs working in the Nebraska cornfields. An adventure. My arms would get all sun-kissed big. I'd be rugged and tough, with pocketfuls of cash.

Randa was there. Get a hold of her. Like lighting dynamite! Think of her skin. Think of her hands. (Palms streaked the ruddy color of an early morning sky. Grease under the fingernails from working on her Vulcan.)

Cara and me could arrive in style. We'd get Angus and his new guy, Jim, to drive us all the way to Nebraska in the long sharp-blue Cadillac. Top down, skinning the highways.

THE NEXT MORNING, after leaving the warm bed of a friendly tourist named Meredith, I headed to the Castro. My hope was to find Cara and Angus at the rainbow church, picking up some free lunch. Instead, I ate my bag lunch on a ledge, and all I got was gay Disneyland without my famileee. Two Sunglass Huts within two blocks. Hairy-chested guys with their Jack Terriers. Suburbanite queers in shorts and tennis shoes on their little larks. You'd think gay people came in pairs. Grabbing hands all casual, but you know in one second, without the other, they'd be lost. Otherwise, why were they always hanging on so tight?

I walked around in circles for a while. I did this a lot. As usual, people ignored me. Averted their eyes.

Passed Café Flore several times, then turned around and went in. It sat at the vortex of the Castro under a huge billboard, usually blaring with a politician's face. Baskets of flowers and vines hung around its edges. Outdoor tables and tiny-paned windows gave it easy charm, but it was really just a pose. It was the too-cool-for-you place. Way too many tattoos decorated the arms of the posing commercials who called themselves people. It was enough to make me hate my dragon.

I had to ask two girly freaks for an extra chair from their table. One looked over and nodded. She had the expensive hair cut, the gym body, the tan. She wanted me ba-a-ad, I could tell, but she was hungry and skittish, not able to hold her territory. She'd already branded me a gutter punk. The eyes gave it away.

A guy with a trimmed goatee and a big-collared polyester shirt sat alone at the corner table, reading *The Idiot*. I tried to talk to him, but he wasn't interested. He thumbed his paperback and frowned because the sun was in his eye. He didn't want to read or talk; he wanted to bend over.

I'd wanted to find a gaze that wouldn't run from me. Everybody thought they were so great. The thing about hanging with Angus and Cara was I felt so easy, comfortable. Without them around I felt like trash.

Where was Cara while I fooled around at Café Flore? Waiting in our underground place?

AFTER CAFÉ FLORE, I escaped back to the Haight and waited around. My lanky, swanky Angus finally came by. He stumbled for a moment when he saw me. Then he ruffled his bleached hair, which always sticks up in five or six different directions. He puts goop on it, and after he sleeps on it it's a big bird's nest. I jumped up and slipped my hands through his belt loops. I tried to sway with him, back and forth, like we always did.

"Adorablicious. Love me, baby?" I said.

"Hey." Angus touched his lip, swollen and cracked from him biting on it.

"What is it?" Something was messed up.

"Cara's dead." For a while neither of us moved; we were like sandbags. I laughed for some reason.

"I saw her today." I was ready to say anything.

"No. You don't get it." Angus flung both his long sweet arms toward the sky. "She's gone."

She'd been real high and got herself electrocuted in the underground tunnel, he said. Near the Castro Station.

As he talked, all I could see was the oozing split in Angus's bottom lip. I couldn't look away. Angus kneeled before me, said it again. "Cara's dead." His skinny limbs, stretched out and still.

"She's around. I know she's around."

"No way. I already called. The tattoos on her legs. No way it could have been anybody else. She's gone."

"You're trying to mess with me."

"I am not, Girl. I am not." Angus was on his knees, still facing the ground. He didn't look up.

It was so weird. Angus was always moving, lanky and swanky, and now he wasn't moving at all.

"See, it was her. Not you." Angus sat up and wiped his nose on his little wrist. He knew how I had always been afraid. Afraid it would be me. "It wasn't you," he repeated.

"What? You're crazy. You're not telling me the truth."

"Girl. I'm sorry. I don't know what to do. I hate this. And every-body is just acting like—*She died. So what?* Fuck people here. I'm leaving. I'm done with cold-ass San Francisco."

"Oh, baby." I took a deep breath. "Where do you want to go?"

"I don't know. Jim said he'd take me back to Memphis."

"Wow." I swallowed.

"He's generous and everything..." said Angus. "He wants to show me Las Vegas."

"I wish—"

"I know... Maybe we can meet up later?"

"Yeah, sure."

All I could think was maybe he was right. Maybe my Cara died so I didn't have to. Took my carrybag and walked, crazy like, away from the Haight and its broken-down hippie hallelujah, not saying anything to anybody.

LONG AGO, HOME FELT mysterious and safe. When I was about five years old, San Francisco was a magic island. It was when I thought I could fly. And did. Late at night over the sidewalk. Floating, yet heavy. Shivers. I stretched my arms to either side and rose right into the air. It felt like when you leave a bath, and your warm skin prickles. The air held me. Flying was not as fast as you might think—a slow, easy ride into the starry night.

I never told anybody about this. Except Cara.

PLACES OF BELONGING

This is the thing. You've got to figure where you belong. Where you feel comfortable. My mom, I figured she belonged in a place called Suicide. That's where she most wanted to hang out, and she probably went through life trying to get there.

If you spend some time on it—say when wandering along some broken three A.M. streets—you can figure where almost everybody belongs.

For Randa, it was on a farm. Every part of her knew what it wanted. You could see it in her callused hands, thickened from sun and work. She was meant to be some kind of fertility superhero with the magic to make everything work and be true to its nature—whether it was clods of dirt, scrambling hogs, or a thirteen-speed hauling truck. Maybe that's why I never forgot her.

Angus was easy to figure. Lanky, swaying Angus belonged wherever he was adored. And that meant the Haight, Polk Street, the Castro…anywhere he went. With the sun going down between Twin Peaks, the passersby dropping coins in our bag, everybody laughing at his jokes.

A lot of girls on the street found their belonging place when they were really young. They were once whole, but then the rest of the world messed with their heads. You know the girly girls who like dancing and bright colors and sha-la-la. They can't live in that place for long because guys use it against them. They get jealous and stamp them out; they won't let them stay soft. A ton of straight girls react by intentionally letting themselves get screwed.

See—the weird thing is someone's belonging place doesn't nec-essarily stay some googly-eyed dream; it's the familiar place they keep coming back to. For one girl I always saw at the Page Street house, it was on her knees swagging a guy. Feeling the scabs form and break again and again on the place where her kneecaps rocked and jolted against the cold floor.

With my Cara, well, I don't think she ever knew her place. She was always yearning. Maybe she wanted to feel protected. She seemed most at home when she had her head on my shoulder and she called her chants, weird and stoned. She always needed to be close. Cara wanted lo-o-ove all the time. You can try to belong to a place of love, but I don't think it works. That just leaves you in a place of yearning. And yearning is a stinking place; no one joins you. Yearning is not having eaten for most of the day and looking inside your granddad's refrigerator, finding sour milk and dried-up meat.

For slammers, like a guy I once knew named Nemo, the belonging place was the fix. The fix stops the pain and makes them belong to the world; it glides them into any situation. That's why they go back again and again. "First, I said I'd never rob for a fix," he told me once, scratching at his abscess. "Then I said I'd never shoot up in my neck. Then, I'd never take dates for dope." Nothing would make him stop.

My granddad was fixing for a while. Then he learned whatever he was using wasn't what he wanted. What he really wanted was to save the beyouteefull world. He tried. He protested nuclear bombs and went to jail. When he gave up, my granddad went back to being a toolmaker in a machine shop. He was happier trying to save the world, though, because that's where he belonged. When he left his place, he started hating himself, hating everybody. He even thought he was a failure when he stopped trying to save me. He thinks I don't remember, but I do. He thinks he's mean and horrible because he let my dad keep me, but he's not. And only I know that. He used to hug me really hard whenever I'd left the room and come back. Then he'd call my dad and yell at him for taking me away, all because he still cared enough to try to save me. That was his place of belonging—being a savior. But he couldn't save his daughter from shooting herself in the head on the Winfield deck, or save the beyouteefull world from bombs, or keep me from being a street rogue. He had gone missing inside. I know that. I just couldn't do anything about it.

Where is my place?

I don't know. It's hard to admit all I see is a freaky night sky. And I love the sky with all its constellations. But when I see myself up there, I am nowhere near the fiery stabs of light. I see myself in the dark places between the stars.

I imagine being lifted and arriving close to my mom. Like two lost birds, we find ourselves flapping our wings, carried by dry winds, no place to land.

FEELING HUNGRY AND EMPTY, I had gone back to Bernal Hill and called the drop-in center from a pay phone. It was true. Cara was getting flown back home to her monster stepdad et al. Just in time for a family funeral. Lots of grief tears there, as if they hadn't already tried to stomp her into a pulp.

I finished the last of the trail mix I'd bought with Cara the day before and wandered around. Like a sick animal, I found myself climbing the hill and crawling underneath the deck of the Winfield house. Kicked my boots into the rocky clay. Dug my fingers into the dank earth. My perverse attraction to the dirt there. It is the closest I can get. It held, it must have, some remnant. A shard of my mother's blasted bone. A strand of long hair. A smear of dried blood.

I opened my jacket, lifted my shirt. I spit into a handful of dirt, dabbed my finger into it and drew an X on my chest.

As I tried to doze, I thought about Meredith, the tourist I'd spent the night with, and her smooth, pale body, about maybe visiting her in Salt Lake... Then I thought about Randa, the farm in Nebraska. My mother's long-ago relatives were out there somewhere. Some place with soft green plains and rolling highways. Cara and I had always wondered about the rest of the country. The land way in the middle. The amber waves of grain and never-ending whatever.

Longing brings a few sprigs of courage. I figure without that we'd just let ourselves compress into nothingness.

redding

I WANTED to be tramping on the road, but Angus had taken off with big-head Jim and left me behind. So somehow I ended up cowering in Redding with Mistah White Socks and his new brood. Sick comfort…as it turned out my timing was putrid. My dad was having a little ceremony that weekend and getting married to Marianne.

He had lined up chairs on the back slope. New white chairs in perfect rows. My dad was in love with his patch of bulldozed earth. The land was once rural but now was being swallowed. The only thing left was the occasional smell of Douglas firs.

After I started on my second baloney sandwich, Mistah White Socks hovered at the dining room table. "Are you okay?"

"What?" I said.

He observed me like I was not quite human. "It's a surprise to see you again."

We couldn't think of anything more to say for a while, and my dad fiddled with a package of dental floss on the counter. Then he crept around the house in his Clorox-bright socks. He is one of those weightless people that the ground repels. His shoulders lift up, his steps have no sound, elbows and knees splay to either side.

When I asked him for cash, he came to attention. He carefully put two hundred-dollar bills on the table. Flattened them with his hand. Money he knew. It both relaxed and excited him. All those years of locking me in other people's homes while he got his law degree, he finally could give proof of the reward.

"If you need new clothes…or something for the wedding. You still have time." His lips spread, quivering nicey-nice. He thought I'd come home for his wedding on purpose, that my granddad had told me the date or something.

I stuffed the two bills in my pouch. "Thanks."

He shifted from one tentative foot to another. "And please…eat all you want."

"Yeah, sure." I finished my last bite of baloney sandwich and licked the mustard from my fingers. "I guess you're feeling fine and dandy?" Fine and dandy, something my granddad would say, but I liked the sound of it.

He shuffled some law papers together on the table. "It's good you managed to come." He squinted as he spoke, still nervous. "Did you see we put new carpet in the outbuilding? The kids are using it as a playhouse."

"I'm glad you're happy. All the best. Good wishes and all that." I gave my best daughter-type smile.

He nodded and his elbows lifted up like a puppet. "Lots to do for our little wedding. Marianne could probably use my help. Time to refer to the all-important groom list." He chuckled.

I nodded. "Right."

I felt lame trying to connect with him. Couldn't believe he wanted to live from here to eternity with all of Marianne's brainwashed kids. None of them had much to say when I got there. They lined up like dough balls, and waited, as always, for something to happen, feet dangling from the TV couch.

I couldn't sleep. Kept thinking about the last time I had been home and how Cara had come to rescue me. Looked around at the chemical-smelling carpeting in my chicken coop, the kids' toys stacked in white plastic bins, and my old books piled in a wire basket. Tried to read some stuff. I found my Shakespeare book and looked for a sonnet to recite at the wedding, a gift of some kind. My dad used to like it when I memorized Hamlet.

Maybe I didn't want to go to Nebraska—even now that I had the two hundred dollars of wedding-clothes money to buy the ticket. I kept the book open to read, but it didn't make me feel any better. The words stayed as separate as islands.

I knew if I left on a bus trip everything would change forever. Maybe I'd never come back. This was it.

I closed my eyes and tried not to think. Felt Cara's head resting on my shoulder. My chanting, blinking Cara, smelling so wild, all alley cat and cinnamon. Still around me, trying to speak. *Gir-r-rl...*, she said, *shh-rr-r-rr-uhhzz*. A ghost's mumbling, a language without a tongue.

The truth was I was fooling myself to think I could stay for the ceremony. I couldn't sit in a shmancy chair, hidden behind Marianne's kids, as if they were the real ones and I was the stinking impostor.

THE NEXT MORNING I waited in the sloping grasses between my coop and the house. A bit of the faraway Trinity woods wafted through the freeway fumes and into early morning. The kids had the TV on so loud I could hear the cartoons: *bang, yelp, screech.* Happy-obedient-bunnyhead Marianne stood at the sink doing dishes and wrinkling her nose. I waved and, for the hell of it, kicked over a couple of white chairs.

The front door was locked. They never trusted me to come and go; I had to pee in the weeds in the middle of the night. So I rang the bell. No luck. Then from the outside of the kitchen window, I gestured to Marianne to let me in. She dried her hands and disappeared. I went through my carrybag, double-checking that I had everything. Got my arrowhead out, held it my hand. Its sharp edges glinted in the morning sun.

When my dad didn't appear, I looked for his car. It wasn't there. He must have been getting ice or something. I guess there wasn't anything more to say anyway. It was goodbye forever. And that suited me fine and dandy.

HOW TO TRAVEL LIGHT AND LOOSE

I often wrote the instruction manual in my mind. While I was vagabonding and spending nights around town, not having too many showers, I needed a system. Eventually, I figured a way to have everything I needed on me at all times.

And I didn't even have to change my system for a journey cross the country.

First, you needed a place to put things, a storage shell. You don't want to feel all empty and exposed. A light, protective jacket with enormous pockets helped. Mine was the soldier jacket that I found at Fort Point, made from light canvas. I dug it from the garbage the night I slept there; it had big ink stains on the pockets. Since I found it near a deserted army barrack, I liked to think it belonged to a military guy. With a marker I colored over the pockets with thick dark swirls. When it was too warm to wear my soldier jacket, I stuffed it in my carrybag.

My carrybag, bought at a street fair, was made from electric-blue nylon. I wore it across my chest and it hung, low and just right, below my hip.

For warmth, nothing beat a thick, hooded (with working string) sweatshirt. The hood provided shelter from San Francisco shivery winds. It also worked as a scrunchable pillow. Angus gave me a dark-navy one he got from a date…all fleecy and new.

I usually kept at least two T-shirts around. My latest favorite was colored an acid orange with a picture of a gun on the back. On the front, an old saying, just right for any occasion: MAKE MY DAY.

Say I was walking up some steep hills on an average ocean-blown San Francisco afternoon: I'd wear a cropped T-shirt and my soldier jacket. This allowed for protection from the weather, but I wouldn't get hot and sweaty. I'd stuff my sweatshirt in my carrybag or tie it around my neck for more wind-shielding. I also had a knit cap. When I didn't feel like trouble, it helped me pass as a boy.

Bad smells are bacteria. If they live on your clothes they grow. Clean your underarms every day, twice a day if you sweat a lot, and it destroys the bacteria. Not having a chance to shower often, what worked for me was a little squeeze bottle of alcohol. In a big Walgreens, it was easy to fill.

I bought new socks at the Goodwill on Haight when my feet felt grungy. And since I didn't enjoy wearing the same boxers everyday, I stuffed a couple of pairs in my jacket pocket and washed them when I could. For my period, I tried to keep several plugs and two small pieces of thick flannel (synthetic blend because it dries faster) in a ziplock bag. Had a black lace bra that hooked in front and took up about a centimeter of pocket space. I wore it to feel more sexy sometimes, but most of the time I didn't need it. I also liked to wear a black bandanna knotted around my neck.

I did have a toothbrush. And Band-Aids to help friends' cuts from getting infected. No comb was necessary for my buzz cut; I could run my hand over my head and detangle my long strip of mane with a few finger crawls. I kept a small tube of my father's old sunblock for my nose to prevent skin cancer. And of course, my shiny Swiss Army pocketknife: something I couldn't resist when I found it on Mrs. Jam's dresser. The knife made me feel ready for anything, like the howling dragon on my right forearm.

Everything I've mentioned, even my carrybag, was able to fit in my jacket pockets.

I carried my real ID in the front pocket of my jeans inside a little zippered Guatemalan pouch. It showed my birth name, Gretchen. In my back pockets were my fake ID (making me twenty-four instead of seventeen and three quarters) and a tiny arrowhead, something I found a long time ago on the banks of the Trinity River.

dizzy creek

ON THE BUS, I threw my soldier jacket over my head. The engine hummed and purred. Comforting to ignore the sights around me after being haunted with everything that had happened. The rumbling, yawning secrets of traveling. Nothing except my private shell encircling me. No wishes even. No wishes other than to make my twenty dollars last, the cash left after buying my good-for-anywhere ticket.

Occasionally I'd take a peek. Houses with peeling paint and strange backyards with laundry on a line. Abandoned plastic toy trucks on coarse yellowed grass. Big rocks near front doors that seemed to mean something. People had real lives out here. It was scary knowing entire towns existed that I'd never seen, and they went on and on. And always had. Without me. Weird.

The bus driver pulled over and disappeared. Some of us risked leaving the bus. I ran in circles outside then curled back under my jacket.

By the dinner rest stop, I broke down and spent some cash to order a piece of blackberry pie. Stabbed the fork in for a bite. *Gush.* Held its tartness on my tongue. Soft fabulicious mouthful. Rolled it around slo-o-owly. Paused after swallowing. Felt it warm and sweeten my insides.

DEEP NIGHT FELL, but I couldn't sleep. The sounds of the bus echoed against my nerves. The smells kept changing, making me nauseous, especially the whiskey on one mother's breath and the piss smell on her little boy. The kid ran up and down the aisle. I gave him a mint from the restaurant, but he threw it back at me. His eyes were Halloween red and squinting; the eyes of an addict before he'd even started school. I wanted to rip him away from his mom, set him loose in the desert, ready to fend for himself...see him gnawing the bones of coyotes and breaking open spiny cactus for their juice. When I'd close my eyes, he'd race back to punch my seat again.

I took the kid's blue marker and drew on my ankle. Tiny swirls. A star.

I GAVE UP trying to sleep and stared at the dirty Naugahyde seat cover in front of me. Its black specks grimy as the pores on an old drunk's nose. The bus tore down the highway, the spooky grime tinged by dim-green panel lights.

By dawn we shot through the bright remaining space of Nevada.

Bone-colored grasses leapt across the screen of my moving window, negatives of movie film. At last we had another rest stop, and I made it over to a Denny's. Ordered blueberry cobbler with ice cream, struggled to open my groggy eyes.

After downing my coffee, I inspected people at the other tables. None had seen a glimmer of what I'd seen—not the tall Douglas firs outside Redding—not the splashing of the Pacific—not the steep hill of Coso Street. They owned their own set of familiars. Memories of comfort and memories of exposure. I wanted to share one of mine, say one San Franciscan afternoon, a day at the Folsom Street Fair where we danced in the streets till the fog rolled down and the cops marched over. I wanted to implant my past in someone else's brainbox. See if it changed them.

Or I wanted to steal other peoples' familiars. The gruff man in a cowboy hat took his coffee in tiny sharp slurps. Where had he hid as a child when his dad got mean? The woman in the low-cut black shirt who pressed close against the table. How had she felt about the hands that had touched her? Were they good?

Freaky, freaky brain waves. After all, none of the people in the restaurant knew me. We were all bags of skin, all the same kind of mammal, but raging different inside. You think about it more in a new place—how people are so-o-o foreign. I longed to know everybody, hear their stories. I didn't have anybody to talk with anymore. No brown-haired, blinking Cara. No sweet, lanky-boy Angus.

In the bathroom I washed up. Changed my underwear, cupped a fountain of water to pour over my face. Squirted alcohol on my armpits and brushed my teeth and tongue. It was too hot to wear my soldier jacket; I put everything from the pockets into my carrybag.

By the time we rambled across the next stretch of highway, I was starting to burn inside. All the rage for the towns of a-mer-i-ca-a-ah. I whispered under my breath, *a-mer-i-ca-a-ah*. A clear, headtrippy blue sky hovered over us all. I couldn't wait. Couldn't wait to hear Randa's big bronco laugh. To have her touch me with the rugged hands that I had never felt, hands that I knew would be warm. And good. I imagined she wouldn't treat me like a kidfreak that needed rescuing once I had made it to Nebraska on my own. I imagined the tall cornfields, the sturdy farms, and the good life that she claimed would change me forever. For once I had a place to go, a home where somebody had actually invited me to stay. It made me feel capable, an optimistic fool.

I sat next to the strangers and talked to them now. Found out where they were going and what they were doing. Told jokes with a fleshy-faced college girl and got her e-mail address. Flirted with a shy American-Indian looking guy. I was ready for anyone and any-where.

Even got the bus driver to talk a bit. He'd driven for thirty years, bragged how he'd had two people die and three people born on his bus. He had hairy, rickety arms and long, bony legs. He said his favorite time to drive a bus was sunset in the deserts of Arizona. I think he liked how the big bus window shielded him from the world.

Not me.

I went and sat with a girl hiding in the back corner. Her eyes gleamed under her fringe of hair and her pointy chin dug into a big hooded sweatshirt.

"Where are you from?" I asked.

"I don't know," she said. She was like a little mouse with a twitching tail, waiting for my cheese.

"I'm from *I Don't Know,* too." Stupid, but I like to say whatever comes out of my mouth.

The girl didn't say anything. I could imagine her at home—in a room with blank walls headbanging to death metal.

"I want to see the cornfields." I raised my forearm in front of my mouth so it looked like my dragon was talking. "That's where I'm going."

"I don't know where I'm going."

"Come with me! I can get us work."

She smiled. She was my age, but somehow younger. Really swallowed up by her sweatshirt. Except for that chin. It scared me a little. Sharp as a knife.

"Can I touch your hair?" She rose up. The little mouse had come out of its hole.

"Yeah, sure."

She walked on her knees along the backseat, then petted my mane. I don't have much hair but when people stroke my one strip I can't help but grow lush. I even whinnied like a horse to encourage her. It broke her up. She got talking. Revealed she was on her way to live with her brother after her mom kicked her out.

I nodded. "My granddad kicked me out. That why I'm on the road."

"Things are going to be different now," she said. "For both of us."

We talked more about our common fates, as if we were the only two roaddawgz in the world. Then she exited at the next stop, and I watched her back as she walked away.

Poof! One more gone-forever person.

THE SUN PRICKED AND FLAMED against the edges of the Nevada desert. Outside the window was a big spreadwide country, and I wanted to make it mine. My granddad would rant about the destruction of america. The slaughtered Indians, the railroad barons, the corporate farm takeovers. But I saw how what was left still managed to sing. The country's history hadn't left. Here it was. So much of what was once called California had started out here. Right here. All around.

I looked for mints for the crying kid and realized that I'd forgotten my soldier jacket back in the Denny's bathroom. It was not a good sign. I used to forget things all the time, but it hadn't happened in a while.

My jacket formed the cozy walls to my own private house. I couldn't get along without it. The ticket was valid for a whole week—for me to stop and go as I liked. A bus back to Reno would get me closer to my jacket; even though chances of finding it were slim.

Since last night, I had been drawing on my legs. Trying to get them just right. Thought they would protect me like Cara's, but I guess that was dumb. Now that I realized I'd lost my jacket, I felt naked and exposed.

SO I USED my stop-and-go ticket to go back for my soldier jacket. Sat on a bench in a town called Leadbetter. Waited for the next bus back to Reno. Hardly anything around. A few burger places, flat land and dry air. Dry and sparse. Car after car drifted by. The faces on the other side of the windshields looked abandoned and on the edge. Alone.

Already I could tell I would fit right in.

And once again, I turned hopeful. Why hadn't I left California before? It was all empty out here, but filled with sky and possibiliteee. I could keep going and never go back.

And it was so hot, hell, I didn't need my jacket.

WHEN I USED TO TALK ABOUT IT with Angus he would tell me I was wrong. Somehow I had thought he could understand, or maybe *not* understand in a way that would be reassuring. So I liked telling him my heebie-jeebie fears.

I remember one night I spent with him in the Pacific Heights place. We rolled around on his clothes-covered nest in the room off the garage. It felt warm and cozy; a velvet robe under my cheek. Angus always lived in the best places, had the grandest daddies.

He kneeled on a pile of scarves and looked at himself in the mirror on the wall. "You're not going to die. Soon anyway."

"I know. I know. I know." I threw a blue scarf in the air and watched it billow and land on my feet. "I'm crazy."

"Girl, you are going to live too long. You are going to have too much life to know what to do with. All this and heaven, too." He stretched his arms and placed his delicate hands on my ankles. "You'll see. We'll be so happy and famous. Famous roaddawgz!"

"Gorgeous thing," I said.

He discouraged my bad thoughts, told me they were paranoid, but I think at some point I did convince Angus about my dark-star future. After all, I had told him about my mom, and how I would go the same way, or at least at the same age. I must have convinced him or he wouldn't have said when Cara died, "It was her, not you." Maybe we both hoped it would break the hex. But Cara being gone just made death more real.

First my mom. Then Cara. Then me.

Can't stop what will come. I decided that for the rest of my trip, I would put it out of my mind. *Just keep going,* I told myself.

WE CROSSED ANOTHER BORDER and then came to a strange left-over place near Ogden, Utah. The bus stop consisted of a gas station and a crumbling, boarded-up brick storefront. Up against its wall leaned a girl, headdressed with a plume of magenta hair, silver gleaming on her fingers, skin busting from balloon-colored clothes.

I couldn't resist this temptation, different than any offered at the places we'd been dumped so far.

As the bus driver took a break and smoked his cigarette, I left the other passengers and made my move.

I ambled over. "Hey."

She looked up, her skin a little ruddy and mottled, her eyes sluggy but alert as she saw me. "You waiting for someone?"

"On a bus break," I explained.

On the highway a car raced by like a desert rat.

I leaned against the scorched wall.

She flashed her colors in the heat. Hot air bounced off the pavement and waved against her chartreuse top and purple skirt. Her top was torn and flapped to either side of her broad chest, revealing little heaps of cleavage.

"Where are you going?" I asked. Knowing I would follow.

She shifted between legs—one looked to be shorter than the other. It needed a boost from a taller platform sneaker. "You got a ride out of here?"

"Do you?"

She told me she was waiting for a friend who was in a band. I asked her if they were any good.

"They have a gig in SLC next weekend. You could make up your own mind." She rubbed her hand along her thigh. As if to challenge me she said, "They also have an acoustic one in Dizzy Creek. Today."

With relief, I retrieved my carrybag from the bus, got a schedule from the driver, and told the passengers, "Cheerios."

When I stepped back onto the road, though, the girl had disappeared.

We hadn't talked long, only a few minutes while the driver smoked, but I had thought she had asked me, more or less, to come along. Maybe I had misunderstood.

Should I run after my bus and bang on the door? It charged past, fumes in my face, engine lurching and whining.

I turned again to the hot brick wall where the girl had been. Now I wondered if she had been a dizzy mirage.

My bus shot away like a bullet, charging until small and blurry, then absolutely nothing. A still highway, a hot parking lot, a blank line of horizon. Everything sank under the weight of the sun. No sounds and nothing around. I felt extinguished.

Across the highway—rocky, garbage-strewn dirt fields, smelling of burned weeds and old cars. It was the only place to go. Dust flew over my boots as I started across the road.

From behind me, a yell. "Where are you going?"

I turned.

The girl's uneven-leg thing turned her walk into a giant swagger. She thrust the tall leg and then swung the other up to meet it, each step propelled by her hips' thrust. I ran back, so happy to see her. We were two girls in the wild west again. It was as if Cara had come back from the dead.

"That was weird. I thought you'd left."

"I'm all yours," she said. Her eyes sparkled and her skin gleamed, no longer so sluggy. "Don't worry."

As we waited for her boyfriend to come, we talked. Jessika was her name, "spelled with a special *k*," she said. The boyfriend's name was Joey, and he had borrowed her car for a week, while she had been doing some work around town. I wasn't quite sure what kind. Next she would follow Joey for a while, going to the concert tonight in Idaho and then to some bigger ones in Salt Lake.

It might all work out. If I got a ride with Jessika, I could stop off and crash with Meredith in SLC. And still be on my way to Nebraska.

As she spoke, Jessika's rings knocked together with a satisfying sound. She propped her weaker leg with its special platform sneaker against the brick. The small, puny leg made the rest of her body appear more full...as if she had started a scrawny winter tree—no leaves, all twig—then broke into bloom, full of summer flowering.

"I have this feeling that people think they can take advantage of you." Jessika paused. "Do what they want with you." She puffed up her broad chest and looked down at me. "Am I right?"

No one had ever said anything like that to me before. It was the exact opposite of how I thought I appeared.

"How about you? Want to take some advantage?" I said it without smiling, so she would think I was ready for her, ready to slide my hand up her short purple skirt and take her right against that wall.

Her lips smooshed outwards a little in response. "What?"

I tried to look away but couldn't. Everything about her was too delicious, clothes stretched tight and riding high to show a small pudge of tan belly and two thick pillars of thighs. Her height made it more majestic, made her gleam, defying this desert and dust.

"Where are you from?" I asked.

She paused. "Reno."

"Yeah?"

"But I've been all over. I'm trying to get to every state," she said.

"Yeah, sure." She was like the people in the Haight, been everywhere and nowhere at the same time.

"You need something. Girl—that's your name, you said? Girl?"

I nodded.

The skin under the hollow of her throat glistened with sweat.

As she stood in front of me and put her hand on her hip, a

magenta tangle of her upright hair blocked the glare of the sun.
"Here's what I think. You need something."

"What you got?" I figured when she had disappeared earlier that
she must have been doing some bright, speedy chemicals.

She swept her arm in front of her face and then opened it out-
ward, palm up. "You hate being lost. Am I right? Maybe you need
the Lord."

JESSIKA TOOK THE WHEEL of her old orange Toyota. I sat in the
backseat with my legs stretched, propping my shoulders against one
window so I could look across to the other. I felt strangely at home,
just going along, not knowing what was next.

Joey, the band boyfriend, wasn't much over five feet, with a dark
curly wedge of hair and a raspy, New York accent that made him
sound like a mobster. He twisted around to face me. You could tell
he felt real comfortable talking to people.

Jessika chewed gum and laughed with him and floored the car,
going over ninety through the straightaway toward Idaho.

Joey told stories about growing up poor in the South Bronx and
stealing food from the corner store when he was five years old. "One
day I wanted an apple, but my hand went so fast I got a tamayta
instead." He made a raspy wheeze. "A little red *tamayta*! It squished
in my hand before I could get it in my mouth."

"How'd you end up out here?" I asked.

Jessika snorted. "He had to go to rehab. Da-da-a-a! And that's
how he got saved. And he hasn't ever forgotten it." She rocked in the
seat and I wished I could see more of her than a little bit of eye and
smooshy mouth in the rearview mirror.

"For real?"

Jessika clicked her tongue. "What?"

"You're both…christians?"

"Is that a problem?"

Joey drummed the front of the dashboard. "It's a need thing. When you are nice and ready, He comes. Be real *desperate*. He comes. You'll see."

I wondered if they were going to kidnap me and make me join some rifle-toting militia. "Yeah, sure."

They discussed whether they thought I was damaged and humbled enough to have the Lord come to me. Jessika thought no; Joey, yes.

Little did they know. There had been a couple of times, very desperate times, I had been lame enough to ask for god's help. No dice.

Next Joey told his band's history. The members of the Apostle Rods first met in Dizzy Creek, Idaho; Joey was doing born-again rehab and the other band members were making pizzas.

"Beautiful." I could just imagine Joey preaching the gospel in a million decibels with his frizzy bat hair. I had heard there was such a thing as christian punk, but the closest I had ever come to it was a recording of an old Berkeley band called Econochrist.

"We've played around. Tons in Omaha. Haven't been back to the Dizzy Creek for ages."

They asked me what bands I liked.

"Fuck brand names."

"*Aay-y-y, muddafucca.*" Joey pretended to take offense and then gave me his intense, beady look. "So name something you do care about. Ga head."

I looked out my window. "You trying to mess with me?"

"What's the deepest? Name the deepest caring you feel—what is it for?"

"The stars."

"Yeah, that's good. Constellations. You like them things. You're into them?"

I nodded.

"Good." He turned even further, all the way around from the front seat and grabbed my hand. "K'mea. Do you have faith they will always be there? Even after you die?"

"Some of them. Yeah." My hand was sweating.

"No matter what you do, those stars, they will be there, right?" He bore down on me with his intense eyes. "No matter how lonely, no matter if you are sitting in jail, no matter if you kill someone, no matter if you stick a needle in your arm, those pretty stars will still be there, right?"

I looked out the window again.

He let go of my hand and took a long breath. "Believe it or not, muddafucca, that's the kind of faith I have. I pray to an angry brown-faced *gawdfadda* named Jesus. He forgives us all."

"That's your theory," I said.

"Right. It's my *theory*. I like that." He turned. "Jessika, you like that?"

"I hate theories and I hate religion. I just like god." She arched her head upward, shut her eyes, and kept driving.

"Fuck, yeah. Look at her faith," said Joey.

"Hey," I yelled. Then closed my eyes, too.

DIZZY CREEK APPEARED: a dung heap of smoking factories, strip malls, and parking lots pitched among smog-coated fields. On the outside of an abandoned department store someone had spray-painted *Apostle Rods*. Local kids milled around, their faces bored as cows. We dropped Joey at the back entrance and parked. When the kids saw me and Jessika leave the car, they stared. Whole miniherds turned their heads in unison as we appeared.

I attached myself to the colorful blast of Jessika and together we glided by the whole line, definitely in our own private Idaho. We went over to the side of the building, waiting to be let in by Joey's friends. As we stood at the door, Jessika showed me some dance moves.

Sometimes a new girl is enough to make me forget myself, but after waiting at the door for a while I turned freaky. And hot. Optimism about my adventure disappeared again into the sky, blank and stinking with Dizzy Creek's chemical overload. Everything beyouteefull was going to be stolen from me; I felt afraid my trip would be about finding the same ole stinking place of familiar. I untied the bandanna from around my neck and wiped the sweat off my back. "Can't you get us inside?"

"Sure." Jessika stopped stretching and knocked harder on the rear entrance. A twitchy Apostle Rods member with a tiny head opened the door. It was pitch black and at first we couldn't see anything, then we followed his flashlight down a long hallway with broken bulbs on the wall.

He took us into the main part of the store. Hangers and stands for clothes were strewn here and there; in the dark the abandoned racks looked like charred skeletons. The signs for merchandise still hung from the ceiling—we passed the sign for KITCHENWARE and then OFFICE. The only light came from a large hole in the ceiling where the sun fell through.

I tried to chill my freaky nerves while the Apostle Rods set up.

Under the broken crown of ceiling, the band and their bouncers gathered. When they let in the kids, you could hardly see their faces. The musicians began to talk to everybody and yell at the crowd.

At last things started. The Apostle Rods tore into a set with a sick fever. No wires, all plain acoustic. Old bat-hair Joey was pretty fierce on the drums. He had twice the energy of the twitchy guys that wandered around the stage and bumped into one another. The lead singer, the pinhead who had let us in, howled about pain, as well as Jesus and bloody nails. Jessika and I threw ourselves into the crowd. There weren't more than a couple hundred of us, and the music was quieter than I was used to, so it was hard to get lost. You bounced against the same people. After a while, the sizes and the rhythms of our bodies got in sync. Some of the boys tried to stomp too hard, but they were mostly skinny kids that weren't big enough to hurt anybody. Each time I slammed against someone, they slammed harder against me. We jumped on one another's backs and crashed around like escaped convicts.

Sometimes we got ragged at the edges of the group and jogged around, or stamped in place, but then another swell would build, and a new mosh would form, with everybody close and hot. It was pretty funny that I had left San Francisco and in less than a day and a half I was in the middle of it again. The thing was, it was even better, because everybody was looking at me in a hungry-interested way, and it made me feel pumped.

Jessika left the slamming crowd to do her own thing on the side, arching that broad chest of hers. As I watched, someone dug into my bare shin with his ankle chain. My leg dripped blood, and I went back to thrashing around. The kids were really laughing that I was bleeding: old school punk, I'm sure they were thinking. For revenge, I hurled my body into a cute, long haired, innocent angelboy.

The angelboy held on to me for a second. We jumped up and down, and a lot of people knocked into us at once. We got squashed by the crowd and squashed more, until we couldn't move at all, held up by the force of their push. We got rolled up high over everybody and I was laughing hard and holding on to my angel.

A girl flapped her arms and ran in a circle around us screaming, "I love Jesus."

Jessika torpedoed into the crowd. "Hey, everybody now!"

I pulled away from the angelboy and ran around with the flapping Jesus-yeller. Jessika skipped in her lopsided way alongside. The big guys protecting the band let her enter the sunlit stage space. She kneeled and raised her hands.

The pinhead banged his guitar and screeched, "Nobody knows my name but Jesus."

I ran up too, but a bouncer guy threw me back. Then Jessika asked him to let me into the stage space, and they beckoned. I rushed again. Looked out at everyone. Raised my fists and shook them. Joined in the booming chorus of the song, yelling, "Nobody knows my name but Jesus!" The sweaty crowd of faces shined with delight, and I soaked in all those staring eyes.

When the music stopped, Jessika talked with Joey, and I wandered around in the dark parts of the store. At some point, I realized the band was leading a prayer. Kids came up to get saved. Joey was putting his hands on peoples' shoulders and the other band members were kneeling.

I found Jessika and we went over and rested against an old cashier stand.

We were far enough from the sunlit ceiling hole that we were in total shadow. I didn't want Joey to see us anyway.

The kids looked relieved as bat-hair Joey touched them. Their faces quieted, like babies being fed. I could see it in how they dropped their heads back; in how, as he blessed them, they surrendered.

I couldn't help but wonder about sticking around with Joey and Jessika. Meredith would probably act like she's never met me. And what the hell would I really do on Randa's farm? It might be better to stay here and be part of something, even if it was all kooky Jesus bananas.

And who knew what could happen if I went up on that stage? Christian salvation appealed to me in some sick way. After all I think my mother joined a religious group before she died.

Maybe if I let gangsta Joey save me I could feel something new. The steady pulse of the world. Or something even better. Go on up to paradise and live forever. Get it over. Death take me now!

"Screw this. God wants nothing to do with religion." Jessika spat into an old coffee cup on the floor. "Look at him." Joey was kissing the top of a pretty girl's head.

I came back to my senses. "Yeah. Who does Joey think he is, some stud christ?"

Jessika put her hands up like Joey was doing. "Muddafucca! I'm Joey, and I'm gonna start da revolution that will save da world."

"Right!"

"Hey, maybe you should go up there," said Jessika. "I want to see it!"

"You go."

"Come on."

I dropped my head onto Jessika's lap and looked up at her face. "Religion makes people do some crazy shit. You better watch out."

"Amen. Don't I know it." Jessika rolled away from me and stretched her weak leg in front of her. She pounded the muscle of her thigh, then massaged it. Her fingers strummed along with their million rings. "So, come on! Go up there before he finishes."

I wanted one of her silver rings. Wanted to put it in my pocket, have a small pretty ring of silver of my own.

"Are you going?" asked Jessika.

"You go." I couldn't tell if she meant it. "What's he think he's doing?"

"Joey says, 'Never stop speaking da truth.'"

"Yeah?" I thrust my hand into her thatch of stained hair.

She leaned against me but kept staring at Joey until the last kid in line got his final blessings. Then Jessika jumped up on her good leg, twirled around in a circle, danced real proud with her own brand of possibiliteee. A showing for me in our dark hideaway. She arched way back and her top spread to reveal more skin between her sweet mounds, a just-right place to plant my mouth, the fabulicious spot where ribs and breath started, where everything, I'm sure, was once first-born.

salt lake

ALL AROUND circled the distant, cradling mountains. They held back from where I stood at the downtown bus station. Not in your face like the Sierras or Trinities. Gray accordion walls, snow-tipped and slatted into high points. Fixed in a distant circle, the mountains gave the city a lonely, promised-land feeling.

After hanging with the Jesus punks for a couple of days in SLC, I'd had enough and made it over to the bus station. From there, I called smooth-skin Meredith, hoping she's make good on her invitation. If she bailed, I figured I'd jump on a bus for Nebraska. I left a message on her answering machine saying I'd be at the station a while if she wanted to come by and say hi. Meanwhile I checked with the clerk about buses to Randa's farm in Bonesteel. He gave me a scare because at first he thought the only town named Bonesteel was in South Dakota, but then he found one in Nebraska, too. The closest bus stop was in Sioux City, Iowa. Northeastern Nebraska was right across the border; I'd just have to double back a little.

I gave up thinking Meredith was going to show and started spanging for food money. Just after I'd gotten a dollar from an older woman, someone tapped my shoulder from behind. "Is that who I think it is?"

I turned around. "Only for you."

Meredith's delicate face looked like it wasn't sure whether it recognized me. Her long red hair covered one eye. "Spare me."

She wore new jeans that were tight around her hips and made her look wide and ready. I love seeing somebody in clothes and already knowing them naked. They can't hide anymore.

In her shmancy white car, I tried to keep some banter going. "So these are the Wasatch Mountains?"

She nodded. Then she gave me a story that she must have told other visitors. How the Great Lake had once been so full it lapped the sides of the distant mountains. Braced by the circle of mountain rock, the water's only escape was evaporation. That's why the salty dried remains were all that was left.

I wondered if my skanky traveler smell was messing with her clean bubble of an automobile. But then maybe she wanted me to mess up her world.

"So there you are! Never thought I'd see you this soon." She laughed. We were driving smack through downtown. "I hope you like it here."

The edge of her cheek had fine downy hair that showed in the late afternoon sun. The memory of her tickled-pink parts heated me up.

She pulled up at a stoplight on a street called South Temple. I was going to say something about liking her town, but I stopped when she looked over. *Bang, bang.* Her eyes got so needy all of a sudden.

"So, it's okay that I came?" I said.

"Oh, yes. I'm in my own world today. Don't mind me. You are going to be either very good for me or very bad." Her fair skin reddened. "I finished a funny little poem, all about you last night."

I slapped my thigh. "Right!"

She swallowed. "No, I did."

"No kidding?"

By the time we reached Meredith's stately tree-filled neighborhood, I felt absolutely Disney. Block after block, we were surrounded by more happy cartoon mothers than I'd ever seen in my life. The women of the neighborhood glided along with their strollers. I'd never seen people with strollers actually *stroll*. No hurry. They took their time. Like ducklings, their toddlers quacked in flocks behind them. Every block, a fairy-tale parade.

On Meredith's own block, trees lunged over the street with leafy branches. Trapped underneath the shimmering green stood the proper, immense houses. I could tell that the religious founders of Salt Lake wanted their neighborhoods to look permanent. The big houses that I had been around in California were new and individual, many of them large-windowed and view-seeking. None of these houses peered outwards. The windows were draped.

Meredith peeled into her driveway and jumped from her car. She'd opened the front door before I had put my carrybag on my shoulder.

As I hesitated on her driveway, she stood on her front step and laughed. "Slowpoke."

The place was much bigger than I had thought. It needed a moat. "Coming, Snow Princess."

I HAD MET MEREDITH that final night in San Francisco. After escaping from the homicidal Nostril Man, I still needed a place to sleep. So I took a bus over to my favorite saviors, the girls at Dollhouse, a small queer party held at a bar in the Mission on Friday nights. Flashed my back pocket ID and kissed Lark, the bouncer.

"Penelope, baby," she said. She spilled over the sides of her stool like a generous raft.

"Your one and only." I liked being called by my other name, *Penelope Huck Crow*, an American-Indian thing I'd made up on the spot the day when I went in for my fake ID. "Who are all these people?" I asked. Lark laughed and pushed me further into the bar. Lots of women wore costumes. Movie-star theme night or something. Gold stars hung from the ceiling of the small corner bar. The worn wood floors were covered with glitter.

I ambled about and started asking everybody where they were from. An interesting thing to do in SF because no one ever says "Here."

"You want to know where *I'm* from, Moon Face?" asked a gorgeous Latin woman wearing a gold hair clip.

"Tell me," I said and sat down at her table. "I'll make a map of the world."

But nobody at her table could give a direct answer. I mean, people move around so much it gets confusing what to call home.

It was Meredith who finally said more than a few sentences. She wasn't cold or distant, just kinda soft, and looked me in the eyes when she talked. She wore a platinum wig with straight bangs, was visiting her lesbytarian sister in town. I hoped she was more than a little queer herself.

"I'm from Salt Lake City." She shook her breasts and laughed. She was drunk and role-playing because that's what people do when they come to San Francisco.

"Tell me about yourself." I moved closer. I suddenly felt dead-tired, like a ghost. I needed a place to sleep. I needed to feel solid and well-founded after almost getting killed in Golden Gate Park. I needed to feel like I had a life. Would have a life. That things would work out. I needed to hear somebody else's words in my ear. I needed to fuck somebody, is what I needed.

I made up questions. I took her hand. "What's the name of your personal devil?"

Miss Platinum gave that a long thought. Too long.

"How about your favorite movie?"

She read the words on my T-shirt and made a gun with her index finger and thumb. "Make my day."

Dirty Harry was my granddad's guilty secret. "Really?"

I looked up from her cool white hand to her arm and over her body. It all was begging for attention. Underneath her act I could tell she had that female desperate thing and wanted to melt. The color of her throat, her bare-arm paleness, reminded me of a patch of snow, a private mound of ice that the sun had missed under some tall tree's shadow. I kissed her tiny cup of a shoulder.

She flung off her wig and let me stroke her copper-red hair. I told her she looked like Julianne Moore.

She invited me to her sister's condo.

HIGH IN THE HILLS above Noe Valley, her sister's place was tucked next to a small garden. We got nice and naked in the living room, our reflection on the couch bouncing against sliding glass doors that led to a cement patio with palms and hanging planters. Meredith liked me being rough with her—one of those women who want it deeper and deeper. If we woke the sister, we didn't know.

I wasn't tired anymore.

By five in the morning, we were talking travel. I told her I was itching to go somewhere. Meredith was sweet, giving invitations, saying things like "You've got to come to Salt Lake." I can't ever turn down that stuff—when people are nice like that.

"Yeah, sure," I said. "You really want me to come?"

Behind us on the couch, I kept looking at Meredith's reflection on the sliding glass doors. To celebrate her invitation, I did a little funkadelic dancing, like some harem boy-girl. Meredith watched me on the glass. I let my arms wave in a hula, and then reached them tall as smoke. Circling her with small steps, I shifted my eyes, cast a spell.

"Listen, snow princess," I said. " Make me an offer."

She yawned and stretched her delicious white arms above her head. "You're welcome anytime. My husband will get you work."

"Husband?"

Meredith lay back on the arm of the couch, arched her torso. "Don't I look married?"

"Fuck you. You're joking."

"You need a home." She took my hand and put it on her breast. "I could show you my poetry, cook you big meals, make you snug as a bug in one of our spare rooms." She gave me a sad, twisted smile.

I could see a blue vein under her smooth temple. "Yeah, sure."

"You say that a lot." She closed her eyes. "Believe me, I need a change. I'm falling apart inside."

I kneeled on the floor by her side and pushed open her thighs, pressed my thumbs into her pale-butter flesh, spread her open again. She ruffled my hair and whispered. "You like to be dared?"

"Okay."

"Hit me."

"No problem."

It was then I took one more plunge into my free-fall life. I need the heat and feel and fuck of them. They call and I follow. It just happens, right? What else are you supposed to do? It's not like I go for some romance of a girl. No, it's the raw hit of skin against skin;

it's my hand thrusting into the wet, swollen, rubbery cave of them. It's the hell-moans, the long stories and whispered lies that come at five in the morning. I like that, okay? The insides of people.

MEREDITH PLUNKED HER PURSE on a table in a long, dark hallway. An old grandfather clock stood in the living room. She called for me to follow into her big Salt Lake fortress.

Unlike the dark front of the house, the kitchen was new and glaring, with greenhouse windows circling the sink. Earthenware pots of leafy thyme and marjoram pressed next to the glass, trying to grab the sunshine. Cabinet after cabinet circled the room, their chrome handles protruding like snares.

She heated a broccoli-cheese turnover in the microwave while I sat on a high stool near a huge island with cutting boards and knives. Every drawer that Meredith opened had contents neatly piled: dishtowels or long spoons or plastic bags.

Meredith said I could stay at her house till Sunday.

"Gonna let me eat you out of house and home?" I took a cheesy bite.

"Go for it."

After hanging for a while, I said I needed to take a walk. Meredith said that was fine because she had to make some phone calls.

I took my chances with being swallowed by a posse of moms and ambled down the block at about the same pace I'd seen them walking their stroller babies earlier.

In Trinity County, way above where my dad lives, you've got your firs and redwoods, tall and straight and full of furry needles. The trees on Meredith's block were elegant, with curvy trunks and sculpted arms. They looked strong, but more because they had to survive being pruned and being in a town, as opposed to firs, and especially redwoods, which are strong because of their fierce old age.

With their showy pillars and wide lawns, the houses seemed like churches, ready to suck me in with big loud choruses of Lord Almighty hymns. Occasionally some live people appeared and stared. One suspicious-eyed girl said hello from the safety of her porch, and later some boys fighting on a lawn stopped to gawk and point at me.

The view from the nearest intersection showed high mountains, dramatic with their late afternoon shadows and brilliant crowns of snow. I wondered how many miles away they were; they seemed near heaven.

Would Meredith let me crash longer than a few days? There was no hurry getting to Randa, really—I would just have to get money for a new bus ticket. I'd never seen any place like this, and I wanted to stay.

WHEN I CAME BACK to Meredith's fortress, she welcomed me as if I'd been away too long, much friendlier than when she picked me up at the bus station. She must have been getting used to the idea of having me. I felt so ready to be had. To live in that big inviting house for as long as they'd take me.

She stood at the bottom of the mahogany staircase. "George, meet our new guest."

His long legs appeared first as they came down the stairs.

"Glad you could come to our neck of the woods." He tottered and his arms hung like sticks. He put his hand out to shake mine.

"Hi. My name is Girl." I laughed for a second. It was so unbelievable.

Meredith asked George to make up my bed while she finished dinner. We went downstairs and I helped him put the sheets on. My room was in the basement with the laundry machines. Its window faced the back lawn, a circle of old trees. Shadows from the peaks of the roof fell across the lawn. I wondered why they needed to hide me down there when they must have had other rooms upstairs, then George told me the guest bedroom had a lot of junk in it because they were getting ready to remodel the upstairs now that they had finished remodeling the kitchen.

"This is just a little basement nook, but sometimes I like to come down here. It's a good place to get away from the heat." He licked his lips and stuttered. "V-v-very nice and cool." Then we went back upstairs to the dark hallway. He showed me the living room with its plump, antique furniture, rose-colored rugs, and the loud, ticking grandfather clock.

I could imagine growing up in this comforting old house. Especially when I sat down to dinner. Meredith had made eggplant parmesan. She had convinced herself that I was a crunchy California vegetarian.

George winked at me as I ate, although it might have been a nervous tick. He had an endearing nerdiness to everything he did. It turned out he was an engineer-contractor and might be able to get me work on a demolition crew.

"Doesn't sound too hard," I said.

"Not much gets by you, does it?" He wink-ticked again.

"I appreciate it, George." Meredith touched the back of his hand.

"No problem."

I dug into my eggplant and scooped up my sauce, turning my insides into a healthy tomato patch. After dinner, Meredith whispered that George would be away the next day. We'd have the house to ourselves.

AT LAST MORNING CAME. Birds chirped. I nestled into the comfort of my surroundings, ready to show my appreciation.

First we made orange juice. Meredith had me take a wooden poker to the small oranges and twirl it inside each half until the juice came dripping. Next she asked if I wanted bacon and eggs.

"Sure. You have the stuff?"

"Or would you like a smoothie?"

"Yeah, sure. Either."

She chopped a banana in half and I added some orange juice and yogurt to the blender. Over the blender roar, she mentioned her poem. "You want to hear it?" She pulled it from the pocket of her loose white dress.

I was distracted when she read it because I couldn't stop craving the smell of bacon. And I craved the sight of her cracking eggs for me—you know, like some farm wife in a movie. I wanted to have that sit-back feeling that a man has when a woman puts a warm plate of food in front of him.

Instead I tried to listen to her poem about how desire was a path and if you took a chance on a windy San Francisco night you might be blown along for the long journey. Then there was something at the beginning and the end about sliding around in a sacred, viscous, life-breeding amoebic fluid, but it wasn't clear how that tied into the striding journey of the rest of the poem. She read it like it meant a lot to her, but it was so goopy it embarrassed me.

After she finished reading, she looked like she had just been punched in the stomach.

"Are you okay?" I moved my chair closer to her. I wondered if she'd offer the bacon and eggs again. "That was really great."

"I get shy when I read. Poems are like my awkward little children." She walked over to the blender and filled up my glass again.

"Really?"

Meredith gave me an aggressive smile, as if she knew it was forced but didn't want to look sad. "You know, George and I lead a weird life." She tilted her head back and took in a long breath. "I wanted a baby at one time, but now I'm glad I haven't had one. It makes me different from everybody. I am enough on the outside of what we used to call the 'frozen-chosen world.' It has allowed me to write. To be a little different."

"I know what you mean." I looked her up and down and smiled. "You have a great kitchen."

"It was George's father's house. Before I met George I'd been a broke poet and living in Minneapolis." She moved a lock of red hair away from her pretty face. "Now I'd never live anywhere else. I love Salt Lake. I take walks all year long. It's best in winter. No one is around." She leaned over and kissed my cheek. "You're probably thinking I'm strange with my ramblings. I get a little nervous with you, but I want to be able to tell you things."

"Why don't you just show me?" I tried to play my cowboy stud role. I was disappointed, though, that the house wasn't Meredith's. She had to get a home through having a husband. It felt stolen somehow.

"Here I am." She pulled her dress over her head. "Go ahead and look."

She gazed at me with the same intensity as when I saw her in the bar and she didn't turn away. That was the look I wanted. Her eyes splintered with need. She sat in a white bra and small white under-wear, her pale skin and wide hips as inviting as ever. The snow patch that I wanted to melt.

"You are beyond beautiful."

"Do you think I should leave him?" Her breasts moved slightly as she spoke.

"Have you brought lovers here before?"

She smiled. "What do you think?"

I didn't answer. What did it matter?

I could have stayed like that, staring forever, seeing her sweet flesh exposed in that big movie-set kitchen, but I knew she expected me to do something.

I rubbed her bare shin with the side of my boot. Put my hand on her cold little knee cap. I wanted to give her something real; her desire was so deep and wide. She was not really like snow at all, much more dry and lonely, like the salt flats we passed outside the city.

She walked down the hallway, then sped up the stairs. "Slowpoke."

"Yeah, sure." I downed the rest of my smoothie and then snatched a red apple before running up the stairs.

THE ROOM WAS LARGE, with windows on either side of the bed. Meredith had already turned back the comforter and splayed herself naked on top of blue sheets. I took off my boots, and then despite myself, because I had wanted to take my time, I put down my apple and propped myself right over her.

Her creamy skin sank into the double layer of pillows. She looked expectant and giggled. I asked her to spread her legs. She didn't do it, so I grabbed her wrists and pinned her. She turned passive and it wasn't a game anymore; she closed her eyes, opened her mouth, and drool leaked out. I touched her shoulders, kissed her small light-pink peaked breasts. I spread her hair into wings on the pillow. Her body fell apart under me.

"If you could have anything, what would you want?" I asked.

"That's good." She lifted her belly. "When you touch me, my body shakes. Every bit of me feels electric."

"Yes! The body electric." I rubbed my cheek on her. Nibbled on her lip.

Meredith roused for a moment. "You know Whitman?"

"I used to." I heard a car pull into her driveway. "Is that George?"

"Don't worry." She started to whisper. "I've been thinking about that night in San Francisco. I want that again."

Then I was sure I heard footsteps in the house. "Meredith. Someone's here."

"Don't worry about him. Don't stop." She held me on top of her.

When I looked over my shoulder, George stood at the foot of the bed. He licked his lips.

Meredith clutched me and I stayed on top of her. "He's harmless. Please don't stop."

"Jesus, Meredith. You look good." George took his shirt and shoes off.

"Hey, we're kinda busy here," I said.

Within a minute, he was in bed with us. I rolled off Meredith and wrapped myself in the sheet. George's hand was stroking my head. It must have had lotion on it; it smelled sweet like flowers. Everything slowed down. His breath had marijuana on it, and it made me feel stoned, too.

It was still morning. A clear, childhood-memory type white light came through the window by the bed. I wondered what the hell to do.

Meredith's eyes rolled back in her head—she was past the point of speech. She rocked back and forth and grabbed George's hand so that they were holding hands over my waist. They pushed into me with their hands and knees, pummeling me like cats.

I kept the sheet tight.

"A little threesome," George was saying. His voice was soft and still geeky. But I was afraid that at any moment he would start with some porn-movie dialogue.

When George went to get the rubbers I jumped from the bed and locked the door. I wouldn't let him back in the bedroom. I've had guys turn weird, and I wasn't going to risk it.

He knocked hard.

Meredith yelled back at him. "All right, already."

"Yeah." I took a breath.

"I can't believe this," George called back. "What are you doing?"

I mounted Meredith.

"Fuck me!" she yelled.

"You want to be hurt?" I asked.

"God, yes."

She was hitting the headboard with the top of her head and thrusting her pelvis down on the mattress. I slapped her cheek. She screamed. The red mark on her cheek scared me but I slapped her harder. She tried to struggle away from me, so I pinned her wrists down with one arm held straight and firm. I reached down with my other hand and worked my fingers inside her and then slammed her slimy insides with my whole fist. He could hear us. I pounded harder. Made her scream again. I wanted to slap her again, but I had no more hands at this point, so I got things going faster and harder by punching my hand inside her like a jackhammer.

She was crying and saying things like, "Oh, god, I can't believe this," and "You're so strong," and he was calling from outside the door, "Jesus, please let me inside." I finally joined the chorus and yelled all kinds of raunchy words that spilled from some twisted place. The three of us sounded like we were recording tracks for arias of Latter Day Sinners.

Afterwards, while Meredith took a shower, I sat in the corner on a stool. It took me a long time before I could think. I wanted to get closer to people, not to get into their private anguish vortex. I don't know. If I had gone even further, really bruised her bad, I knew she would have liked it even more, and that made my brain freaky. For a moment there, before George came home, I had felt so close to Meredith, like she was going to open her soul door. I had misread everything.

The hardest thing of all, though, was that my lamebrain had thought they liked me.

I unlocked the door and looked around. I slinked toward the kitchen to get a knife in case timid George turned even more psycho.

Meredith had said some of the Mormons were literally crazy, and maybe her husband was included. I heard him breathe nearby in the hallway, so instead of getting the knife I fled downstairs to my lair and locked the door and put a chair in front of it.

Soon I could hear both of them in the kitchen—the pipes running, a radio playing, feet shuffling. Outside the basement window, everything was still there—the sturdy trees, the big yard, the shadows of peaked turrets on the grass. It didn't comfort me any longer; the place taunted me.

I slept, trying to escape the whole thing. After I woke, I packed my stuff and crept upstairs to the hallway. George looked at me from behind the butcher block. I saluted and clicked my heels. "Hello, George, my man."

"Hi. We're getting some dinner ready here."

I figured he wasn't going to kill me. "Go right ahead."

Meredith was making a pizza, using a premade crust and sprinkling tomato sauce and cheese on top.

As George chopped some garlic, I turned away and left them. I had to do something, and now was a good time, while they were cooking. I crept down the hall and found Meredith's purse on the table near the grandfather clock. I got her wallet, opened it, picked the one bill inside—a twenty. Then I heard a phone ring. When no one appeared, I looked further and found a MasterCard. As Meredith sang along to Natalie Merchant on the radio, and George talked construction jobs on the phone, I stuffed the credit card in my back pocket. Meredith had told me she might help with some money for my trip, so I was letting her make good. I also snatched a photo of a young schoolgirl, somebody special, I guess, because it was old and wrinkled.

I went back in the kitchen.

Meredith turned around. Her hair was pulled back in a ponytail and her eyes were pleading for some kind of understanding. "Well, that was a trip."

"I don't get you guys," I said. "Did you set that up?"

"I'm sorry I came home and interrupted you two. I guess I'm a wee bit lonely sometimes." George checked his cell phone and then put it down. "I'm not really a j-j-jealous man."

"Since when? You talk like we do this all the time." Meredith looked at the floor. "You know I always want more, George. Always more. Oh, it's so endless. Like the Buddhists say, desire brings suffering. Or maybe…it's the opposite. Maybe they got it wrong." She giggled. "You know, maybe it's our suffering that brings desire. A kind of rippling, endless stream of desire."

It sounded like the start of another poem.

"Where's the pizza cutter?" George asked and clucked his tongue. "Oh, here." He set it on the table.

Meredith took the pizza from the oven. She walked over and placed both hands on the back of a dining chair. "Girl, will you eat with us?"

I asked for my pizza to go.

SEVEN TRUTHS I WISH MY MOTHER HAD TAUGHT ME

Don't be afraid to leave; it's the only way to get strong.

Don't settle, and never marry. Love dreams will choke you with tighter hands than loneliness.

Always talk to strangers. They will be the ones who will help you in the end.

If you are a woman, don't tell anybody.

Never want anything you don't have. Look at the sky. It's as big as a dream. Want the sun and sky and you will be okay most of the time.

The body has the sweetest secrets; it's more real than money or religion.

Mothers are always ghosts. So don't go looking for one.

I WALKED AROUND the leafy old Salt Lake neighborhood, got lost, and ended up not knowing what to do next. It was a familiar dizzy feeling. Circles. Round and around. I couldn't stop thinking about Cara, and how things would have been different if I'd gone to look for her in our underground place.

Then at some point I came back to my senses. Realized that Meredith might call the cops when she found out I'd taken her credit card, or drive around and find me. So I broke down and asked a strolling mother the way to downtown.

By the time I left Meredith's coiffed territory, I felt better. I started fantasizing about living in a genuine farmhouse. Randa's land of the prairie started to feel less a dream-hole and closer to real possibiliteee. It was time to stop messing with shake-and-bake poets and get on with my trip. The purpose of it. Randa was my fate, after all.

THE FIRST TIME I MET RANDA I didn't think she was a solid type of person, not at all. I thought she was a maniac. It was when I was back in Redding soon after being arrested the second time for Being Beyond Parental Control. I was only fourteen or so. Randa and I had crossed paths around town a few times; we had some weird ghostly connection.

Cara had been staying with me at my dad's house. She wanted to go back to San Francisco, but I was too depressed to do anything. Up in Redding my eyes always locked closed. We were taking a day to ourselves, had some good drugs, and were looking for people we knew. We stood on Route 99 at the intersection downtown and put our thumbs up as a joke. Randa stopped in a huge green Chevy.

Whatever I thought I was becoming, I saw it in Randa's eyes right away. I sat in the backseat of the big green Chevy, Cara got up front. Randa hooked her sturdy fingers on the bottom of the steering wheel and stretched back as she drove. She had been on a hand crew, she said, and had just finished yesterday fighting a fire near Trinity Center. "A mother of a fire. It spread uphill so fast you'd have thought it was after us."

You could tell how much she needed to talk. And she just kept going.

"We were lucky to have the helicopters. Those grasses are dry. California, I tell you! Not like where I'm from." She rested her hands on the steering wheel in a way that made it clear she was in control, one small rocking movement for each curve of the road. "It was insane. We ended up diving at the embers, trying to catch them."

"Wow," I said. "You caught the fire in your hands?"

"We used mitts."

I could see the side of her cheek, her hair pushed behind her ear.

"God, yesterday I thought I was going to die. And today everything looks so beautiful. You know?" She looked at me in the rearview mirror. "Everything." Her lonely, deep caves of eyes changed as she laughed. She gave a wild guffaw that started as a chuckle and then purred for a while before turning into a roar. Cara looked at me like she thought Randa was whacked. Me, stoned already, thought Randa was from some long-ago era. I thought that maybe she was some country singer. And I hated country music, all those people dancing around like they had crap in their pants.

Eventually, though, as I sat in the backseat, I started getting crushed out. The swing of her hair, the thick ends of her fingers. The way tar-black grease made crescents in her knuckles. She had an outdoors glow—like persimmons and dirt mixed together in a blaze.

The thing I loved most, I have to admit, was her motorcycle. A
sleek black Vulcan Kawasaki cruiser with a low seat and buckhorn
handlebars. It tore right through the Trinity Mountains.

The first time I rode on the back of her Vulcan, I remember how
scared I felt. We stopped at Jerry's Gas, and I went to the restroom
to see if I was still all there. My eyes looked clearer than ever, but I
shook all the way down to my heels. We had ripped down Route 99
so fast that the vibrations wouldn't stop shaking my knees. Later,
when she dropped me off at my dad's house, I couldn't speak and
walked away without looking back.

When I ran into her some months later, a friend had taught me
how to handle a motorcycle. I was ready, and the Vulcan couldn't go
fast enough. I leaned behind her, right into the turns. Nothing else
mattered; I was flying. Even though she wouldn't let me drive it, I
would get so excited when she would drop by. After we rode I felt
just back from heaven.

And then there was the day we lay out in the woods on the Lower
Canyon trail. Sunlight pierced the redwoods in fairy shafts, tall
magenta foxglove with bells of flowers in the shade. We sprawled
over a rise above the creek, ferns around us, deep earth smell, her
head resting on her boots, my bare feet still wet from wading in the
creek and tucked under me. I remember turning to Randa, asking
anything and everything. She sat up, throwing rocks into the water,
opening beer after beer from the cooler pack. So I asked her if she
had done it with women.

"You could say that," answered Randa in a low voice.

She held herself back because she saw me as so young, which
hurt because it meant she saw me as different. After a while, Randa
finally told me about her dyke past. She had drunk so many beers,
she didn't know what she was saying. She told me about some older
butch women in Chicago, where her family had moved after losing
the farm. She made taking her clothes off sound like a humiliation,

and she never forgave the women who made her do it. At one point I wondered if she was going to lift her shirt to show me where her lovers had put in their knives, and how she still had the scars.

The next year, when she and I were both living in San Francisco, I ran into her at the Wild Side West bar. I tried not to think about when she had first met me. How she had gotten mad so often and thought she should take over my life because my dad had failed. I suppose it embarrassed me how young I had been when we met. How stupid.

By then she talked only about how she wanted to move back to Bonesteel, Nebraska. She was convinced that I'd love it on a farm. Still tried to take care of me, like I was an orphan. Had me over to watch Giants ball games and to handle her collection of antique saws and carpenter planes.

When she left, I made sure to keep the phone number she said to call in Nebraska. Kept it tucked around the corkscrew on my pocketknife. It took me a long time to get the nerve to call.

road to bonesteel

NORTHERN NEBRASKA JUMPED with green. The grassy crops sparkled as if the sun had licked each leaf and stalk. Everything needing sun to grow and everything was getting it. It was July and it was hot and it was magnificent.

"What a spread." I had the wheel and hadn't said anything for a while, so I said something lame.

Jessika bounced her colorful body about, as restless as I was to leave the car. "You could say that. I mean it goes on. And on."

I found her at an Apostle Rods hangout in Salt Lake after fleeing Meredith's. Joey had taken up with somebody else, and Jessika was ready to bail. When I suggested going to Randa's farm in Nebraska, and told her I had the plastic to pay, she said let's do it. To get ready for our trip, she chopped off some of her flame-colored hair, and the remainder sprang up like she'd been plugged into an electric socket. With her ragged sparkly blue nails, her big flying body, and her godspeedy old orange Toyota, she was everything I needed.

After we got gas and loaded up on food, maps and stuff, we bought sleeping bags at a nearby sporting goods place. Jessika said she'd always wanted to see Nebraska, and I felt relieved. Her goal was to see as many states as possible before she hit twenty-one.

We used Meredith's MasterCard all the way through Wyoming; at self-service pumps it's no problem to find out if your card is still active. I was surprised we got more than one day out of it. Maybe Meredith let me charge her husband's card on account of guilt, or poetic fantasy, or something. She might have needed to stay connected in some way. I could understand that.

Jessika and I used maps to get our states straight, but otherwise we liked never knowing where we were heading. Things were working out. I might not have my famileee, but at least I had my kooky dancer.

We were on a grid and I could imagine it from a plane, one square after another. *Don't end*, I thought. Nebraska was definitely my favorite place so far.

Jessika pointed to the county road ahead. "Take it. It's getting stranger and stranger. I can't stand it."

I grinned. "Telling me what to do again."

As the flatness took over the horizon, the green came tumbling more and more. I turned off where Jessika wanted.

At the side of the narrow road, wild grasses bent in loose crimson arcs. Harvested hay lay heaped in miles of rows, and piles of corncobs dried in open containers. Dark silos poked high into the sky. Then at last. The first of them. About two feet high. I stopped the car.

Cornfields!

The stalks grew in long bunches. The leaves branched from the base in limp dark green, and at the top, fronds waved around like soft, fuzzy antennas. I wanted to leave the car and walk among them, but fences contained everything. There was no place to go and curl up into it all.

"I feel so empty," I said. "In a good way."

"I know. I get that. It comes over you when you don't expect it." Jessika snapped her gum.

"Zap!"

"Zap!" Jessika sat back. "I like the ways out here. Corn for days and days."

"I know."

Actually I was getting to like Jessika a lot. After all our time in the car together, we finally started to talk. The kind of talk I used to wish for with my granddad, where you said stuff, and you didn't argue, and people listened, so you said more, and no one goes away.

"The person I stayed with in Salt Lake," I said. "She was a joke. She didn't really like me. Some kind of body, though." I drove slower. "I was a fool. She just wanted a little S/M stud muffin."

Jessika stroked my arm. "You're such an innocent. What was it really about her?"

"What do you mean?" It felt like Jessika and I were alone in the world and everybody else had vanished. "Sometimes it hurts that I love bodies so much, cause everything else is messed up." I wondered if I could feel close to Jessika without fucking her.

"Oh, I despise people's bodies." She paused. "It's weird, but dancing gives me a chance to forget. Forget about bodies, I mean."

"Yeah?" I said. "When I was younger I thought sex made magic and would take away my skin so that I could forget about myself, stop thinking and worrying. And then I could be lo-o-oved forever. I didn't know anything. I was stupid." Jessika was really listening to me, so I kept talking. "I thought wishes made in someone else's body would stay there and come true. Now I know they disappear. Zap!"

"Wow. Zap."

"It's like your dancing. There is no record. Everything goes away."

"I don't know if I ever wished for something when I was with a guy. Maybe I wanted to feel *nothing*. That's good sometimes. A really good wish."

The car moved like a drifting raft. I drove even slower. "Not really."

Jessika stared at me for a while. "You have this hard look, but your face is round like a little kid's. I could see why people go after you. You give off these twisted looks and wear these torn-up clothes and have these deep, deep-set eyes. People probably think they can scavenge some secret from you."

"Not you, though."

"Well, you know. I just want to save your soul." She whooped. "My big fat mission in life."

"I know what you mean. That's what I'm trying to do."

"What?"

"Save my soul."

I SUPPOSE MY GRANDDAD had wanted to save my soul, but it never really worked.

I must have been at least twelve. We sat outside in the patio area of the McDonald's in Redding. When he drove me back to my dad's, I always made him stop on the way. My dad had custody, and I was only seeing my granddad occasionally. He wore one of the white T-shirts that showed his big arms.

"You've got to realize it was bad times." His voice got a little higher when he tried to get his point across.

I ate another few bites of my True-Happiness Meal. When the people next to us left, I replied, "So, that explains everything." I handed him one of my napkins to sop up the mustard dripping down his chin.

"Gretchen, my Gretchen. People act as a result of so many factors—their genetic code, their culture, social pressures. You've got to realize that when it came down, Reagan had just been elected. A lot of people were depressed. I sure was. It was not a shining moment."

"Did my mom care about who was president? Wasn't she a Jesus freak or something?"

He slurped his extra-large Pepsi. "I don't know. I'm just saying it was awfully weird times. Take that in as part of the picture. We aren't only individuals. People manifest their historical moment."

Kids were yelling and sliding down a big colorful tube in the fast-food playground pen.

"Reagan's election doesn't explain why she did it."

He finished his last bite of burger. "Oh, hell. When I think back, even I wanted to shoot my brains out when he was elected. It seemed the end of the world. Really. Here was the Hollywood actor, a reactionary buffoon, suddenly in control. He wanted more nuclear power, pumped up the military budget, it was intense. Star Wars, and the weapons he got going. The start of an evil era." He sighed and furrowed his brow with his oh-so-serious look. "We may be still in it, really. And these things affect us. At some point most people will think about killing themselves."

"Yeah, sure." I stood. "You think so?" I wanted him to tell me more about why she did it. But he never would. All I knew is she had been part of some religious group for a while. I could never find out the details. He'd just keep taunting me with long political lectures. He hated recounting personal memories, about Oregon where he came from, or anything from our past. And especially about my mom. He discounted that, said it didn't matter. We had to look forward, he thought, not back. He had a point, but maybe he took it too far.

"Okay, we'll talk about this. Sit back down. Don't crook a snook about it." He finally wiped his chin. "Let me say this. On the other hand, just because a person thinks about doing it doesn't mean they have to do it."

"So, why did she do it?"

"She was overwhelmed, I guess. Unhappy. I think she felt lonely in San Francisco, and your dad didn't help. She was young and dramatic. Had some hyperactive demons inside her, like we all do."

I needed to know how she felt about me, but he would never tell me that. "Didn't having a baby make her feel less lonely?"

"It was bad times."

"But you admit that Reagan didn't make her do it?"

"No. Damn it." He shoved his food tray down the bench. "You want to be like your father? Jesus. You're being a goddamn lawyer with me. *I don't know why she did it, okay?*"

I kicked the table leg. "Well, you must wonder."

"Don't you get it, child? Calm down. Think a little. I'm trying to give you some historical context. No one studies the basic facts anymore—even you, smarty thing, you don't respect social context. We are products of our culture. It's that simple. We don't always determine the path of our own lives. Some things are way, way beyond us. They push us in ways we can't control. It's the truth, Gretchen. I want you to know the truth. It will help you accept things. Make things easier for you. Might even make you happy."

I stared at him and didn't blink. "Are you?"

"What? Happy?"

"Going to kill yourself?"

"No. *No.* It would be pointless. You know me, the optimistic dodo." He hung his head down, lifted his elbows, dangled his forearms, doing the broken-winged bird act that he used to do when I was little. "Hold fast to dreams!"

It made me sad seeing him do that again after so long. I'd forgotten our old poem-game. I gathered the unused mustard packages, put them in my pocket, and waited by the car.

"SOMETIMES I WANT TO SCREAM when I see the sun go down." It was late in the day, and Jessika had most of her head out the window.

"It's escaping us." Down down down. I knew this. "Is it because, in some way, you're not sure if it's ever going to come back?"

"Fucking exactly. That's it. I never knew why. That's it. That's it!"

"Nothing we can do to stop it."

She leaned further out the window and gave her war cry. "You ain't going down. You ain't going down tonight."

"You remind me of a friend I had. This girl Cara." She wasn't like Cara at all, I just said it.

"Oh, sometimes I cry when a sunset goes off. I call it having a *So Really Much*."

I wondered if she did cry about the colors in the sky or if she was making it up. What if I believed these things she said but she was just putting them on like a costume? It made me feel lonely that I always wondered if people were real.

I pulled the car to the side of the road. "Do you like doing lap dances?" I kinda whispered it.

"Why?"

"Because I want you to shut up about the sky."

"Get over yourself. I'm not even into girls."

"Kiss me."

"Bad girl." Jessika slapped the seat with her large, ringed fingers.

Then she leaned over and gave me a big tongue kiss. "Come on, get on the road."

AFTER WE FILLED our tank at the next gas station, I told her we couldn't use the card again.

"Why not?"

I got another piece of gum and stuck it in her mouth. "I don't know." Meredith was bound to notice the card missing or get tired of giving me a free ride. I pulled the credit card from my pouch. The photo was in there too, the one I had taken from Meredith's wallet. I left it alone for now. Using the tiny scissors on my pocketknife, I sawed the card in two halves and threw them out the window. I had to rely on good luck now, so I took my arrowhead and placed it on the dash.

"You! My Secret Agent Girl! You are freakin' insane." She closed her eyes and smiled.

We rode a long time more. The clouds turned orange and lavender and I ached from somewhere I couldn't name. I knew Jessika came from a real family. There was something careless about her, as if she'd had things taken care of in the early days and now was just playing. She was so pretty and gigantica and godspeedy and jeweled, and I felt slow and subhuman. My deep slits of eyes felt like cracks in old cement.

At some point the sun dropped so hard and fast that we had to think about where to sleep.

"What about here?" said Jessika.

"We better find a town with some food." I felt tired of seeing everything from a window. I was sick of being trapped inside, and I was sick of not being close to the land we drove through. After a while, even the beyouteefull places became a distant, untouchable blur. It wasn't real.

I wasn't sure where we would sleep. Not smack in a farmer's field. The farms were big and flat, so our car would stand out for miles. And it was all fenced, so there was no little nook or dale or bluff or grandmother's woods or anything. I took another county road, another number not on any map, and we headed further away from the falling sun.

mars

AT LAST I FOUND US a town and we parked near the Pizza Dog Heaven Café. Jessika scooped up her spotted leopard purse, I got my blue carrybag, we each tucked a sleeping bag under an arm, and we were finally out in the air. We walked by the Swinging Doors Lounge and a tiny American Legion Hall. I was a little dizzy and plucked-out inside from not eating, but I had to get to know the land around us. It couldn't be just a view from the car anymore.

Jessika came along behind me. She could keep a pretty good pace even with her leg. In a couple of minutes we were out of town. Without talking, I crossed over to another old county road. Number 54.

We had talked a lot of wild stuff on our trip, but now, finally, we were talked out. We walked for about fifteen minutes, until I saw Jessika really dragging herself. I stopped. The fields were still except for one thing: a machine rolling across a cornfield and getting closer.

A monster machine blew something from a funnel at its rear. It traveled in a straight line away from the horizon and toward us. We hid our sleeping bags in the drainage ditch and watched.

The summer twilight lasted forever. It smelled like hay, and I knew it would be beyouteefull to sleep in the fields. People had been telling us that it was usually hotter by the beginning of July, but it seemed plenty hot to me, just right really.

We waited for the huge tractor-thing to come face us. Glass enclosed the driver, and we saw only a strange, blue reflection where he must be sitting. As the machine crawled closer it paused at the edge of the row, rose a few feet and hovered, exposing the parts underneath—like a robot insect showing its legs. We waved. A human being appeared, tilting from the enclosure, poking out an arm and a head. An old guy with headphones and a cigarette stuck in his mouth. His robot-arm saluted, slow and steady. Then his machine turned and left.

Free from the spell, we shook our heads and howled.

We explored a little further. Hopped a fence. Landed in a wet gully, a tiny bit of leftover land, too rocky to be plowed. Careful not to sink in the slush, we chose a dry place to lie back. Because we were on fallen ground, no one could see us from the road. We used our sleeping bags as pillows.

"It's still making violet." Jessika hummed. "A *So Really Much*."

"Yeah."

She rocked her torso back and forth. Hummed louder. "I say dings and more dings and I don't know what's coming out dah my big mouth." She laughed. "See, Joey's voice."

A couple of red-winged blackbirds flew onto the power line across the road.

"Muddafucca," I said, imitating Joey, too.

"I do things and don't realize I'm doing them." She flicked her fingers. "Am I moving right now? Is that me or something else? Is it something inside me exploding that I have nothing to do with?" She stretched her arms as far as she could, made fists, and pulled them down to pound the middleplace of her chest. "I'm not in control. I should be, but I'm not. I have a real problem sometimes. Sometimes I wonder if anybody notices."

"I wouldn't worry." I placed my hand where she had pounded and rubbed the spot gently.

In the last of daylight, her balloon-colored clothes dimmed into pale shimmers, and she seemed more dreamy outline than real person.

The blackbirds flew from the power line and disappeared into the darkening sky.

"This is stupid. I wanna fly," said Jessika. "Flap, flap. It would be *incredible*. Go straight up and never come down."

"Be gone, gravity, huh?"

I lay in the weeds and looked up. Imagined Jessika doing a warrior dance in the sky. I imagined her dancing just for me.

I felt content to listen and watch. So content that I passed on the cannabis that she offered. I decided, as I had many times before, that I didn't need sluggy drugs.

I watched her arms and cheeks and skin mix with the streams of smoke she blew. The violet dusk caught her plume of hair to give it a crowning glow. I could understand her need to fly. Maybe it either belonged to you or didn't. I longed to help her and keep her close at the same time.

I didn't know how.

No roof. No cars. No guys. A girl stretching her arms into the sky, a girl I liked a lot. The hot pressured colors of her presence exploded and smeared around in a sad kind of way. I knew even if we made it to Randa's, Jessika would soon fade away and I would leave for my next place. Zap! And that was the truth. It wasn't some spacey Cara theory. Just the truth.

I put my arrowhead on my belly and closed my eyes and wondered what it would feel like to be old and solid, to feel part of the warm earth. To feel like nothing could ever come and crash my life into pieces. Somehow I had to make my longings into something real. Maybe then, and only then, I wouldn't have to disappear like my mom.

"RANDA, IT'S A GIRL," I would say.

"God darn now!" she'd say.

I could see the big farm-dueling boots, the beer in her hand. Randa's voice would flood through the telephone wire—the rumbling, echoing, make-my-day laugh. I'd make her guess where I was and she wouldn't believe I had found my way out here. "I'm really here," I'd say.

She'd say, "I miss you, Girl. I want you to know."

Then I'd be silent. And she would speak again.

"I'm sorry, Girl. I'm sorry I didn't take care of you. But I've got my head together now. It's going to be okay."

I don't know why she apologized in my fantasy, but that's the way it went.

THE PIZZA DOG HEAVEN CAFÉ was the largest building in Mars, and empty except for two girls drinking Cokes in the corner. Jessika and I sat near the huge windows, almost on top of the highway. We'd left our sleeping bags and packs hidden in the field and come back to town to get some food.

One of the high school kids asked if we were in a band.

"She plays guitar." Jessika jackhammered her platform shoe into the floor; her own private drum-roll. "And I'm a Hollywood actress."

"I was in California once and saw the Hollywood sign." The girl who spoke bounced in her seat and her strawberry hair bobbed against her cheeks. We found out her name was Melanie.

"I like your tattoo," said the other girl, called Bo. Black eyeliner oozed from her eyes and her emaciated body was draped in a T-shirt that said OMAHA SKILLET-THROW. My type of kid.

"Don't listen to Jessika. She's in fantasyland. I look the way I do cause I don't want to be part of your regular american world," I said. "Hey, Bo. Try to put something over on me."

"What do you mean?" She and Melanie came and sat at our booth.

"I mean, you can't."

The girls liked that a lot.

The fleshy waitress nodded at everything and smiled, hovering at the edge of our table. She was big as a pile of pillows, and starved for company. Her white shirt was stuffed down in front but hung out in back. I let her run her hand over my mane and examine my dragon tattoo.

Feeling tired of being on display, and tired of our long night-day-night of traveling, I went to the phone near the restroom and called my granddad collect. He wasn't around. So I took my pocketknife, unwrapped the paper around the corkscrew, and called the number.

Some older woman answered who I figured might be a Randa relative. Except her family was supposed to be in Chicago. Whoever it was said Randa wasn't there.

"But she is in Nebraska?"

"Oh, no. She's in Chicago with her mother. But she'll be back in town by the Fourth of July." There was a pause. "Would you like me to take a scrawl?"

"A message? Tell her Girl is coming to town."

"Coming here? When might that be? We are taking off for the Fourth, of course."

"I'll be there soon. Soon as I can get there. Thanks."

WHEN I SAT BACK DOWN, the kids asked where I was from. I told them San Francisco. They couldn't hide their glee.

"Everyone here hates us. We aren't part of anything you could call regular," said Melanie, the cute one.

Bo, the ghost, said everyone in town called them the druggies. We asked if there were any farmers around and they said there weren't many. Everyone worked in the Blue Basket factory making Caramel Fudge Bomb-Pops.

"What about these fields?" I asked. "These tower-things with corn in them? Somebody has to be doing the work."

"It's all done by machines." They laughed in a deep, bitter way, like I could imagine their parents doing.

"What about that?" I said to Jessika. "Here we are in Nebraska, the All-American Heartland."

"Woof, woof." They turned their hands into limp paws and rolled their tongues to the sides of their mouths.

"Woof," I said joining in their private joke for the hell of it.

Jessika flattened her drinking straw with her back teeth, chewing further and further, till I thought she would choke. "Come on? Really? Where's the farmer's daughters?"

"Well, yeah," said Bo. "If we went to San Francisco, people there would think we were all farmers." She jutted her chin out over the table. "I'd say screw you." The girls smirked as if they had won my challenge and gotten one over on us.

"Well, you think we're all a bunch of queers, right?" I said.

"No, no. Not at all." Their eyes got big and respectful.

Jessika howled. "All right then. Do you have anything?" Jessika looked at Bo. "I want to get iced."

They went to the bathroom and did who knows what. I munched my curling grease-cup of a hamburger. Melanie smoked. She was desperate to know about my scene but didn't want to seem too curious.

When they came back Jessika's eyes and skin were lit with energy and she wouldn't stop talking about Sioux City and how she would get a job there. Sioux City was all the way in Iowa, but she said it wasn't much further than Bonesteel, right on the border of Nebraska and Iowa and South Dakota, where the rivers meet. This was the first I'd heard about her plan. We were supposed to be heading straight to Randa's farm.

Jessika said Joey had a friend who could get her a job stripping.

"Taking your clothes off?" said Bo.

"Why not?"

"So you want men to look at you?" I said.

Jessika shook the ice in my water glass and took some out and licked it. "Why not? We need the money."

"What about Jesus?" I asked.

The girls laughed, thinking I was the religious one and pulling the christian card on the table.

"Jesus can look, too!" Bo and Melanie pounded the table so hard that the silverware shook.

"Jesus Freaks A Go-go," I joined in. "Fifty bucks and we will pray for you. Down on your knees!"

"Scum. Go to hell and rot!" Jessika trotted out of the restaurant, leaving her little leopard-spotted purse to glower at me.

"Your friend split?" Melanie said. "Sorry."

Bo hung her head down and drew a skull with horns on her place mat. Her nose was running, and she was definitely high.

I told them I'd insulted Jessika and should probably go apologize. "Would you watch our stuff?" I asked. They smirked and said it wasn't the kind of thing you had to worry about in Mars. No one even locked their cars.

"Mars is a vicious name for a town. You guys are lucky. After all, you could be stuck on Earth somewhere."

"Yeah, right," said Bo, the skin-and-bones alien. "Ha ha."

IT WAS JUST ABOUT DARK in the sweltering parking lot. The truck lights sped over the highway like bright bugs trying to escape.

"Maybe you should let me take care of you," I said to Jessika. "You could take it easy. I'll work on Randa's farm and get money for both of us. Then we could take off somewhere else."

"Don't bother, okay?" Jessika paced as best she could. "I have to do things in my own way. No one ever understands."

She seemed so proud and defiant, and it was making me mad. "You think you know everything."

"I don't know anything more than you."

"I guess you don't want to go to the farm with me," I said. "Unless you still want to save my soul?"

A car pulled into the parking lot and an older couple emerged. They didn't look over, just wobbled into the diner.

"I should keep my mouth shut," said Jessika. "No one ever understands me anyway, so sometimes I just say things. But you, muddafucca, you had to listen."

"I like listening."

"Well, don't."

I let her stew for a bit while I kicked the gravel. "I thought christians felt they were better than everybody. I didn't know it could be just one more thing, something real, but messed up."

"Yeah. I am one mess of a wasted christian."

I looked back in the diner. The kids were dragging hard on cig-arettes, keeping their faces bored, sneaking glances our way. I want-ed them to enjoy being kids while they could, enjoy getting cooked for and having their rent paid and their choices made. Instead, here they were drugging themselves and holding on to a big tangle of nowhere. Shit. Just like home. Why did kids get so caught up in being stupid?

"I'll always listen to you." I put my arm around Jessika's waist. "At least you try to believe in something. You're kind of like how my granddad used to be. Only he wasn't a christian. He wanted to have faith in things and tell people his ideas. Like you. I mean, I think. Unless you're lying to me."

"You're the one that lies all the time. Don't put that on me. Like you said that credit card was okay." Jessika sniffed and rubbed her nose. "You're so innocent and so amazingly twisted at the same time. I can't figure you out."

I kissed Jessika, right in the center of her broad warrior chest.

She cried a little while she drilled her chin round and round into the top of my head.

WHAT THEY CALLED "THE PIT" was a man-made pond in a sorry little park that was a short walk from Pizza Dog Heaven. Since all of town filled two blocks, I wondered where they hid the Blue Basket ice cream factory. We walked into the parking lot, where a few beat-up cars circled the edge of the park. Some flabby, sweating boys sat on their engine hoods. A cop drove in at the same moment we arrived.

"It's the pigs," Bo mumbled.

Pigs. That was what my grandfather used to say.

"Yeah, Five-O." Melanie turned around. "I got to leave." Her little cupcake breasts and strawberry hair disappeared into the dark.

Jessika was restless. She fidgeted with her nose ring and stamped her big platform sneaker into the ground.

When the studly cop came over, Jessika started smiling. "Hey, officer, I'm new in town."

I crept away with Bo. The last thing I needed was a conversation with an officer about my whereabouts.

Bo knocked on a car windshield. A guy without a shirt named Curly had his bare back pressed against the passenger window. I was nervous and asked Bo if we could get in the car. We stuffed inside with the guys. Bo giggled.

Curly turned around from the front seat and gave me a lazy smile. He was mountainous with flesh, enormous shoulders and belly and cheeks. Long Indian black hair flowed down his back.

"Need anything at all, just call me." He wrote down his number on a piece of paper cup. "I'm the mayor of Mars."

"Mucho thanks." I gestured to Bo that I wanted to leave the stuffy car. At last she got the message when I put my finger against my head to shoot myself.

Bo asked Curly to tell Jessika we went to look at the swan babies.

We took some cement stairs that led far down into the pit. The girls had told us earlier about some new swan ducklings; one of the highlights of their summer. Bo and I walked around the pond, through bushes and trees, looking for them. Most of the pond was dark and out of view of the cars, but portions were lit bright from huge fluorescent lights.

As she shuffled along, Bo hunched her shoulders way over so her stringy hair fell forward and covered her forearms. Her chest was concave, scooped out like a ditch. She told me in her gravely voice that years ago she had seen an eight-year-old boy named

Zachary get pulled from the pond after drowning.

"His body was bloated with water and his eyes were open."

"Yeah? So what?" I hated death stories. "Do you ever want to leave here?"

"I wouldn't know anybody anywhere else."

"Why don't you come to the farm in Bonesteel? You'd know me."

The park's tall trees and spotlights now circled around us. Distant sounds of boys' grunting and a wailing radio guitar came from above.

Bo didn't say anything about my offer.

Something moved in the center of the pit. "So you're going to stay forever in Mars?"

She shrugged. "Look!"

A swan flashed by in the murk, her crooked neck guiding her ducklings, small as flowers. They disappeared around a marshy bend.

"Let me know if you ever want to leave." I tried to tickle her.

"You're weird." She moved away and kicked a rock into the water. "I'm spinning, man."

The orange electric lights surrounding the pond made the whole place seem a bit like a morgue. The swans were little god gifts, but everything else was pretty close to a horror movie. I couldn't imagine the kids coming here night after night, then going on after high school to work at Blue Basket, and that's that.

Bo chose that moment to tell me she felt like puking.

"Lie down and be still. Breathe normal." I tried to see if she could still hear me. "You'll be all right."

At the edge of the pond, she curled in a ball near my feet. I pointed to the wings of Cygnus the Swan. Then showed her the bright golden star of Arcturus, one of my favorites.

After a long silence, Bo sat up. "Those starfires are thousands of light years away and are already dead." She dug both hands into the dirt at the edge of the pond. "We just see their light. But it's not really there, right?"

I could see her spending her whole life feeling lonely without even knowing why. "Yep. The stars are going to die some day, just like you and me and everybody else." I splashed my hand in the water. "Sneaky death will come and find us all. Big and dark. A creeping thump, thump, thump."

Jessika and I had left our sleeping bags in the field. Now I wondered if we would even find them in the dark. And if we could ever get out of here with the cop hanging around.

What I wanted to say to Bo, but didn't know how, was that even though most of the stars are probably long gone, I liked knowing their names. The names were a way of having a memory of something, even if it wasn't around anymore.

"All right!" Bo yelled. She stood, suddenly sober. "I'm going swimming."

"That would feel good!" I threw off my pants, left on my T-shirt and underwear, and ran in.

Bo kept on her clothes. She raised her arms like Frankenstein and lurched into the water. She giggled as the weight of her heavy jeans sloshed against the marshy weeds.

My feet sank into the soft mud, and I slapped my arms against the glaring orange reflections on the water. Just a little farther and I was in up to my neck, and no more bottom. I sidestroked to the center. "Betcha can't get me." Being in the pit was the first time I'd felt cool in days. I turned on my back and floated.

Jessika stood at the top of the stairs, a long cement row of them. "Hey, baby baby." Galloping down the steps to us, she dropped her strong leg first, then plunged her other leg to meet it. Her arms pumped in jogging motions. Jessika's own stumbling, private dance channel. None of her moves were what anybody else would do.

"Don't let them hear you," said Bo. "I hope you told Curly not to come down."

"He's gone. Mr. Nice Man in the Uniform told them to leave."

"Oh, they're around. I can hear them."

Music still wailed from somewhere in the dark fields.

Jessika took off everything but her scarlet bra and lavender underwear and got in. We splashed one another near the willow trees on the far side of the pond, hidden from the stairs and parking lot.

Bo and Jessika played games, climbing on top of each other. I swam around and floated in the cool relief.

When Jessika slipped and fell from a rock, Bo asked about her leg.

"I was born with it. God gave it to me."

"That's cool." Bo pulled her T-shirt away from her concave chest. Eyeliner dripped down her cheeks. A real Goth maiden.

"I was just thinking about that," I said. "God's gifts."

Jessika climbed onto Bo's back again.

Maybe this was all I wanted. Us three female-beings bobbing around a pond in the town of Mars, with the swans loose, and the stars high.

Glory Be on Us Freaks.

I walked deeper. Dug my toes further into the velvet mud. Hoped the boys wouldn't come.

Sioux City

TWO O'CLOCK IN THE AFTERNOON and the place was packed. A big room with lots of stages. Jessika slowly took off her top. Her chest gleamed like armor, invincible after so much gazing. Pudgy and perky, her breasts were smaller than the other dancers' silicone missiles. She was also thicker in the legs and belly and had scrapes on her knees, but her tranced-out belief in her own private dance-channel glory made her magnetic.

The men gave her dollar bills to hang from her skirt. It was hard for me to see her share her priestess powers. I wanted to do something like spit on the floor, show the men not to mess with her. But none of them looked my way. They were hypnotized.

The worst was when Jessika did a special dance for a big tipper.

Under the bright clown lights, she made a creepy, little-girl pouting face. She stroked her rear, and did a fast hip-grinding thing to the blood-curdling music. The men drooled over the whole cripple thing, which was too weird. It was a summer day in the prairie and here I was in the dark with scores of panting hogs. They couldn't help themselves; they had to get fed. But knowing this didn't make me feel any better.

When we couldn't get a hold of Randa on the phone, Jessika had insisted we forget about the farm and go to Sioux City. I hadn't wanted to come, but I didn't know where else to go. I felt invisible, just one more watcher. After sitting with the crowd as long as I could bear it, I escaped to the parking lot.

The lot was set up in the back to keep the townsfolk from seeing the parked cars. One car was really fine, an ancient Dodge with lots of rust and character. When I saw it had the keys in it, it just seemed too easy.

After getting my stuff from Jessika's dressing room, I looked around the lot again. State lines are magic when it comes to warrants. Once I left Iowa and crossed the border, the police wouldn't bother with or even receive a bulletin for a stolen car. And the owner of the Dodge must have been some old lurker watching Jessika. This was the cost for seeing her dance. The cost for getting a look at her bare statuesque being. One fine car.

DINNER IN PARADISE

It would be in a really faraway place, near a waterfall. Some tropical island with palm trees and smoking volcanoes.

We split coconuts and fork whole fish and slurp mango-banana crèmes. Yes! My mom's long ghost hair falls to her waist, and plumerias circle her neck. She wears bracelets with charms, and they chime as she picks up her drink. Ghost tattoos cover my sun-kissed island body. I whisper every question I ever had, and she answers in slow lava murmurs. Or better yet I won't have to ask. She answers each unspoken question with a story about the world before I was born.

THE DODGE WAS FUN. Definitely from the don't-fuck-with-me sixties. A solid, cast-iron, slant-six engine and goofy push-button controls for the automatic gears. I took the highway straight west from Sioux City and back into Nebraska. Then veered onto a small road alongside the Niobrara River. I hoped my half tank of gas would last.

After I made some real money on Randa's farm, I would go back and get Jessika. Rescue her from the panting men waiting for their main meal, their naked-woman gruel.

To the blast of country music, I stuck my head out of the window and yelled into the liquid blue, my own swim-ocean. Red barns sailed against the super-size skies. Yes! I took a parallel offshoot, the road fissured in so many places it looked like the puzzle-piece bark of a tree trunk. Fences marked every stretch of land. Long soft green fields in the sun. Big towers. Houses set way back. No people. I wanted into the center of this open space, the exploding blast of color.

The wind rippled the grassy fields; the movement, like waves crashing.

"Come on," I yelled. "Come on."

Randa had told me about the Great Plains. A long time ago, she said, the middle of the country had been true prairie, meaning wild and unbroken. So when I saw a sign outside Bonesteel—WILD PRAIRIE PRESERVE 2 MILES—I made a quick turn and followed the rough road. It led me to a piece of land marked like an exhibit. It was wild grass, and they had to save it like whales.

Enormous bright puffy clouds covered the late afternoon blue sky, just like in the movies. I parked my car and walked along the road. Had Randa, her mother, or her mother's mother ever walked nearby?

A man pulled alongside in a white pickup and stopped in the center of the road. It seemed funny, meeting out in the middle of nothing, like lost boats in a big ocean. He was freckled and his head fell to one side.

"That your automobile?" His voice surprised me, it didn't fit the calm around us, but sounded cartoon-like, dubbed onto his freckled face by a bad technician.

When I said yes, he nodded. "Stretching your legs?"

I told him I had relatives from here, and if he didn't mind, I'd keep watching the clouds. He stayed for a little and then left.

bonesteel

THE TOWN HAD FOURTEEN AVENUES and twenty-six streets, most named with numbers. I passed the fairgrounds, a high school, an Elks Club, an old library, some historical markers, and several signs on Central Avenue that pointed the way to a museum.

When I stopped at the Food and Fuel, Freckle Face was sitting on an aluminum chair outside the gas station store. I didn't want to deal with him, so I parked and scavenged some change from the glove box and floor boards. At the pay phone, I punched in Randa's number. When there was no answer, I called my granddad collect.

"Hey, Grand Papa."

"Where are you? You're not arrested again?"

"I'm at a gas station in Northeastern Nebraska. Just calling to say howdy."

Freckle Face walked closer so he could hear everything I was saying. That pissed me off. I hung up.

"You going to keep staring?"

He kept staring. I went in the store to buy a soda. Freckle Face followed.

"He giving you trouble?" asked a tall skinny man, grinning.

"Kinda."

"Like the hair."

I bought some orange soda and a bottle of water and told the storekeeper I was a friend of Randa Franklin.

He was grinning. "I'll be damned."

"She's pulling your chain, Floyd," said Freckle Face.

"Maybe," Floyd said.

"Darn right."

"She's the wildest chicken who's ever flown into my coop." Floyd shook his head and stared at my tattoo.

The two men spoke about some Franklins who once lived in town—I hadn't thought they'd know Randa's family since her folks had left a long time ago. Then they asked me about myself.

I told them my name was Girl.

"Just that?"

"Just that."

"Well that ugly-looking man is Elmer, and I'm Floyd."

"Randa's coming back to town tomorrow," said Elmer. "I think she'll be back out country with Irma and Flint for Independence Day supper."

"I've never been in a small town, you know, seen any old farming stuff." My voice started to twang a little. This was fun. "Maybe I'll check things out while I'm here. Go to your museum."

"Farming, huh? You want to know about it?" Floyd smacked his lips. "Mrs. Dottie, Irma's mother, she'll talk to you. Her family was one of the first to settle here."

Floyd called Dottie on the phone, but there was no answer. "I'll try again later."

"I'll tell you, sir," I felt my voice slowing down even more, getting into Floyd's way of speaking. "Don't bother. I'll just be on my way." Then I couldn't resist asking one question. "So, do you know, sir, if Randa is, well, settling in Bonesteel?"

"I don't know. Is that what you hear, Elmer?"

"That's what I hear. I'll tell you what. Go down and talk to the elderly fellow at the museum." Elmer nodded. "You go down there and you'll learn a lot about Bonesteel."

"Yes, and come on back later," said Floyd. "We'll take you over to Mrs. Dottie."

A SEARS ROEBUCK–TYPE DUMMY from the fifties with bright orange nail polish on her rubber lady hands sat in a glass cage marked PIONEER. Old silver brushes, pairs of eyeglasses, and washboards lay around her in cramped displays. The heavy coats of paint, the lifeless dioramas, the glass knobs on the cabinets, and the musty pipe smell made me remember my kindergarten classroom. It smelled just like that, creepy and glue-filled.

A tall stooped man in short sleeves came over when I stood at an illustration of a tractor.

"Howdy," I said.

"See you found something."

The guy must have been near eighty. His nose was big and red, like it hadn't wanted to stop growing. I asked him about the picture of the big machine. It had huge wheels with blades and a storage bin.

"That's a combine." He whistled. "Around out back we have a whole barn of farm equipment." He raised his eyebrows and teetered from foot to foot, like a friendly giant.

After some trouble with the key, the old man finally unlocked the padlock. "Always showed the fellows before. Never a young lady. You aren't a boy, are you?"

"No, sir."

"Yep. I knew that." He smiled at the ceiling.

Sticky cobwebs clung to old metal parts, tractors, buckets of tools. The air was dry and earthy smelling. I picked up a rusted horse bit on the table in front of us. "Do you know who owned this?"

"Couldn't tell you about most of it." He wouldn't look me in the eye.

"What's this thing?" I raised a wooden handle of a long pointed beak.

He told me it was a plow, and I asked what it did.

"Well. That gets things ready."

Randa would have been in heaven here, I thought. She loved old tools, went to flea markets to buy antique saws and planes. I asked him if he knew her. Said he knew a Bill that had a fiancée named Franklin, was that the one?

"A fiancée?" This was news.

The old man walked farther back into the barn and the equipment got bigger. A machine with a shark-jaw in the shape of a W. Behind it, a car-sized mower had a paddle wheel twice my height; the cutting blades stuck out, low to the ground, about five feet of teeth. He let me climb on an old tractor.

"Didn't use padding on the seats till the '40s." He smiled at the ground.

I sat on the high-seated tractor and kicked it like it was my horse.

"I never was a farmer. I was a surveyor." He rubbed the wrinkled skin on his forearm with his other hand. "Looks like you might take to it, though. Never did see a gal so interested in the stuff."

"Everything in here had a purpose."

"Ye-es." He said the word in two parts, starting low and then ending high in a question.

"Do you ever wish the old tractors could talk?"

"All the time." He moved his tongue around in his mouth. "May I ask where you are from?"

"California."

He kicked the tire of the tractor. "Always in a hurry then."

"I'd stay here all afternoon if I knew what to ask." I laughed.

"Ye-es. Some old farmers have come by, though." He still wouldn't look at me, but there was a fiendish pleasure under his words; he had nabbed a passing stranger and kept her by his side for a while.

"The farmers know about all this?"

"They like it here. A couple of 'em have explained, told me about every last thing in here. Just like you said, everything had a purpose. Ye-es, ma'am, it all had a purpose."

Before I knew it I was sitting around having milk and home-baked Norwegian cookies with the old man and some doddering ladies gathered in the back room, the library of the museum. It was as if people thought they owed me something because I was a visitor. In San Francisco people come and go; no one cares. Here it was like I had beamed down from outer space.

Floyd and Elmer came over from the gas station and found me with the old folks, but I told them I had to get going.

"Always in a rush." The old museum guy offered me another sugar cookie.

I took it. "Thanks a lot."

Floyd and Elmer asked again if I wanted to talk to Mrs. Dottie, the old time farm person. I told them another time.

I SPENT THE NIGHT in the wild prairie preserve.

I hid my Dodge as far back from the road as I could. Other cars might be newer, but it had more soul, and I was happy I had taken it from the lurker panting over Jessika in the topless bar. He must have reported it by now, though.

Before sleeping I took some time to clean my underarms and brush my teeth. I felt restored and lay back on my sleeping bag, stretched over the tall grasses, thick as a mattress. It was fiercely hot and that helped me from hunger panging. I was getting to like the feel of the thick sweltering air, a warm, drowning flood of night. My only choice was to sink in deep and final. I hugged my carrybag on top of my chest and pretended it was my old stuffed animal, Flopsy. The crickets and locusts chattered. I wasn't really alone.

Away from the lights of town and with no moon out, the Milky Way was thick and dense. Millions of stars filled every patch of darkness. So many that I couldn't find the familiar ones. If Bo had been by my side, I could have pointed to at least fifty shooting stars.

THE HIGHWAY WENT ON AND ON as it does until at last stood a group of tiny people circling a picnic table in the distant heat. I pulled alongside the cornfields onto a long gravel road and drove to the only solid thing around, an odd lean-to suburban house, looking as if it had flown in on a cyclone. And there she was. In silhouette, the sun behind her, arm stuck high, waving. I could imagine a big sharp scythe in her hand, like some heroic action figure. Randa the corn-slayer, bloody husks at her feet.

She hollered when I leaned out from the window. I cut the engine and jumped from the car.

"You came to me!" A smile lit Randa's face.

"Couldn't resist." I laughed. Her blaze of tanned persimmon skin fit here in the dirt and sun and sky. She was the first thing I'd seen that seemed to belong among the amber waves of grain in the great big middle.

Randa opened a beer at the picnic table. "You of age yet?"

I grabbed it. Took a lovely cold swig and nodded at everybody around. The group consisted of guys in sweat-stained tractor caps and muddy boots, women resting their cigarettes against pastel shorts. The bright late-afternoon sun made them squint, and they looked cold and hunched, even in the July sun, as if used to standing in winds.

A man with mirrored sunglasses stepped closer and tipped his head at me. "So you must be the thing she found in San Francisco."

"My name's Girl." The women were veering away from me, but the men were getting closer.

"Hi. I'm Randa's," said the mirrored sunglasses.

"Randa's what?"

"He'll be what ever Randa wants to make him," said a woman chewing gum.

"Don't listen to these people," said Randa.

"Oh, yeah?" I winked at the guy. He was wiry, slightly bow-legged, and strung tight, like a rodeo cowboy.

"How'd you get all the way out here?" he said. The guy laughed at my beat-up car and took a long drag of his beer.

I shook my beer and sprayed some foam over Randa's feet. "Congratulations, Randa. You got your farm."

She grabbed the beer away from me.

I reached for a barbecued rib from the picnic table and started gnawing.

"You still a troublemaker?" She nodded her head at the group. "Think Bonesteel can calm this kid down?"

"How about all of you. You all farmers?" I asked between bites.

"When God lets us," said the gum chewer.

These people weren't joking. They were for real.

Randa and I stood grinning at each other, while the women started talking again. They squeezed out words in small dry bits, as if it cost them.

"It smells good out here, smells like burning sky." I said. When no one answered I turned to Randa. "How'd the fuck you end up here?"

She slapped my back. "You get some more food."

RANDA OPENED THE DOOR to the seventies-style ranch house. It had a concrete stoop, but that's all that was around it, except for weeds. As if it landed by chance. The door swung funny because the foundation tilted. Inside it smelled of mold and decay.

"I told you I was going to do this. Don't act so surprised."

Randa had the same strange fire in her eyes. She looked even more maniacal than in California.

"What are you really doing here?" I asked. The house didn't fit what I'd dreamed up.

She showed off the place like it was gold. The shag carpet was pressed down in waddles as if buffalo had slept there. The curtains were threadbare at the bottom, windswept. One room was stained in the corner, flooded from something. Randa was thrilled because the rent was only fifty dollars a month. And fields all around it.

In her bedroom, we stood close to each other, almost touching. Over her shoulder I saw a man's boots were on one side of the bed. "Looks like you have some company."

"I've known Bill since I was a kid. We're mainly friends." She pointed to a soft leather case by the side of the bed. "That's my real sleeping companion."

"What's that?"

"I decided my .22 wasn't quite enough. I'm happy with the new one. It's a little more powerful."

"Show me."

"*Hmm—mmm—uh—hauh—hau-u-uh, yeah!*" She raised the unzipped leather cover to show me the thick metal gun engulfed in sheepskin.

I laughed too, but I hated seeing it. Guns reeked of evil. Yet Randa was so proud.

"So…"

"So. You know it's my birthday?"

I'd forgotten. "Yeah, that's why I'm here."

"Yep. Twenty-four on July Fourth."

I couldn't believe Randa took me into her bedroom to show me her damn gun and let me know she was sleeping with Bill. "So. It's good to see you."

"I knew you'd make it someday." She crossed her arms and sighed with satisfaction. "Didn't know it would be this soon. You're here for the wheat harvesting. It's great. Just great!"

WHILE RANDA CUT HER CAKE and talked with the women, I sat with Bill on a couple of hay bales under an umbrella.

Bill's mirrored sunglasses reflected a cloud, a car, my face. I wondered about the way he talked to me, drunk and not caring what the other people thought.

He coughed. "What I want to know is if I came to San Francisco, would you have a place for me? Is there somewhere I could sleep for the night?"

"Sure." I nodded. "Lots of couches to surf."

"You have the life. Randa told me. You just don't care, do you?" He stretched one of his wiry legs and kicked his heel right back into the hay bale. "Ever seen a real farm?"

Bill took me up into a huge combine. It was as if the rusty farm equipment I'd seen in the prairie museum had magically changed into space age equipment, all glass, buttons, and shiny metal. Bright red paint and a big glass enclosure with funny mirrors stuck to either side like insect antennae. A see-through horizontal rocket ship with big sharp cutters out front.

I sat on the one seat inside the big machine, Bill stood on the side, and we looked over the green fields. A little perspective on the rows and rows of crops.

He told me how after college he'd gotten a computer job helping set up the Farm Relief office. Then a couple of summers ago, his dad started needing him. So he'd fallen back into working on the farm as well as part-time working in the office. "Yep. Nothing's ever what you expect."

"Are you and Randa getting married?" I asked.

"That's the plan." He laughed. "If she doesn't go chasing fires again in California."

Did he really think that's all she was chasing? "Right."

"You have a boyfriend back there, in Cal-i-forn-I-ay?"

"Kind of."

"Ahh." He rocked his head. "Don't let Randa scare you away. We could use you around here."

"She scare you?"

"I wouldn't say that." He adjusted one of the mirrors on the combine. "She was born out here, you know. Her farm wasn't far from here."

"Where was it?"

He pointed behind us.

I turned. "Heard her talk about it." Nothing but more and more farmland around us in every direction.

He draped his arm across my shoulder, and I could smell soap. "Think you'll stick around, Pony Girl?"

"Why not?"

He squeezed my shoulder. "We'll see, huh? Nothing turns out the way you expect.

I HAD ONCE ASKED my granddad about my long-ago relatives, but I didn't get much info. We were channel surfing and I made him stop when there was a country song on MTV, and there were pretty pans of blue sky and clouds. The video flashed on a South Dakota highway sign. So I asked about my mother's family and where they lived before Oregon. When I was a kid he'd told me once, but I'd forgotten most everything except something about a town called Independence. My great-great-something grandmother traveled there from Germany, a real pioneer. "Out there in the big middle, where no one knows what spells they cast. Where everybody believes in god and country and hates commies." He was quiet for a moment. "It was a farm."

"What did they grow?"

"Well." He blinked a few times. "I'm not too sharp on that."

WHEN BILL AND I got down from the combine, we found Randa still drinking, alone on the picnic bench. The sun was setting and everybody else had left.

Randa knocked an empty beer bottle against the table edge. "Left the birthday girl all by her lonesome?"

"Well, sweetheart." Bill stuck a fork in a leftover piece of cake. "Not for long."

They talked back and forth about when to take his parents to the drag races.

"Fuck if I'm going," said Randa. She took another fork and stuck it in the same piece of left-over cake.

"Okay, then." Bill stomped away, but called back before getting in his truck, "Nice meeting you, Pony Girl."

Randa shook her head. "Bill's desperate for company."

"Desperate people always like me." I took her beer bottle away and put it in a barrel of trash.

"I won't let him mess with you." She stood and swiped away a fly. "It's great you came here." The smile was off her face now. "Really."

"Never thought I'd come?"

AFTER BILL DROVE AWAY to pick up his parents, Flint and Irma, Randa took me into the cornfields. We walked quietly, like the times we used to leave the Wild Side West bar to see the sunset on Bernal Hill.

She was thinking about it, too. "A little different, Girl?"

The green corn was low, about to our knees. Randa said Flint's corn wouldn't be harvested for a while, but the wheat was near soft enough for cutting. We walked till the house became a small dot in the distance. I raised my hands and spread my arms, trying to reach the field's edge.

"Why did you really come?" said Randa. She stood a few feet away.

I moved closer. "I couldn't wait to see you."

Her body shook as she held me. She closed her eyes. "You mean so much to me."

She gave me such a long hard hug. It reminded me of my grand-dad. Then she talked in her rumbling way, the words sounding as if they came from deep in the lonely blue cave of her insides.

I stuck my finger under her T-shirt on the sleeve, felt the little hard muscle on the side of her arm. My hips were a touch higher than hers, so my hipbone pressed on the flesh over hers. I felt strange, standing close for such a long time, so I pushed her to the driest piece of ground, hoping she'd wrestle me.

"Whaddaya doing?" She tried not to fall, but she had been drinking and wasn't steady. She pulled me down. We spun around, as if rolling in a tunnel. She locked my forearms. I twisted on top of her. My leg between hers, both of us covered in the lemony, summer-smelling dirt.

She pushed my hand away when I tried to touch her. I was obsessed with her skin, having wanted to see more for so long. I wanted to know everything about her, the colors of each part. Hoped I'd at last found somebody that was a similar kind of beast as me.

She grabbed my wrists, didn't let me inside her clothes. I suppose I shouldn't have been surprised after what she'd told me about her lovers in Chicago.

"Okay," I said when she reached for me instead.

Her breath changed as she lifted over me. I felt something shivery around her edges.

"I always wanted you, Girl."

I let her in.

She touched me as if I was fragile. This scared me about getting older. What was it you thought you lost? Why did she think she had to be so careful with me?

"Something wrong?" She sounded scared.

I pulled the hair from her face. "Go harder."

I let her pound me, felt it go to the root of my insides, hoped it would never stop, or at least that I could always remember.

THE DAY FINALLY COOLED a little. We both lay back. Her skin lost its color as the sun left and before long everything around mixed into the fading silhouettes of the small cornstalks and their growing leaves.

"Are there going to be any fireworks?" I asked.

"Out here? Maybe a few." The gentleness of her voice disappeared.

I zipped up my pants.

For years I had been imagining sex with Randa. I had dreamed of some loving tractor driving over my insides and making pulp out of me, some sort of gut-numbing, depth-charging, thrust-fucking. Instead her hands had been strong but reverent, giving me the same kind of precise attention that she did when she worked.

I never know what to do when people don't fuck me hard or crazeee enough.

"Happy Independence Day." I grabbed her. "Let me take you."

She raised her eyebrows. "I'm not ready for that, okay?"

I sat up and fanned the air to get a breeze. "What are you going to do with me?"

"Flower Girl." She took my hand and stroked each finger. "Let me get you some work. It will put some sense in you."

"You think so?" I thought back to the last morning I'd seen her in San Francisco, when I had helped Randa load boxes into her rental truck. Her pleasure in simple work.

She put her head on my arm and again closed her eyes. "There'll be no slacking. Dust and bugs and heat. But you'll know what real work is. For the rest of your life."

I let her hold me tightly again, let her think I was content. Soon Randa dozed, her breaths even and deep.

Out in the hot, jumbo-size Nebraska night, my desire felt stirred and wiggy. I wanted to explode. What would happen if I did? A gun blast of feeling. My insides shattering, flying apart, zillions of bits of fucked-up gobs of brain and blood-smeared shards of bone.

THE WINDOWS were the only things that made Randa and Bill's kitchen a room. Otherwise it was like Dorothy's house after the tornado. A strange collapse of a place. Cabinet doors ajar, an old avocado-colored refrigerator with no shelves and a busted freezer. A stove crusted up into one black cake of burned grease. For fifty dollars a month, though, I could think of people who would love to have it. I wanted to e-mail my friends from the city and tell them to come out and rent the slew of bankrupted farmers' houses around us.

The door leading from the kitchen to the pantry was crushed in the middle; it had a hollow core. Bill bragged to me about Randa's temper and told me how she threw a fist into the door. He said it was because her mother had got sick back in Chicago, and she couldn't do anything about it. Something about her anger made him excited. Like Randa had said, Bill was desperate for something, anything, I guess. He was one of those guys who was real tough and strung tight with sexy muscles, but all collapsed on the inside.

My first morning at their house, Randa showed surprise when I asked about work.

"So you're serious? You going to stick around the farm?"

I nodded and looked out the window over the sink, where I could see the highway.

Bill crunched away on cornflakes, his lips and jaw really going at it. He vibrated at a high speed. A fast guitar-picking type rhythm. "Stay here as long as you want."

The situation between him and Randa deserved some thought. When I met Randa she had seemed one-hundred-percent dyke. I could see she had found somebody with a farm, but why the hell would she actually hook up with him for good? She seemed to like what we did the evening before pretty well.

"Bill will want to show you his computer games."

He looked up from his bowl. "Randa calls using computers a game."

"Do you go online out here?"

"That's how Bill gets to look at naked women."

"Bobtail hauling trucks is more like it." He stretched. "All the time I have."

"You find the 24-horse? 13-speed?"

"Sure did. Fair price."

I pushed my chair away from the table.

"This weasel." Randa pretended to shoot him. "Why didn't you tell me you found the truck?"

"Randa sure makes a nice tyrant, yeah, Pony?"

"Why does he keep calling me Pony?" I asked Randa.

"Beats me. That's more than he's said to me in days." Randa looked from one to the other of us and winked. "This is going to be interesting." She jangled some keys and went out to Bill's truck.

Bill stood. He walked over to a hook where his crusty cap rested, on the wall by the door, leaving his bowl on the table. "What you doing today?"

I told him Randa was going to put me to work soon.

"Okeydoke." He made a fist and knocked it into his other hand. "I'm off to raise hell. Randa makes me work Sundays. That's the pits, huh? Later, my Pony Girl."

I helped myself to a second bowl of cornflakes.

Then I walked over to the door. Bill and Randa were getting into an old flatbed truck. "Who cooks around here?" I yelled.

"Feel free!" Bill waved.

They peeled down the gravel road toward the highway.

THAT EVENING we went to Bill's parents' house for Sunday dinner. The house looked like Randa and Bill's, but everything stood upright, not buckled or broken. Your basic suburban-style house, but in the middle of beyouteefull cornfields.

"An awful lot of mud is finding its way in here," mumbled Flint, looking at the carpet and my dirty shoes.

"Why are you doing this to us?" Flint said to Bill as we sat down to dinner. He seemed to be referring to me. His words were garbled, as if something was wrong with his mouth.

On the large table our empty white plates shined like UFOs. I expected to see them lift off while we waited for Irma, Bill's mom, to finish preparing.

I liked watching Irma trudge back and forth with the food. She had a great playing field of a body—wide and flat. A round belly stuck up under her waistband, a pitcher's mound. Her hair was colorless, and her large glasses floated forward on her face.

I wondered when Irma's mother, Dottie, would join us, but it turned out Irma brought Dottie her dinner. She ate in the TV/living room with the five o'clock news turned loud. After feeding Dottie, Irma slung lots of chicken and corn down for us.

Then she shouted a booming grace.

I closed my eyes. "Amen!" That was the part I knew.

I bit into my chicken thigh, but kept looking around. Randa's hair fell into her face and covered her cheeks. I tried to imagine her as a shy little girl.

I chewed into my corncob and wanted Randa to look over, give me an encouraging sign in hostile territory, but she stayed hidden and mute as she swallowed her food.

After a few minutes, Irma shuffled over to get more fried chicken, then flung the plate on the table again—she could have been feeding the hogs. All the while she ranted about how the gangs from Los Angeles were coming to Nebraska. From the lack of response at the table, I figured this was a common topic for her. She talked louder, as if it would make people listen.

"Bill, now, I *still* wish we'd home-schooled you. More and more that's the way. What with the school closing down."

On the drive over, Randa had told me all about Irma. Back when Randa had lived in Bonesteel as a kid, she remembered how Irma had drunk beer and drove fast. Before she turned christian.

Sure enough, the Bible sat on the table. At one point, when Bill and Flint talked about the farm, Irma opened it and smiled over a passage. A slightly slobbery smile, as if plotting revenge.

Back in San Francisco, I had always wondered where the born-agains lived. I hadn't even believed they were real people. Now they seemed to be crammed in every corner of the Plains. I left for the bathroom.

On the way back, I stopped in the living room and said hi to Irma's mother. Dottie looked up with scared, blinking eyes, as if no one had talked to her in a long time. She had finished her dinner and her hands shook over the TV table.

"I won't bite." I smiled and stood there until she calmed down. "I'm not the devil. Just his daughter, maybe."

She nodded at me.

When I came back to the dining room, I stopped out of view from the doorway.

"You guys," Randa was saying.

"Us guys know a joke when we see one. Where'd she get that

thing on her arm?" Flint had stopped eating. His words still sounded garbled.

"She's seventeen. That's how they grow them in California," said Bill.

I walked in. "You have such a nice house." For a moment I caught fear in the air, as if I had taken their house from them by merely talking about it. "Really nice."

"We heard you, firecracker." Randa leaned back in her chair. Her body looked small compared to the tall, hard-pulled figures of Bill and Flint.

Irma said, "The Shulls said the storm got them, too. Thirty or so lots."

They talked about how cornstalks had been broken in two, but their wheat was fine.

Randa slowly stroked the knife on the table with her finger, as if she was measuring its length. "So what do you think?"

"It's not soft-soft," said Bill.

"But is it ready?'

"Could be."

"Could be another couple days, then?"

"Bill should get the thrasher working tomorrow. It's still acting up." Flint didn't so much answer questions as stick to his line of thought. He turned to Randa. "You git out there and help him."

THE WHEAT HARVEST was a big deal, from early to late. Randa drove the grain trucks from the farm to the big bins where they stored it. That was the only job Flint let her do. I came along.

We'd pull to the side of the field and everybody would yell at Flint as he drove the combine right up so its snout would flood grain into the back of our mammoth truck. Meanwhile, Bill and the crew would be trying to clean the gunk that fouled up the mouth of the snout when it got stuck.

Irma brought the cold drinks, the chatter, and later a big lunch.

We drove all the way to the grain elevator and unloaded our grain, turned right around and came back to do it again. The crew would be sweating and hollering again when we arrived. They'd stored all their coiled desire for this season, the days of reaping.

IF YOU WALK HIGH ENOUGH in the Trinity Mountains you'll find snow even in the summer. You need a car to arrive at the good trails, though, because the logging roads twist for miles before offering a hiking path. Once there you can hike for hours and get past eight thousand feet.

Randa liked fighting fires in the Trinity Mountains; it was what brought her to California. But when she was walking the mountains with me, she got wiggy from being so high. Afraid I'd slip or fall, she always looked back to make sure I was still around. Couldn't sit still even when we rested—she threw rocks to hear them fall, or picked at granite boulders with her knife.

Once in Bonesteel I finally understood how strange it must have felt to be in the high mountains after growing up in level country.

I thought nothing was better than an outlook from a mountain. The air was clear and fresh and you felt on top of the world. But even in the Trinities, you never saw as much sky as from a field in Nebraska.

WHILE THE OTHERS were working, I went over to visit Irma's mom. When I rang the bell the first time, Dottie sputtered as if her voice was a cold engine. "What's your name, dear?"

"I can get going. I'm sorry to bother you." There was a long silence. My voice had cracked. "I don't know what I was thinking."

"That's fine, dear." Dottie stood, her shoulders bent. She took a shaky step and then another. I felt lucky I wasn't that old, shut up in a house, ignored all the time, maybe for years. I wanted to give her a big hug right then except there was something so frigid about her that I was afraid I would stick to her like ice.

When I told her I wanted to see pictures of her life as a kid, she pulled out an album from a cardboard box in the pantry on a bottom shelf. "Don't know why they keep them here." She wiped her nose in a funny way, getting a little twitchy and excited. The album looked like it was going to drop from her grasp, but I didn't help her because I could tell she needed to do it on her own.

We sat at the kitchen table and she opened the big red album. The pages were old and near falling out. In the front was a group of photos not pasted in, and one of them was a combine photo.

"There it is." She poked a shaky index finger at it and then tried to pick it up, but her hands were gnarled and she couldn't.

Lots of men and a handful of women stood in front of a machine as big as a Mack truck and three times as long. It had sharp wheels for cutting and a big open bin for storing hay.

The faces were not happy. No old time photos are. No one ever looks like they have a life. They always look pinned to the world, flat.

Dottie asked me why I was there.

I explained again that I was there to see Randa. "Do you have any pictures of her?"

"I see. Irma said that, didn't she?" Now she seemed to remember again. "But why did you come *here*?"

"I guess I got tired of California."

"California." She said it was like some fairy tale.

"You know, I was curious about the middle of the country."

"The right choice. You coming here."

"Why do you say that?"

"I don't know." She chuckled.

We talked around the kitchen table for a while, and I felt her relax. I imagined the kind of comfort that a stranger might give to someone locked inside a small town. The best part was when she showed me the china figurines in the cabinet, brought all the way from Norway. Milk maids and apple-cheeked boys, delicate white sheep and flame-beaked hens. Her favorite was a wishing well, painted with tiny brush strokes, made to look like old stones, with a wooden bucket the size of a jewel that swung from a ribbon tied to its crank.

I HAD A BABY-SITTER who lived on what must have been a farm. Mrs. Dowell. She was old with white hair, let me sit on her lap, gave me orange and cream popsicles. Loose roosters clucked around us. And my favorite thing, a couple of sheep. Their fleece felt scrunchy and I would sit in between them and grab a handful of each. The sheep shook nervously in a tiny way, vibrating against my hands. I always think of them when I hear the song "Old MacDonald." The place smelled like manure. There was a big tractor and some near-by orchards. I'm not sure where the hell it was. My granddad took me out there when I was really young; or it maybe it was my dad getting rid of me for a few days. It all seemed like a dream now. Dottie reminded me of that nice old baby-sitter.

Maybe that's why I stuck one of her tiny little china hens in my pocket.

MY ROOM had skanky shag carpeting and nothing else but a kid's desk that had collapsed. It must have been some boy's room from a long time ago—a moldy Hot Wheels poster dangling from one tack on the sliding closet door. They had gotten me a mattress, but I still had trouble sleeping. I couldn't get used to the sound of the dryer fans in the nearby grain elevators. They went on all night long and sounded like monsters breathing.

One night I crept along the hallway to the door of their bedroom. The curtainless windows let the moon shine on the bed. The sheet was half down. Bill had one arm stretched above his head. Randa was curled up next to him, her back along his belly. I stepped inside. On her nightstand, as always, lay her soft gun case. Unzipped and ready for her hand to slip inside.

I kneeled by the nightstand. I wanted to take the gun, but I was afraid even sleeping, Randa would get there first. I moved silently and placed my head on the side of the mattress.

Randa's cheekbone gleamed, the skin on her closed eyelids smooth as a baby's. I could feel her breath tickle the skin on my throat. Her hair fell away from her forehead and the space above her eyebrows looked raw and precious. I thought about how mothers bend down to kiss that part of their sleeping children.

"Randa," I whispered.

She flinched. "What!" She grabbed the edge of the bed and sat up. "What's wrong? You need something?"

I stayed on my knees. "I'm going to suffocate in that room."

She got out of bed. She wore only a T-shirt and white underwear; her legs looked pale as roots compared to her tanned arms.

We went outside together. It was still hot as anything.

"You want to sleep here?"

She set me up with a tarp under my sleeping bag behind the house.

"Can you make those dryer motors stop?"

"Sure, baby. Just for you." She yawned. "Night."

Nebraska got a lot of rain in the summer. So sleeping outside didn't always work. Like the one time it thundered and started to pour. I ran inside and knelt by the bed.

"Come on in," whispered Randa.

So I got in the bed. Randa put her arm around my slippery, rain-wet waist.

Bill raised his head. "I've always wanted two women in my bed." Then he started snoring again.

Randa held me. I felt both safe and deprived at the same time. I stayed awake for hours.

Once I got my corn job, I became as dead tired as they were at night.

I WANTED to ask Bill if I could use his computer to e-mail Angus, but somehow I was too exhausted to get around to it. And I wondered whether I should be asking things from Bill. Especially the week Randa went back to Chicago to be with her sick mom.

"I sure do feel lone-ly tonight." Bill twanged a song as he came in the door with his beer. It was our first night alone. I considered him from the waist down. His legs were real working legs, and his jeans were worn smooth from kneeling and bending and heaving crops. But then—there was his face. All bony and hiding around the eyes. The skin was white around them, like a raccoon, from wearing sunglasses all the time. His eyes were slits, kind of like my mine, only they were dull. There was no real self left under there.

So while Randa was away, I slept in my stranded Dodge with the windows open for air, but the doors locked. Just in case. Just in case Bill got too drunk and we did something stupid.

MY JOB, once the wheat harvest was finished, was corn detasseling. It meant yanking the tassels off the corn to help them cross-breed. It helped get things going, made the right kinds of corn pollinate with each other. Randa's teenage brother had done it back when she lived in Bonesteel as a kid.

A lot of the cornstalks were broken in half from a June windstorm, so it wasn't going to be a great haul this year, Flint had said. And the wheat was stuck waiting in storage till the trains would come get it. Flint wasn't happy because there was a glut, and he couldn't get the price he needed. Bill told me that was the farmer thing, to always say what a miserable year it had been—that's the way things were most of time, miserable. All the farmers had second jobs to survive. This year was particularly bad; last June, two farmers in the county had shot themselves.

But somehow there was always work enough to go around.

It started early, way in the dark. I walked to the highway, got picked up by a couple of high school guys, and got driven to downtown Bonesteel. Then we rode in a school bus for an hour with about thirty other kids. We got dropped off, divided into squads, and dispersed in a big, waiting field. Every four-person squad took a row. We had to reach, pull the tassel, throw it on the ground, step forward, and repeat. Soon the sun rose and made what had been a dark tunnel fill with green. The moisture from the leaves was all over us, and unless we wrapped ourselves in plastic bags, our clothes became drenched. We were wet and cold and ready for the warmth of the sun.

By the first break at eight-thirty, we were parched. The water break was like getting good drugs; people took as much as they could. The next few hours passed in a rhythmic trance. Then it was lunch and we still weren't talking much. By afternoon we joked and helped one another when we had finished our own row. After a couple of weeks, it was the happiest I'd felt in a long time. But I have to admit that when I started, I felt like somebody on a prison work gang.

The first day, they put me on the beginner's squad and I sang made-up slave songs and wanted to stop after only about fifteen minutes. I worked some more, considered running to the highway and stopping the first car that came along, getting the hell out of there. It was dusty and the insects buzzed around just like Randa said they would. My hands sweated in the gloves and rubbed and burned, and I got cut along my forearm from sharp leaves. If I stopped, I imagined the others would say I was a lazy, homo city kid.

We had to pull off the male flowers on the tassel of every fifth row. The farmers planted two different kinds of corn that would crossbreed and make better corn. Left to self-pollinate, corn isn't as yummy I guess. We helped female silky threads catch their neighbors' corn seed in the wind and tuck it safe into their husks. Our corn detasseling guaranteed good farm-approved corn sex.

Step, reach, and yank off the sucker. I could hear Joey's voice in my head—take that you muddafucca! Go! The tassel made a popping sound as it was ripped off. Now again. Reach, pull, pop. I kept my kerchief tied at the back of my head and wrapped around my mouth so the dust wouldn't choke me.

"Hey, there's the bandit," said the main captain.

"Watch your mouth." I wiped some sweat off my temple and shook it his way.

After a few days of it I wondered what I had ever done to deserve this punishment. But I wanted the money. So I kept it up. I got so I could do hand over hand over hand. Pop, pop, pop! Throw the tassels down. After a few more days I started feeling strong. My hair had grown some, and I got sunburst skin and was swaggering and joking like everybody else. I kept the bandanna tied around my mouth and before long, my squad became infamous. They called us the banditos.

I didn't get any glorious welcome home, though. I wasn't wanted again for dinner at Flint's house, and that's where Randa and Bill ate. So my meals were canned chili and tamales that Randa dropped off. By the time Bill and Randa came home from Irma's dinner, I was already dead tired and near gone. They said hello if I was out back looking at the twilight. Or if I was sitting in the kitchen finishing my chili and listening to country songs on the radio, one of them might chat a little as the other took a shower. Within about twenty minutes, they'd be in bed. So I didn't see them much. I began to look forward to work each day and dread the coming home alone part.

I SUGGESTED MURDER as a solution when Randa and I went food shopping together on the weekend. "You should be running this whole operation! You should own the farm." I paused. "I can tell Bill and Irma both hate Flint. He controls them. The three of you should poison him. Then you could be empress and own all this land."

"I have to be patient." Randa drove Bill's pickup, an old Ford. "You think this is a movie for you to direct and star in."

"How can you be so patient?"

Her hands gripped the bottom of the wheel and she leaned back. "I'm proud of you. Pulling your weight here."

This was the first time we'd had alone together in days.

"I want other jobs." I tugged on my mane and wrapped it around my neck.

"I don't want you messing with any spraying. It's bad enough you working the corn after it's been sprayed." She nodded at some guy in a pickup coming the other way on the road. "Some kids had to go the hospital from pesticide poisoning recently."

"Could we get on your bike sometime soon? I'd like to take a ride."

"Your problem is you like trouble." She looked at me with that hungry look, like right before we had sex in the cornfield. But all she said was: "Just relax. Work is good for you. I can tell."

First we had to stop at the grain elevator and find out what the latest prices for wheat were. I waited in the car. Lots of grain was waiting till Flint felt they could sell it for the right price, the highest price. Farming had a lot of gambling about it.

Back in the car, Randa went on with her farm talk: figuring yields and no-till methods, whether she wanted to do beans or hogs, and what kind of equipment she could rent from Flint. Whatever she did, she couldn't make enough from the land to live. She'd have to have another job. She was looking into working at a shop where they fixed the farm machines. This time of year farmers didn't have enough time for repairs. Plus there was a big farm nearby that was setting up a year-round shop soon.

I asked her about Bill's dad's, why he talked funny. She said he had a disease that made his tongue swell up.

"So maybe he'll die."

"I wouldn't count on it. It's not fatal." She spoke softly. "It's not cancer."

For a moment I thought she was finally going to talk to me about her mom and what kind of cancer she had. I guess the whole thing made her too upset though, like Bill said. Too upset and angry. I was scared to bring it up because I thought about the fist hole in the kitchen door.

"So what are you going to do about Flint?"

"He'll get used to me. He thinks I'm marrying his son." Randa squeezed my thigh. "You know, having a little firecracker like you around here may just about drive me crazy."

"Yeah, sure."

"Let's get a farm of our own. What do you think?" She paused and then let it rip. "*Hmm—mmm—uh—hauh—hau-u-uh, yeah!*"

FOR OUR PICNIC in the wild prairie, Dottie wore a bright yellow bonnet. With her tufts of white hair, she looked like a little old lady Easter bunny. She sat in a folding chair under a parasol, and I lay at her feet on a blanket. I wore the all-american shorts that I'd bought in Salt Lake and a nerdy baseball cap that the crew had given me for work. After we finished the last of Irma's fried chicken, Dottie and I watched the bright puffclouds. They were the most generous thing about the country out here. I thought of Jessika dancing, and I wanted to spin into the soft clouds for an entire afternoon, such a big place to disappear.

"So, what do you have to say for yourself?" I said. It was the same question Dottie greeted me with when I visited on Sunday while the others were at church.

"I can't say much, dear." She laughed. "I don't have half a brain left."

She closed her eyes. I closed mine, too. I wanted to hold her hand, but she wasn't a touchy-feely person.

When I first hung out with her, Dottie had been wary. She had an old-person's tremble and looked as if she was rising from a grave. But she loved showing me old photos, especially the combine one. It was amazing that her family had been on this land that long.

As we sat together in the fields, I made believe that I was protected under that big sky, as if Dottie was my grandmother, my people. Thinking that I belonged to this land, as much as anybody did.

Then as Dottie dozed, I decided to explore.

The grass crunched—snap, crackle, pop—as I stomped. The tall stalks didn't bend like California summer grass. Prairie grass flattened with a snap, than bounced right back up after each of my footfalls. Stiff, hardy survivors.

The clouds at the horizon, the only border of all this space.

For some reason, I could imagine Irma praying in the wild prairie. It would be her place of belonging. On her knees in a dip of a meadow. Wearing the turquoise stretchy shorts featuring her mound of belly. She'd be grinning her evil, plotting smile and wishing the weird tongue disease on her husband Flint. Maybe like Randa and me, she was waiting for her husband to die. I wouldn't put it past her. A voodoo christian.

WHEN DOTTIE WOKE from her nap, I asked her about her memories. She told me that when her grandmother was alive they didn't use money. Everyone traded stuff. People relied on one another. It sounded good, like some fantasy. She said even the Indians had been friendly. They had worked hard and helped one another. She talked like a propagandist, in that way old people do when they don't really tell you the truth. I asked her more about her own life. Most of what she had told me before was about the cooking at harvest time; the big meals they baked, the roasted chickens, the pies and biscuits. She repeated that stuff again. I didn't mind. I liked the sound of her voice.

"Did you know Randa when she was a kid?"

"Randa moved away when she was very little. She had been so unhappy to leave the farm. Of course, her father had already rented out most of it by the time the kids came along."

"Really?" Randa always talked like her dad farmed hundreds of acres. "Have you ever wanted to leave?" I pulled my baseball cap down so the sun didn't glare in my eyes.

"Where, dear? Leave Bonesteel? Oh, I suppose." She sniffed. "Never did."

Next she told me that all her grandchildren had left Bonesteel except Bill. "What is the price for a bushel, now? Might as well get a

city job as get that. Or some people say worse." She whispered.
"'Might as well be a whore as a farmer,' they say."

"Yeah? You've seen a lot of change."

"Oh, yes. Nothing stays the way you'd want it."

"How would you want it?'

"Couldn't say." She snorted. "Somehow you always want it different!"

"Yeah, I know that feeling." I stared into the sky as she spoke, listened to the calling blackbirds. They sounded so far away, as stranded as Cara's long-ago chants, flying into the wound of blue.

Maybe everybody on the whole planet felt kind of strange, as if life didn't quite add up. It sure was there, even in Dottie's eyes. Little pink bunny eyes, tiny and strong. Alone.

SPACE IS INCONTROVERTIBLE. You can't argue with it. After a while, being on all that land made me stop fooling myself. I slowed down my trains of thought, paused my rambling brain. I started to admit there were things I still longed for. I felt a strange yearning that reminded me of when I was a kid.

I got the yearning when I saw Flint drive his tractor into the distance, when he had one row to travel and another row after that—even if all he was doing was spraying Round-Up. When I looked at him I knew he had a place to be. I felt so lonesome in comparison.

Or I got the pain when I thought of Randa and how she wanted to farm, and how she always knew what she wanted.

Randa's only cure for me? Work. And more work. She thought it was the pill for whatever disease I had. So each morning I went back to this kids' summer job of detasseling corn, stripping the husks, feeling the silky tassels in my fingers. The sun beat on my nose and my underarms chafed and my feet grew imprints into my boots, and one thing after the next just to prove to these Nebraskans that I could do it.

No one had ever given me a job before where my body had to do actual hard stuff. I'd shelved porn magazines in the Tenderloin and mopped floors at CookieMonster, but I'd never had a job that depended moment by moment on such back-straining rhythm. The muscle flexing and heart beating and the step, step, step of it, all there in each reach for the corn. It was the kind of job that couldn't be faked. Sometimes I worked fast and sometimes I worked slow—I didn't care how many corns I got done, not really. The whole thing was: I had to keep going. Each day, usually in the afternoon—after the slaphappy lunch jokes passed—I would go into a trance. I would move harder and swifter and get crazeee with work fever.

Sometimes I got overwhelmed by all those cornstalks and their floppy green leaves. When I looked down at the dirt under my feet, I felt something vicious and excessive in the way the earth pushed up stalk after stalk, over and over again, more and more life. And there I was, helping it continue. Me, making life fuck into itself. Stripping the tassels from every fifth row of males and leaving the females ready to pollinate. Making growth, covered in dirt, hot fingers reaching. Fertility, right? The earth didn't produce life because it was beyouteefull; it had no choice. It had to keep going. Water plus seed plus soil plus sun equals life. No choice. The corn couldn't stop growing. At night you could even hear the ears pushing into their new sheaths. A bubbling, gurgling sound. *Roo-oo-oo-sh-sh-k-k-ee-ee-k-k-ee-ee.*

At the end of every workday, I walked back to the truck to get my ride home. My crew was mainly high school boys, a couple of college girls. Sometimes we talked about the fact that everything we touched and helped to produce would soon be cut down and gone. Death in the name of popcorn.

Each night I got dropped at Randa's empty ranch house, and I had never heard such quiet. I was so outside of everybody and every place of belonging that I knew I wouldn't be able to stand it much longer.

"HEY, JESSIKA?"

"Yeah, is that you?"

"You want to take a trip?" I asked.

"Where are you?"

"In Bonesteel at a pay phone. I want to come get you." It was so good to be able to say those words. To be ready.

She didn't say anything.

"How are you, Jessika? I miss you."

"I'm okay. People here are really weird. They don't listen to me like you did." Jessika's voice was shaky.

"Yeah?"

She coughed and said something else that I couldn't hear, with all the club music in the background.

"Are the guys paying you and everything? Are you making it?"

"I can't talk." She covered the phone for a moment and said something to somebody. Then she paused. "You took the car, didn't you?"

"What?"

"Oh, boy, oh, boy, oh, boy." She took a long pause and her breathing was loud.

"You're tweaking." I said. "That's fucked up. I want to come get you."

"If you come back, the owner will embalm us both."

"You sound weird."

"I gotta go. Take care."

I slammed the phone down.

BILL, RANDA, AND I chomped and slurped away at our three bowls of Sunday morning cornflakes. It was one of the few times that we had all sat around the wobbly kitchen table.

The sky was pink, and Randa said it looked like a little rain would come that evening.

"Yep," said Bill. He already had on his mirrored sunglasses. There was an empty beer bottle on the kitchen floor that I was rolling back and forth under one foot. I'm sure it was his. They occasionally turned up in weird places.

I told Randa how I once had relatives in South Dakota.

"No joke? You must be of good ole farming stock, then."

I asked where South Dakota was and she said the border was less than an hour away. We both slapped palms, grabbed fists, and twiddled thumbs. One of those handshake things I'd taught her in SF.

"You girls are two peas in a pod," said Bill.

"Blood sisters," I said.

Randa walked outside. I could see her through the window looking at the clouds and sniffing the air. She loved the rituals of morning. She always was anxious to test the day, smell the coming weather. Couldn't wait to get her hands into the farm work, and never took a day off. An obsession, it seemed. Whatever it was, I figured I had no place in it. I was starting to feel that in my bones, as sure as she could feel rain coming.

She came back inside. Her hair was tucked behind her ears and swung below her jaw. "Well. We got to go on a ride."

THAT AFTERNOON the weather turned humid, cloudy, and gray. On either side of the highway were long, damp furrows that smelled of manure—their color rich and brown like used coffee grounds. Randa kicked her sleek cycle to over a hundred miles an hour, the road ahead narrowing to a pinpoint. I grabbed on tighter and tighter. Happy as a big gazooney fool. We were soaring. Yes!

We stopped at a roadside historical marker for lunch. It said that Lewis and Clark's long-ago campsite was nearby on a conical mound. According to Indian legend it was a place of devils. "The devils are in human form with remarkable large heads," I read. "About eighteen inches high."

We took our lunches from Randa's saddlebag and walked far into the fields to search for the conical mound.

The land undulated slightly, and a hill or two rose in the distance, but no identifiable cone shapes. The grasses were grazing ground, Randa said.

"I don't like the feeling that anybody can see you out here," I said. "No place to hide."

"No problem for me."

We plunked down on a small rise and munched our peanut butter sandwiches.

I looked around. "Can you imagine being a pioneer? When there was nothing but the wind and the 'devils'? Dottie told me they had to build their houses from mud because there were no trees."

"No. I can't imagine that." Randa tore her sandwich into quarters. She never paused when she ate, and she always looked like a shy kid, letting her hair fall into her face.

We both lay back under the dome of sky. I wondered where the blue stopped, at exactly what point the stratosphere ended and pure empty space began. All we could see was the blue, the refraction, the sun's gift.

"So why do you like farming so much?"

"You're full of it, Girl. You are a piece of work. Just you wait. I'm gonna get you later."

"As far as I can see, *later* is never."

She grabbed me and I grabbed back. I held her forearms and moved a knee into her. She pulled me off balance and wrestled me down till her shoulder was on my chest.

She jumped up. "We got to get back."

Randa was pricing hogs today. Flint had sold his lots some time ago, but she was looking into the business.

On the walk back to her Vulcan, she admitted she was getting restless. Flint still didn't trust her with any of his big machines. They were expensive and if operated wrong, stuff could happen. Bill wasn't teaching her, because he didn't want to anger his dad. A neighbor farmer who owned some of Randa's dad's old land had let her go out with him a few times.

Randa relaxed a little as she told the truth of her situation to me. I figured she probably hadn't admitted to anybody, even herself, how frustrated she felt.

She whistled. "Not everybody has your heart, Girl. If you got to know me, you'd learn I'm not what you think. Down deep I'm a d-e-v-i-l." As she spelled out the word, she placed her hands behind her head to make horns and flared her eyes.

"I like devils."

"You don't know the least of it. In Chicago, I had a dog that I once beat the shit out of." She looked over at me and shook herself. "I'm not myself living in the city, feeling so crammed next to people."

"Yeah." I couldn't imagine her not feeling like herself.

"And I don't like working for anybody else. When I do the farming stuff, I'm a better person. I'm clear-headed. I have to keep busy. It's a simple, lonesome kind of thing, but farming keeps me occupied. And when you grow up here, land means something. Look at Flint. It's the deepest connection he has—to his land. He doesn't need anything else." She stopped and then looked away. "Besides, I'm not a drifter like you. I can't just float."

"I don't want to float either. I want to feel solid."

She smiled. "Right."

"You haven't always wanted to stay put. You must have gone to San Francisco looking for something," I said.

She pointed at me. "That's right, and I found it."

I grabbed her hand and placed it between mine. Felt the thick wrap of her calluses, the pulse in her well-worked skin. "I want to get out of this place."

"You do what you need to do." She looked up at the sky for a second out of habit. "Don't sleep outside tonight. There will be a few more showers."

I smiled. "You could come travel with me for a while, have some fun."

"I can't tell you what to do, but I hope you stay." She got the helmets and handed me mine. "You're something. One of a kind."

"Yeah, sure."

I asked her to let me drive the Vulcan for a little on the way back. I had told her many times that my friend had a motorcycle and I had learned how to handle them.

She stood absolutely still for a second. "Go ahead."

"Really?"

She handed over her keys. "Take it down the road for a piece."

I got nervous as hell. "With you on back?"

"Sure."

As I struggled with the strap on my helmet, she grinned. My impatience with inanimate objects always gave her pleasure.

"Get that thing tight."

"Right-o." I straddled the monster and started the engine. Randa got on behind, and I could feel her body nearly trust me.

I revved it and howled in delight. Randa joined with a big ripping guffaw.

And we took off.

ONE MORNING, the blowers started getting to me. More wheat still had to dry, so the dryer motors in the grain elevators blew nonstop. I worked to the sound, slept to it, woke to it.

I wiped the sleep drool off my mouth and started to groan. I howled to the back beat of the churning blowers. Jumped up naked and thumped my chest. Let me be a dragon with fire coming from my mouth! The rows of corn, the work rhythm, the sweat, sweat, pluck, and pull, and tear, and on to the next. The blisters, the dirt, the flying bugs, the orbiting sun beating down. I had wanted to know if I could do it. I did it. Do-o-one.

Had some googly-eyed part of me bought into the notion of a little house on the prairie? Randa wasn't really interested in me. Face it.

Let the warm shower water run. Soap my body clean. Abracadabra. Couldn't believe that this awkward being of skin covered bones and muscle was me. My tanned, scraped arms, my long hairy toes, my knobby breasts, my big bony knees. The hungry, concave belly. Randa was a human being sufficient unto herself. She was an island of a person, but I lived in a starving beast of a self that wouldn't shake away. I was a roaddawg who needed more adventures.

Besides, the more I got to know those rows of corn tassels, the more I didn't want to be part of any razzamatazz mass-murder agriculture. Farmers controlled and cut and sprayed and planted. Corn was chattel, oppressed little stalks, all slaves to the popcorn manufacturers! It seemed a joke to plant, sow, and then chop, chop, chop. Say I'm a fool, but whatever drove a farmer, I knew I didn't have it. I couldn't be part of the picture.

After dressing, I strolled down the flat highway. The land was too splayed out. I wanted forest. Protection. Some unruly growth and ferns and redwoods and the smell of flowers. Some nature that was not grown to be used. Some pleasure and overflow of sweet-smelling vines, untouched by plow, combine, thrasher.

My Dodge felt too marked and dangerous to drive back to Iowa and pick up Jessika. I had kept it hidden behind the house and wanted to leave it there. No more stolen cars. It was time to explore

South Dakota, find the town of Independence, where my ancestors had homesteaded. Ready to go looking for my big ole craggy roots.

But how?

One thing I knew, I couldn't manage this freaky longing without hearing the sound of someone's voice. So instead of going to work, I hiked all the way to the farm to have a visit with Dottie.

NO ONE was at the house. Only Flint, it must have been him, hulking through the fields on his machine, blowing fumes to kill the weeds.

The big combine Bill had showed me on the Fourth of July, the one they had used for the harvest, hid behind one of the barns. Strange as ever, a bright red vehicle with a bumper full of knives. The slide tube for the grain was detached and the machine sat there, alone and useless. I climbed the ladder hanging from the door and got inside.

It was a relief to be raised from the stuck flatlands. From above, I could see the furrows stretching into straight lines, primed for the next thing to be planted. Felt the caked stiffness of my jeans, the worn grooves in my everyday baggy pants that I'd long ago cut off into shorts. I wanted to say, *You go, clothes. Walk off my body and carry on.*

Flint's cell phone lay on the floor of the cab. I wasn't sure why he didn't have it with him today. The lone farmer plowing his large fiefdom—connected by cell phone to anywhere in the world. I liked the image and imagined him in his big machines having long gossip sessions with his fellow farmers, swollen-tongue wagging.

Since Randa and Bill still didn't have phone service, I felt starved for the feel of it in my hand. Rubbed my fingertips over the buttons, as enchanting as science fiction. Punched in my granddad's number and hit the talk button.

I knew how the conversation would go.

"Hey granddaddy-o."

"Yeah. Where are you? You're not in trouble again?"

Every time I call my granddad he thinks I'm in jail. He spent a lot of time in jail himself back when he was younger—for self-righteous protest reasons—and I think the idea of my getting arrested always gets him preachy.

I could hear the ring of the phone, and I became excited thinking how it was actually ringing in his apartment in San Francisco. I knew my response when he would ask what the hell I was doing out here. "What am I doing? I'm doing america."

It rang and rang.

Finally I pressed *End*.

I looked at my heebie-jeebie, overexposed, spacious-skies view.

Which direction was Independence? I knew it must be somewhere north. It seemed useless to wonder about my mother's long-ago family because my granddad had told me so little. I only wanted a hit of the past. Just a small piece. Finding roots wasn't really the point. It was simple curiosity about people who held an invisible connection to me. All I wanted was a memory of somebody. When you had a mother you'd never really seen, it made you stuck on that. It made me recognize the way that life and history and families are filled with empty places. I saw them and felt them all the time.

THE NEXT DAY I packed up my carrybag and got ready. Decided to chance going to Sioux City and picking up Jessika. I really didn't want to take the rest of the trip by myself.

At the last moment, I tried to think of a goodbye note. What could I say?

Randa, I wish you could come with me, but I know you are fine and dandy and happy here. Then what? *Thank you for everything. I love your crazeee laugh, your warm hands, your fast motorcycle…?* The more I thought about writing a note, the more lame it seemed to try.

Instead I picked some grasses and put them on her pillow in the shape of a lopsided heart. That's all.

WHEN I STOPPED in Bonesteel to get a soda, Floyd and Freckle Face were hanging around and happy to see me. I nodded and let them jabber for a bit, then hot-footed it right back to my Dodge. Except when I turned the key, the engine didn't roll. Only a click. Again. I waited, unable to believe I was having trouble already.

"Piece a junk, huh?" A familiar pair of mirrored sunglasses appeared at my side. Bill had come to town on Randa's bike. "Where were you off to?"

"I like this old Dodge. Don't say that," I said. "It has character."

"Well, I was getting some things for Irma." Bill parked the Vulcan and ambled over to look under the hood.

Probably getting more beer, I thought, and left the car to join him.

"Maybe it's dust in the gas," said Bill. "Get back in and try again."

Still dead.

"Is the battery okay? Need water?"

He was irritating me. "The battery is fine. I just checked it this morning."

"Yeah? It could be the fuel line then." He whistled. "This won't be hard. Old cars fall open like ripe fruit, it's so easy to get to anything."

"Yeah. I know."

Bill waved me off when I tried to look under the hood with him, so I sat down on the side of the road. I hate when men do the car know-it-all thing. Crows looked down at me from their high perch on the telephone wires. Randa told me most of the birds would leave by August. It was now the end of July and so hot that I put the can of soda on my forehead and let it rest there in between sips.

Bill hummed as he worked. I daydreamed. The sky seemed to recede and then fall closer, back and forth, making me dizzy. For some reason I thought of old *Lassie* reruns I'd watched after I'd gotten arrested the first time and my dad had hauled me back to Redding. Late, around two A.M., I'd sneak out of the chicken coop and through a window into the main house. The first time I did it, I felt incredibly comforted, like all I wanted to do was watch TV for the rest of my life.

A pickup came by with two men. One had a missing tooth and long dirty hair, and the other was unshaven with bloodshot eyes. They leaned from their car and asked if we needed help. Yeah, right.

Bill didn't say anything to them, but they talked anyway. They were real proud of themselves, making sure to tell us stranded fools that they had jobs with a Wild Bill rodeo show in South Dakota.

I took the opportunity to use the pay phone to call Dottie. Told her I was hoping to be leaving as soon as I could get my car to work, and that I'd be sure to write.

"I'll be waiting for your scrawl," she said. I could hear a loud motor in the background.

Floyd and Freckle Face saw me and followed me back out to the car.

Now there were five men around my damn broken-down car.

"I think I see what it is," said Bill. "Floyd. I need you to find me a nut, about an 8-32. The ground wire on the distributor is loose."

But then, even after he attached the loose wire with a nut, the engine wouldn't turn.

So I wandered over to check the battery. Whoops. I had thought it was a maintenance-free one and wouldn't need water.

"Thought you said you'd checked that." Bill spat.

I shrugged. "Well, I did a while ago."

He walked over to the store to get some water.

Next the sheriff car came by and stopped, because my hood was still up. He lumbered over like a cowboy with a big old gun belt. He started snooping, looking in my car right away.

"It's just my battery. I need water."

The sheriff's bunched-up ass stuck out over my fender. I hadn't seen hardly any skunks out here in the Great Plains. As he leaned over I was tempted to snitch his gun from its holster. When he asked for my ID, I pretended to search my carrybag, then told him I didn't have it with me today.

He started some radio checks. I was done for.

Bill came back just in time to hear the cop tell me there was an outstanding warrant on the car. It had been used in a robbery in Minneapolis.

"Hey, the car is borrowed. It's not mine. I mean if somebody did a robbery with it, it wasn't me."

The sheriff kicked the tire of my car. "If I don't see some ID, miss, you're going with me."

"Where'd you get the car?" Bill asked.

"From a guy I met in Omaha. His name was Moe."

Bill and the cop talked. I rubbed my arrowhead and then got out my real ID and handed it to the cop. "I haven't done anything. Really."

Bill went to call his parents' house so they could get a hold of Randa. He left the Vulcan with the keys in the ignition.

The sky cleared as I waited for the cop to finish his radio checks. The clouds had left the sky open and fresh. It was getting to be a beautiful afternoon.

I got back in the car and waited.

Skunks. It must be a strange job to always be looking for people in trouble. Except I really didn't have any sympathy. You should have seen the slime of green happiness spread over the woman who searched me the last time I got arrested. But the worst part of the YGC was being in a room with no door knob. Till you've had that experience there's no way to describe it. All I can say is it made me feel inhuman, they made me into an animal. Something switched inside me in that locked room, and I've never felt the same. I would do anything rather than be locked up again.

Bill strutted back from the phone and stood by Randa's motorcycle.

"Look at you. You're sweating!" Bill chuckled. "Don't worry. If you done nothing, the police got nothing on you. No way they have you." He leaned on the cool slouchy Kawasaki, posing like some kind of gangster. Suddenly Bill was just loving being my howdy-partner-in-crime.

"Yeah, right." My voice didn't come out too well because I was pretty near tears at that point, thinking I'd ruined everything by not checking a stupid battery.

I could run faster then that huge sheriff, I knew I could. I could race him in the fields, the tall green cornfields. Hide in the stalks till he went away. Then run to a farm. Maybe a sweet farmer's wife would give me dinner. Biscuits and gravy and apple pie.

But I looked around and there were no cornfields. Around town there was only wheat fields, already harvested. He would see me run. He would shoot at my back. It was going to be a beautiful afternoon in the wild west, and I would be the thing the sheriff caught. As he drove me along the highway, I would give the thumbs up sign and smile to the people in the next towns, like I was a celebrity and getting a police escort. But then there would be the getting locked up part. Staring at a blank door with no doorknob, no way to get out.

The more I thought about the wild west the more I thought about what I could do.

He was not going to get me.

I sat very still in my Dodge and collected myself. It was simple. I reached for my carrybag and hung it crossways over my shoulder. I heard Bill say, "She's all right. She's staying with us. She'll give you the car and won't make any trouble. She's working with the kids on the corn crew."

The moment I left the car, I didn't wait one blink.

"Later," I yelled. I jumped on the Vulcan and turned the key. The bike lurched and then accelerated. In twelve seconds, I would be flying at one hundred thirty.

Unprotected, my skin was exposed to the wind. My bare arms and face took a vicious thrust. I squeezed my mouth closed and squinted so there were no openings for the air to rip into me. Holding on with every life-or-death muscle; this was exactly what I'd always wanted. Go. Tearing through the wind. Godspeeding. Wing flapping. Fuck me, world. Give me more!

The siren was far away.

presto

THE EARTH on either side of the South Dakota highway had been abandoned long ago, lots of hard dirt, scuffed up with patches of burned yellow grasses. The outskirts of reservation land. A place, finally, not controlled by some farmer.

There weren't many choices of turnoffs once I got across the border. The fences, the towns, the signs became seldom. My hands sweated and lost grip, my vision blurred, and I couldn't see much of what was ahead of me. I don't know what I thought I was doing. Hoping to grow wings?

Randa had bragged a couple of times that her bike accelerated much faster than a cop car. It was no contest. Left him in the dust. Left everything else, too. Even my skin felt ripped away.

The Kawasaki burned fuel like mad, and within no time after leaving Nebraska, I ran out of gas. As I pushed Randa's bike along the road, a few pickups slowed down to offer help, but I put my hand to my sweaty forehead in a salute and waved the drivers on.

The road was forever long, the sky forever big, and I was on my own. Hot as hell, but free.

I needed a hat or a tree shadow or some kind of protection and thought of a joke I'd heard about a plains farmer. He took an afternoon nap in a crematorium fire and lived to say what a cool day it had turned out to be.

The sun didn't seem to be moving any closer to the horizon. To pass the time, I sang anything I could, even Apostle Rods songs. "Nobody knows my name but Jesus...." At last even my words disappeared, swallowed by the parched land. I was sweating out my insides and there was nothing to drink. No town in sight.

I wondered if Randa would come looking for me.

My hands started to blister from gripping the handles without any gloves, and my knees were buckling. If a cop came, I could drop the bike, but once again there were no crops to run through. The police must have some bulletin out about me, and they had my real ID now. But thank god, once again I was in a new state, and I hoped that would lose them.

The blue of the sky was the only relief in sight. I looked up again and again, trying to drink it in, a big pitcher of cool water.

Like any city-born kid, I had romanticized open space as something that spelled freedom. And it had for a while. But after pushing that bike for what seemed like hours, I started to feel like I was on a big shooting target and couldn't hide. I mean, the only thing around, the only thing to break up the horizon, was me.

At last. Ahead was a sign. PRESTO, POPULATION 56.

THE BUFFALO TRAIL MOTEL offered me a cramped cell. Three steps across, and even then you had to lean away from the walls. It wasn't the kind of motel room escaped bad guys found in the movies; they always had thick bedspreads, a television, and a shiny phone by the bed. Mine just had a bed with a plastic mattress cover, a sheet, and a rough army-style blanket. I wished I still had my sleeping bag and could have slept outside.

My legs and arms and brain were long numbed and over-tired. I was hungry, but afraid to be seen by the skunkers, so I stayed imprisoned. The weak air conditioner, sitting where the window should have been, didn't cool the air. It only whipped up the disinfectant smell.

To get to sleep, I tried to remember a truth list I had made back when. See what still fit…

Don't be afraid to leave; it's the only way to get strong.
I don't know. Am I brave or just a fool?
Don't settle, and never marry. Love dreams will choke you with tighter hands than loneliness.
I guess. Maybe. Probably so.
Always talk to strangers. They will be the ones who will help you in the end.
Whatever.
If you are a woman, don't tell anybody.
Yeah.
Never want anything you don't have. Look at the sky. It's as big as a dream.
Okay. I'll keep trying.
Want the sun and sky and you will be okay most of the time.
Fuck it. I'm not okay.
The body has the sweetest secrets; it's more real than money or religion.
Yeah. I hope so.

Mothers are always ghosts. So don't go looking for one.

Shit.

The air-conditioning motor kept waking me when it kicked against the window frame to recharge. At some point the sound became rocks falling on top of me in my dream.

I NEVER TOLD anybody this, but once I spent the night at Fort Point, in the military ruins near the foot of the Golden Gate Bridge. Right after the first time I ran away. I used my sleeping bag and slept in a broken concrete box in a wall. As I dozed, I could smell the beach. In the middle of the night, I woke and couldn't fall back to sleep. I made long lists in my mind. Then I wandered to the edge of the water, stood under the bridge. Not many stars, just blowing mist, moans of foghorns, the bridge rising over me like some sea serpent.

I stood there clinging to the edge of the city. The Pacific, a black sea lapping at my feet. Could have been killed right there, but I didn't believe that. I hadn't yet run from a gang of skinheads. Or jumped from a moving car. Or fought a man trying to rape me. I was a kid needing freedom. Doing anything that seemed loose and unharnessed. All I knew was that I wanted to be brave.

THE HASH KNIFE CAFÉ, across the highway from my motel, was the most ugly-ass restaurant I had ever seen. The walls were covered with adhesive paper made to look like fake wood paneling. Barn shaped, with very high windows, the long room, even at high noon, had no real light. Two industrial fluorescent tube lights hung from chains overhead and gave off a ghoulish glow. Most of the customers were worn-out, hairless, and hungry looking, shoulders raised as high as their ears. They stooped over their lunches and chewed in unison like strange, long-necked birds. Plucked, boiled vultures.

I sat down for breakfast across from the only oddball, a man wearing tight fatigues. He had the beaten-down look of someone who had driven too long or watched too much TV. He told me that he was on his way to hunt prairie dogs at the nearby Rosebud Indian Reservation.

"Really? Do you eat the dogs?"

He blinked. "No, darling. It's sport."

I took a sip of water. "What do you use?"

"Enough, well," he coughed, "enough to splatter them into a few million pieces."

"Want to take me along?"

"You a shooter?"

"Occasionally." I nodded. "Have killed a few people."

His eyes froze while his mouth rose in a weak grin.

The one saving grace of the Hash Knife was the raised, illuminated pie box behind the counter. A slanted mirror in the back of the box reflected five noble pies, each with slices cut to reveal the gooey berry or lemon or cherry inside.

With pie at one dollar and a motel room at twenty-eight, my corn detasseling money would last a while.

I FIGURED I'd better call Irma and try to leave a message with Randa. I used the pay phone in the parking lot of the Hash Knife.

They were watching baseball, but Irma accepted my collect call and got Randa for me.

Randa didn't talk long on the phone after I told her where I was.

"You stay there. Don't go anywhere."

"Randa. I'm sorry I took your bike."

"You're a fuck-load of trouble." Her voice was strained and low.

"I didn't do anything. It was someone else that did the robbery."

"We'll see you soon."

When she hung up, I stood with the receiver in my hand and listened to the dead connection.

I had meant to leave Bonesteel without any fuss. With my pocketful of cash, I figured it was time to have some more adventures. I had planned on ditching the Dodge in Sioux City, rescuing Jessika from her topless gig and going off to explore the place where my mother's people were from.

Nothing turns out the way you expect.

BILL AND RANDA hadn't gotten to Presto by late afternoon. So I went across the highway to the fabulicious Hash Knife again.

I slithered through a smooth piece of lemon chiffon pie and pondered my situation. Meredith didn't know my real name, so there was no way she could report my identity to the police. The cop who now had my Dodge also had my real ID, but my record should've been clean other than the Beyond Parental Control stuff.

How was I to know the Dodge had been used in a robbery?

For my second piece I ordered the blackberry with ice cream. Deelishousssnesss. My favorite.

Everyone in the restaurant ignored me entirely. Even the kid waitress with the long bangs didn't look at me. She stared at her pad, took my orders carefully, and gave a little private smile after she finished writing. As I ate my last bites and the other customers left, the kid waitress looked over with her big scared eyes.

"Ja-care-fir-anythin-else?"

"Tell me about Presto Land."

Sweat broke on her forehead. She brushed aside her bangs and sat down on the seat across from me.

Turned out her name was Pammy and she was a true-blue farmer's daughter. She said her dad had fallen asleep on the tractor last night and almost fell off.

"So, Pammy, do you think you'll ever leave Presto?"

"Haven't gotten to that yet!"

Once she started talking she seemed unable to stop. She told me the county name, Burnt, came from a long time ago when some Indians threw themselves on a prairie fire. They were able to quench the flames and managed to live, except for the sacrifice of their crispy skin.

After she finished giving me her report on the linguistic roots of her county, she got a little more personal. She was in tenth grade and wanted to go to college and study art. She said *art* like it was a word tasted only in private.

"I draw my friends sometimes. And things like goblins, which my mom hates." She sat real still and didn't look around at all, answering my questions like she was in school.

WHEN I LEFT the diner and got back to the motel, my saviors had arrived. Randa was filling the motorcycle with gasoline from a big tin container and wouldn't look at me.

"We'll see you back home. Bill, tie her up if you have to." With that she got on her dusty Vulcan and took off.

Bill seemed kind of amused and charged by my predicament. He even took off his sunglasses. I asked him to help me pay for another night at the motel.

He kicked the gravel parking lot where I stood waiting. "What you going to do for me?"

"What do you mean?"

"Just kidding." He pulled up his jeans. "Well, word's out about you. I think you're going to have to turn yourself in. If you didn't do the robbery in the first place, well, it doesn't seem like you'd be in too much of a pickle. You come back to Bonesteel and it will settle out."

I had Bill to thank, really. If he hadn't been using the Kawasaki that day, I wouldn't have had my lucky chariot out of Bonesteel.

"I didn't do the robbery, but the Dodge wasn't exactly mine."

"Oh, really?" It was getting near dusk. "You may have some explaining to do."

Sweat dipped down my back. "I'm not going back."

"Yeah?" He coughed.

"That's right."

"She won't be happy." He was staring at my breasts.

I crossed my arms. "What do you think Randa is doing with you anyway?"

He wiped his sunglasses on his shirt. "Wants the farm." His raccoon eyes looked really sad.

"Good luck, Bill." I kissed his cheek. "Don't tell the cop where I am, okay?"

He nodded. "Right, Pony Girl."

I laughed. "I'm not coming back with you."

"Right."

After I closed the door and locked the push button, I listened for the sound of his truck. I heard his motor cough and the wheels turn in the gravel and then the scrape onto the road and roar into no sound at all.

The room was so white and so stinking of cleanser I thought it would scour me away. So the only thing to do, the only place to walk, was across the highway to get more pie.

WHEN JEHOVAH'S WITNESSES came to my granddad's apartment, I always let them in. The first time, I was really young, and I let them read to me from their Bible. One was horse-mouthed and wore a tiny checked dress. We had a discussion. I told them humans had been around a lot longer than the five thousand years they claimed. So the next week they brought me an official Jehovah's Witness pamphlet that explained why the science of carbon dating was mistaken.

It was before I thought much about girls—but I remember the shy one's legs. From beneath the Bible in her lap jutted two tiny, caramel-colored knees. She touched them a lot. I argued hard, and she had to argue back, but in a soft voice. I never told my granddad, but I let them take me to a church in Bay View. There were more dressed-up black people there than I'd ever seen in one place. One Big Happy Church. I loved it. But I never went back.

THAT EVENING as I waited for Pammy to come over from the Hash Knife, I dug some stuff from the bottom of my carrybag—the photo I had taken from Meredith's wallet, the little girl in a silly school photo. The figurine I took from Dottie's shelf. I felt bad that I hadn't returned it like I planned. It was a tiny china hen with a smooth red head and flat blue eyes. I had a few other things—like a ring of Jessika's that I had pocketed—and I placed them on my belly. Wondered whether to throw them away. They embarrassed me. But somehow I couldn't get rid of them.

Then I felt restless, pathetic. What the hell I was going to do with myself in Presto? Took the Bible from the top of the air conditioner and started reading from the beginning. "The spirit of God moved upon the face of the waters. Let there be light in the firmament of the heaven." I wondered if my mom had ever read the same words.

The next pages listed men who had lived for hundreds of years. Then god got angry and decided to destroy everything he had created. "The end of all flesh is before me." It made me feel like burning a few pages, but I didn't have any matches. I rolled the flat motel pillow under my head, tried to get comfortable, and skipped ahead to find more comforting examples of god talk.

The air conditioner growled over my head. I hadn't read anything in so long. Books offered so much baggage; I stopped trusting words a long time ago.

What if god didn't talk at all, but was just some headbanger, a sweaty dancer up in the sky? Stomping around the stratosphere making clouds.

But if god didn't have language, what good was that? I needed a god that could hear and respond.

I tried pressing and digging the corner of the Bible into my chest. "If you are up there give me a sign."

Nothing happened.

"Help me."

I opened my door and looked across the highway. Shadows in a low hanging cloud formed a cross. It freaked me out. Someday I'd end up a stupid christian. I could just feel it.

PAMMY'S WIDE-OPEN GAZE filled the no-color blankness of my motel cell, her brown eyes all shining. When I got claustrophobic, I suggested we sit inside the doorway. I pulled a joint from my wallet that I had gotten long ago from Jessika.

"You ever smoke?"

"What do you think we do in Presto?" She spoke in a high, little good-girl voice. We broke into giggles.

I lit the joint and handed it to her. The motel clerk walked out and put some garbage in a bin. She walked like a stiff skeleton. I suggested we walk around behind the room.

"She don't care." Pammy's lips drew on the joint with the same careful attention she used when penning orders on the waitress pad.

I took a hit and slowly blew it on the top of Pammy's head. She took the joint from me, dragged, and as she released the smoke, another joke spread inside her.

"So, you find me funny?" I asked.

She looked at her feet, shy again. She wore dusty white sandals.

When I had asked Pammy to hang with me after work, I was hoping for the scene in every road-trip movie where the charming rogue finds comfort with the lonely, sultry waitress.

"Are you really from San Francisco?"

God, I wished people would stop asking me that. "No. Actually I'm from Hades." I crushed the roach with my boot and stepped inside my room.

"I have a cousin who went to school in California." Pammy tried to walk around me, but there was no way to fit two people against the bed in the cramped room. "I'll probably go to State or something."

I closed the door and turned on the rattling air conditioner. "Do what you want, Pammy. I won't stop you."

She clasped her hands together. "You are a girl, but you look like a boy."

We both sat on the bed. She took a pen from her pocket and started drawing a butterfly on my forearm next to my dragon tattoo.

I was hungry and my mouth was dry from the dope. "You think you could get me a whole pie from the Hash Knife? Maybe boysenberry?"

"You should try the peach. Yummy."

"Why didn't you tell me before?" I looked at her, and she laughed. I rolled around on the bed trying to get comfortable. "Girl. Boy," I said. "Sometimes I think if we didn't have to use words, things would be better."

She talked faster. "Words, words, words. I hate the way things get named. Like paintings." She twisted her bangs. "I like drawing creatures that aren't human, weird things. They have no names." She drew spots on the butterfly on my arm. Then she pointed to the dragon on my forearm. "I could draw a better dragon than that."

"You're cool, Pammy." She wasn't my fantasy waitress, but she was kind of sweet.

"Why do you call yourself Girl?"

"Did I say that? My real name is Penelope Huck Crow."

A motorcycle roared and we heard it pull into the parking lot. I pulled away from Pammy, sat up against the wall.

I heard talking in the office.

Soon Randa opened the door.

Pammy stood up and tucked in her shirt. "Hi!"

"What the hell?" Randa stood there in the doorway.

Pammy looked at me.

"Don't worry," I whispered to Pammy. "She's not my mom."

We both burst out in giggles.

It was dark outside, which made the loose hairs around Randa's head flicker in the fluorescent blue of the parking lot.

"Don't make a big issue out of this, man," I said. "This is Pammy. She would like your acquaintance. To make it. That is. Your acquaintance." I pulled Pammy so she was back down on the bed, and put my arm around her shoulder.

"You are some piece of work, Girl." Randa hit the side of her fist on the door frame.

I stood up. Pammy rushed into the bathroom and slammed the door.

"What's wrong?" Both my hands closed, ready to fight if she got any closer. "You want me to come back to Bonesteel, but you don't give me the time of day. Well, forget it!" I stepped around the bed so I wasn't flush against the wall. "I borrowed a credit card in Salt Lake.

Your sheriff might have all kinds of charges up against me. I'm not going to let it happen. They'd have me. They'd own me. Is that what you want?"

Pammy was running the water. It sounded high as her voice. I thought of going in the bathroom with her and locking the door.

Randa's chest heaved up and down.

I was cornered. I wanted to say something brave, but instead I found myself under the bed, curled in a ball so that she couldn't kick me.

Instead she kept yelling. "Who do you think... What do think... I can't stand... Doing this to me..." I covered my ears. When she finally stopped, I moved my head to where I could take a peek. She was in the doorway still, but now turned in profile. Her eyes looked puffy and bloodshot.

I whispered, "Were you crying?"

"No!" She walked away. Leaving the door open.

I yelled from the doorway. "Don't ever think about hitting me again."

When Pammy came out, I told her things were okay.

"Are you sure?" She was using the little-girl voice again, wringing a wet hand towel.

I walked Pammy to the highway. Randa glowered as she stood near her bike.

We said goodbye, and Pammy walked away with the motel towel draped over her shoulders. She looked like a tiny, white-cloaked nun pacing into the darkness.

ALL THE SUN'S GLOW had gone from the fields. The only light around was from the fluorescent motel sign. After sweating in the heat for a while, Randa started to talk.

"Hey." She swallowed.

I wanted to go look at the stars, and leave her, but instead I felt stuck in our tableau of mutual hate. "Yeah?"

"I'm sorry."

"Yeah, sure."

"You're a fucking handful, you know that?"

"Yeah." I let out a laugh.

"Hey. Don't leave me again."

She got her .45 from her saddlebag and put it in a holster that hung at her side. Then she suggested we take a walk.

"You going to shoot me?" I asked.

"Come on, let's go." Her eyes still looked really red and upset.

I let her put her arm around me. It felt good; she'd never done it before.

We walked down the highway and within five minutes were out of the range of the motel's electricity and alone in the dark summer heat. A car's headlights looked miles away. When it got close, we moved onto the nearby field. In the passing light we could see each other's faces.

Randa reached down and grabbed some of the fallow dirt in the field. "Just tilled. Bet somebody's planting beans."

We walked in between the furrows and up to a small rise where a sign stood. We couldn't read it till we got close: CABLE UNDERGROUND. Behind it was the large circle of concrete.

Randa pulled her gun from the holster and placed it on the ground. We lay side by side next to the gun on the warm ease of cement.

Constellations pierced through the black. Because we were farther north than San Francisco, Pegasus was high. With no moon, the sky was much clearer than when I'd star-watched with Bo at the pit. I kept thinking about how the starlight was traveling in hundreds of thousands of miles per second.

I found myself telling the story of the time my dad had pointed out some constellations. A week later I looked at the sky and the stars had changed places. The Big Dipper spun higher, and I couldn't find the tail of the Scorpion. I was terrified and had gone running back inside.

Then I showed Randa the constellations I knew.

When she didn't say anything for a long time, I said, "Maybe our devils have nothing more to say." I looked over at her. "It's so quiet out here I can hear my heartbeat. It's weird."

"I have my .45. No one's going to bother us. Don't worry."

"Which stars do you think are dead and gone?"

"What do you mean? They are all here." Randa tucked her arm under my neck and stroked my shoulder. "Tell me you don't like it out in the Plains."

I could smell Randa's sun-toughed skin mixed with the dead-twig smell of the plowed earth. "Yeah, sure." I sat up. "If it wasn't so hot. If people didn't think I was a freak." Randa had never understood how much of an outsider I was on the farm.

I needed to touch her tonight or I was going to burst. She had wanted me the first night I arrived, but only cause she thought I was leaving soon. When she found out I was going to stay and work on the damn cornfields, then she pulled away. But now everything felt different. If she did want me again, what did I have to lose? Not much.

"Do you think it's easy for anyone here?" Randa sat up, too.

"I don't know."

"Maybe you'd be happier following the wheat harvest. There are so many big places that need to hire out. It's cash work. You'd like it."

"The Wheaties."

"Yeah, that's what they're called. Bill tell you about them?"

I tapped my boot against Randa's ankle. "Why are you always telling me what I should do?"

"Because no one else ever has."

I fanned the air to feel a breeze. "We could be two outlaws together."

Randa didn't answer.

"So why the hell were you ignoring me the whole time I was in Bonesteel?"

"You're a trip. You don't get it, do you?" Randa was quiet again for a while.

I turned on my back. "Well?"

"I want you to love it without me making it happen. For you to take to it here. The life. The land. The sky. I didn't want to get in the way."

"You could help me." I couldn't believe I said those words. How was Randa supposed to help? She thought I was some free-spirited California girl. Randa didn't know half the stuff I'd done. If she did, this would be over fast. I felt envy for the girl that Randa imagined I was. Somebody young and careless and happy.

Arcturus flickered bright and blue. The summer triangle soared. It made me feel way too needy, like a Lifetime movie. Some doomed small-town girl hooks up with a handsome bad seed and ends up having to murder him with his own gun. The last shot is the girl alone in jail.

"We could start our own farm."

"You never know." Randa put her arm around me. "Girl, you should be thanking me."

"For what?"

"For saving you. Getting you away from the city."

"Yeah, sure. The big bad city."

It was way past midnight. Very, very quiet everywhere. I pointed out what looked like a planet.

Randa sighed. "It sure is something."

"I don't want to be called Girl anymore. I like the name Penelope Huck. Or just Huck would be good."

"How about Huckleberry?"

"Maybe."

We fell back again, close now, and watched the constellations move slowly across the sky. It appeared as if they circled the North Star, but I kept reminding myself it was really Earth spinning.

I had been avoiding asking Randa about her trip, but now seemed the right time.

"So, what happened with your mom in Chicago?"

"Well, she has breast cancer, you know."

"Is it bad?"

Randa felt for her gun for a second and then placed her hand on her belt. "Oh, I don't know. I got in a big blowout with her. I haven't called her since."

"Randa, what's your mom like?"

"All being alive is doing for my mom is making her more bitter. I think she wants to die."

"You never know what someone really wants."

Randa whistled. "The woman hates me. She knows I've fooled around, done what she calls immoral acts, and it ruins her." She stroked my shoulder. "I realized something in Chicago. She's going to die. Just like everybody. I wish I could help, but I can't." She paused. "None of us can help our mothers. When I accepted that, I stopped feeling guilty."

I'd always felt guilty about my mom. As if I could have kept her alive. Was Randa right? Was it impossible to help someone? I didn't want to believe that. "I know what you mean. Even real mothers seem unreachable. Like ghosts."

She squeezed my hand and then pointed to a cluster of stars. "What's that one again?"

"Cassiopeia." I lifted my hand and circled the fingers around Randa's forearm. Whenever I touched her, I was surprised to feel how small she was. Rock hard, but smaller than me.

Face it. I needed people so much. All the time I needed them.

When I stroked the back of Randa's hand, the skin felt so thick and real, a hand entirely shaped by sun and work. The hand I admired back when. I rubbed the skin of my own hand. Looked at the silhouette of my legs. My body felt foreign, as if I didn't know it at all, hadn't grown into it yet.

FINALLY, WE LEFT the starry night for the air-conditioned room. Randa wanted to watch TV, but there was none in my room. She thought there would be some bulletins about me, like I was an escaped convict or something.

"All I heard yesterday was a news report of a missing kid. Some ten-year-old from Reno. It happens all the time."

I took off my shorts and lay in my T-shirt and underwear on the bed. There was only one pillow so I pushed it to her side. "The kid will probably be okay."

"Look at you." She got in the bed and lay silent for a while. "See, there was no way I could leave you. You are a fucking orphan, and you don't even know it."

She moved around on the bed, and it felt like we were rocking together on a tiny boat.

"Randa, why did you ever think you could be with Bill?"

"It's simpler with men. They don't take your soul."

"Since when? You've never let anybody take you."

"I know I'm being selfish, wanting you. I've always known that."

"Get over it."

It was totally dark so I had to feel my way. I put my hands on either side of her hips and used my knee to push open her legs. Even women hard and screwed shut like Randa, even them, when you find them in the dark, they have to give it up, and they always have that part that can't help but be wet and silky.

I felt her for a long time with my hand, kneading her. She made sounds like it hurt, but I knew she was only trying to let go.

Then she flipped me on my back and took me. Pretty hard.

She fell asleep holding me. I lay there waiting for morning.

One thing I always knew was that sex means nothing but the moment. I never trust it to be more, and that's why I can ride it so far. Randa trusted it and now I see how I must have hurt her. She thought our sex that night made the bonds between us permanent. I just hoped it made them real.

THE FIRST MORNING after Randa came, we went for an early breakfast at the diner.

"Blueberry, huckleberry, lemon," said Pammy. She used her little girl voice and tried not to look at Randa when I asked about the day's pies.

Randa growled at me. "Have some protein, kid."

I ordered two pieces of blueberry pie and relished every bite.

Randa ate her eggs and bacon quickly. Then told me she was going to go for a ride to explore the area.

I told her I wanted to stay in Presto.

"Don't look at her like you are ever going to get near her again, Girl. I mean Huckleberry. Because you aren't."

"She's a cream puff, and you're my life," I said. I was playing our romantic fantasy for all it was worth. It felt pretty good, too. But Randa just nodded and left to go take a shower.

I stayed and read the paper and looked at the retired farmers. I apologized to Pammy for the drama of the previous night.

"You in some kind of trouble?"

"Would you mind keeping it quiet?"

She nodded, serious and excited, used to keeping secrets.

When I came back to the Buffalo Trail, Randa was in the shower and had the door locked. She had the key. A used rubber lay by the next room's door, but we were still the only vehicle in the lot. I wandered over to the office. No one was there. So I walked around to the bathroom window and knocked. It was about one foot square and seemed more like plastic than glass.

Randa let me in. She used a T-shirt to dry off. Her breasts were very white compared to the dark tanned hide of her arms and lower legs. She reminded me of a centaur, with a white human chest and tanned bestial limbs.

Her gun was on the bed. I picked it up.

"Put that down." She combed her hair, pulling hard on the knots. I knew she must feel weird not going to work on the farm in the morning.

"I'll give you some money." She took out a five. "I don't know how long I'll be gone. If we're going to stay here, we need some cash. I'm going to scout around for a bit. And call Bill."

I couldn't believe that she'd decided to stay in Presto.

I pointed the gun out the window.

"If you want to practice with that thing, I'll take you out. You should know how to use it."

"How about today?"

"Do you always get what you want?"

RANDA AGREED TO A QUICK LESSON. We went back to the cable marker, the big cement circle in the hay field where we'd watched stars the night before.

We walked out and stood there, exposed.

She let me handle the gun before she loaded the magazine. It looked like death itself. Black and solid with a big gaping hole for the bullet to charge through. I'd fired rifles before, but never a heavy .45-caliber pistol. A former army gun, she said.

She showed me how to hold my arm straight and firm, how to focus.

I held it down by my leg and practiced bringing it up fast and aiming. There was nothing to shoot, but then I realized that's exactly what I did want to shoot. The dry empty space. The sun with no breath in it.

She loaded the chamber and showed me how to use the hammer and keep the gun ever ready. Cocked and locked.

"Go ahead."

I took a breath. Aimed.

The kick of it went into my body. Rather than a release, I felt an implosion. As if the charge went straight back. It made me gasp.

"You're doing fine."

"Let me watch you."

Randa took the gun and walked to the side. "Stay there." She turned toward the highway and slowly raised her arm. She fired at the cable marker road sign. "See that!"

"Pretty good." I didn't smile. I hated this dry plain. I hated that there was nothing alive around for miles.

"You don't like guns, do you?"

"Yeah, right. I'm just a flower girl." I crossed my arms, suddenly ready to get my hands around the gun once more.

"You know, babe, there's no need to worry. You can learn how to protect yourself."

I wanted to do more than that.

UNLIKE MOST PEOPLE on the street for the long haul, I'd never had the really horrible stuff happen. The sick thing was that sometimes I wished somebody would try to beat me. So I could kick and mash them until they were pulp on the floor.

When I met Cara, she had escaped her family after getting beaten so hard that she was still in bad shape, her pelvis crushed and her leg pulled from its socket. My granddad let her stay for a while. I read aloud from his books and she got better.

It made me furious to know that they had flown Cara's body back to Seattle, returned her to a sadist stepfather and pill-infested mom. I wanted at least to have buried Cara. I had to live with the fact that I would never know where her remains were. If the monsters even buried her. Maybe they just let her rot.

At least my mom didn't get flown back to Oregon. My granddad and father told me they'd taken her ashes out on a boat near Angel Island.

Cara was gone, either way, anyway, so what could you do?

It's like when a pet dies. You looked in the eyes, felt the fur, but it's really gone. No breath, no soul. Whether you buried it in the backyard or took it to the SPCA, in the long run it didn't matter, because it won't put light back in its little glassy eyes. There's some poem that asked how a body as small as a kitten's could ever hold such an immense thing as death.

I never had a pet, but my baby-sitter, Mrs. Dowell, did. One afternoon we found her little cat strangled in a bit of old volleyball net. So lifeless. When the soul disappeared, it didn't leave shit.

AFTER MY SHOOTING LESSON, Randa disappeared again. When she got back that night, she told me she had found a job. She found work at one of the farms that had a machine shop on the property. They repaired tractors and equipment for many of the other operations. She would work for a while till we got enough money to go somewhere else, some place where I'd have less chance of getting caught. She also had called Bill again and told him she definitely wasn't going back.

"What did he say?"

"He said, 'That just goes to show.' "

"Show what?"

"He didn't say. Remember, Nebraskans are naturally laconic. They don't like to talk much, especially about anything personal."

"I know what laconic means." I punched her on the arm. "So, he wasn't mad?"

"Couldn't tell you."

THE NEXT DAY, she went to work and left me her gun. I considered flushing the bullets down the toilet or putting them in the garbage behind the motel. Instead I took them out and hid them in my bag.

I wanted a gun that was invincible, better than any police gun—always faster, always the best. But that's the history of the world, right? Everybody kept trying to get a better weapon. Look where that led.

Randa was working till she got enough money for us to leave and become outlaw Wheaties together. We needed money to get on the road. Meantime she wanted me to be her wife or something, so I had nothing to do during the day. I read my Bible, ate pie, or bugged Pammy at the restaurant. Eventually Pammy started asking me over to her house in the afternoons. I didn't tell Randa because she had made it clear that she didn't want me hanging with anybody else.

What I really waited for was the nights.

I got to like the way Randa touched me, the craftsman accuracy of her hands. I felt like an object underneath her, which excited me.

It was as if she owned my body. I couldn't wait for her to say at the moment that I was going to lose it: "Go ahead."

Afterwards she would finally let me touch her. And I was ready to take her, again and again. Especially after those nights sleeping in the same bed with her and Bill in Bonesteel, all the times I'd wanted to lift my hand and slide it between her legs.

Seeing people fall apart; it always got me. And Randa had such a long way to fall. I would kiss her on her cheek. Smell the blaze of sweat and outdoors that I loved. Or sit on top of her and make her peal with on-and-on purring rumbles. Rock her back and forth till she got dizzy. Tease her crotch—just a little to get her high—and then make her wait in the ache.

Once I even tried to fuck her with her .45. She rumbled out a big bronco laugh and told me to put it away.

WHEN PAMMY wasn't waitressing, we spent a lot of time messing around on her computer. We surfed through boy-rot punk sites. We posted on some of the roaddawgz bulletin boards and sent e-mails. I sent one to Pedro, a high school boy in Miami. I contacted a homeless guy named Rex who sent e-mails from wherever he landed. Everybody wanted to know about SF. All these bored people thought that if they could get to San Francisco everything would be cool.

Angus-Face ------- !

Cuteboy. Where are you? I don't know where the bejeesus I am. Some place far far far far far fucking awaaaaaaaay. You couldn't find me in a million zillion years. Hey, I'm gonna be working away on the wheat harvests!!!!!! I'll be following them all over with Randa (remember the butch woman with the 750 cycle who liked me?) and I may end up in your neck of woodsiness...the big ole state of Texas. I'll be tanned and rugged and no one will mess with me!

Stars are great out here. Yes!

I hope you get this message. I miss Cara. I think she talks to me sometimes. Not that I can understand what she's saying.

What are you doing? Are you still with Jumbo Jim? I reeeeeeeeeally
hope you get this. I miss you lots and lots.

Peace Outta Here--------

Girl-Face

THE LINDFLOTTS owned six hundred and forty acres. Pammy
told me property was the thing here. It was handed down from family to family and when people died or went broke, the family farms
got bigger. You had to be a big landowner to survive. Although the
weather played havoc with anybody and everybody. It had been too
wet, then too dry, and so forth. Whatever was happening up in the
sky, it wasn't making things very abundant.

The Lindflotts lived in a hideously clean ranch house. I still
hoped to find some charming old farmhouse, but this land had
not been settled that long and I guess most structures hadn't lasted. The only homes around were low-slung and perky suburban
with ugly paint jobs. What was unique, to me anyway, was the fact
that the Lindflott house had so much land around it, lots and lots
of amber waves of grain, or in their case, soy beans. The most
interesting part of the property was the machines that hunkered
around nearby. The hoppers, thrashers, wagons, and grain trucks
circled the outer perimeter of the house and pointed the way to
the barns and silos on the property. The driveway scooped
around, and unlike the Bonesteel place, the house was not far from
the highway.

Pammy hadn't told me, but her mom was in a wheelchair. She
wore a lot of powder on her face, which made it very blank: like a
slipcover on a couch, it seemed to be hiding something. Other than
that, the family did not seem unusual. You never saw the dad; he was

always working. It just happened that he worked on the farm and not the law office. Status Quo America.

Pammy's bedroom was very neat. Her mom still helped clean it for her. You could see the wheel chair tracks along the clean blue carpet. Against the wall with the door stood an older bureau where the only bit of chaos flourished, a hairbrush clumped with Pammy's hair and piles of pink and yellow terry-cloth hair bands. On the bookshelf sat a neatly placed box of Ultra-Soft tissue, three fantasy books, and notebooks of drawings. The bookcase also showcased Pammy's My Little Ponies and Garbage Pail Kid cards collection. It wasn't so surprising that she would still have those around because Pammy still pretended she was a little girl to her parents. She even talked in her high voice with them, like a doll in a horror movie.

With me she was pure devil, or tried to be. Unlike Bo, though, she had substantial curiosity. (She wasn't high most of the time, so that helped.) Pammy was her own person somewhere deep; I could see her being an artist one day. I wished she were a little older. She acted how I did when I was about three. I mean seriously. I probably had a squeaky voice like her, and I was probably still trying to please people.

One day we sat around her bedroom. She had tried to get online, but the connection was busy. She leaned against her bed and I lay on the floor.

"I wish I'd been born in San Francisco," Pam said. She took a match and set fire to the threads at the bottom of her jeans. "Did you know the Haight Ashbury?"

This was one of Pam's big talk topics. Hippiedom. She had done research on the web. I tried to tell her about what the Haight was like now, but she didn't quite get it.

Before I could say much, though, Pammy went on to another topic. Eventually I learned to answer without much effort. In her room I became very passive and yet on active duty at the same time.

Kind of like a mom in the park with a toddler. I had to follow her meandering, couldn't keep my own agenda.

Pammy twisted her bangs with her hand. "I think my mom's gay."

"Really?" I looked over to see if she meant it.

"She had this friend for a long time. They slept in the same bed sometimes when my dad was sleeping on the couch. Before the accident."

"Really? Did your dad push her in front of a combine when he found out or something?"

"Yeah, really. Like my dad would notice. It doesn't matter, right? I don't think you'll go to hell." She took out a cigarette. She couldn't smoke in her room because of her parents, but she liked to hold cigarettes in her hand and tap them against her leg as she spoke. "Do you think I should leave home now and go to art school?"

She blew at her bangs. Then sucked on her pencil, like a baby sucking on a pacifier.

I lay on the rug and listened to her. What else did I have to do?

AFTER LIVING WITH RANDA a week in the cramped Buffalo Trail motel room, I had a dream she died. We had launched a tiny wooden canoe into Stow Lake in Golden Gate Park. Stroked deep and hard because the bluish-black lakewater was thick as oil. Pulled hard with our oars to get our canoe around the funny island in the middle. We got right up close to the dusty, broken-limbed cedar trees, the long-ago archways, the stairs leading to the hill. When I stood up, we both seesawed back and forth. As I looked down to get my balance, Randa disappeared. I saw the splash and ripples from what I knew to be her fall, each circle of her wake. Eerie and quiet; one big hush. No one around, and for some reason, I didn't jump in to save her. I woke sobbing, and reached to touch Randa's back. The thick cords of muscle were even warmer than my sweaty palms. I didn't mean to wake her but weird sounds escaped from my chest, like a kid's deep whooping cough. She rolled over and told me everything was going to be all right. When I started telling her my dream, she pulled my head to her chest and whispered, "Sh-h-h."

ONE AFTERNOON I left the Hash Knife and wondered what to do till Randa got back to the motel. I saw a familiar guy bent over the engine of an old silver Buick. He had no shirt on, and his belly fell over his pants like brown dough.

"Hey, are you Curly?"

"You the hobo, the California hillbilly?" He laughed.

"I met you at the pit. You're Bo's friend."

Curly smiled. "Pleasure's all mine."

I took Curly back to my air-conditioned room, because after he fixed his car he wanted to smoke.

We sat on the edge of the bed. He took a bag of ganja from his pants.

"So, you know Bo well?"

He struck a match and lit up. "They come to me. I take care of them." He sighed, like he had such important duties. Then he got sweet and told me about Tiffany, the girl he loved in high school, a girl who had already married and divorced. He took a photo from his wallet. "Here's her babies."

I took another hit. "Are you the daddy?"

Curly winked. He still had his shirt off and his skin was the color of perfect toast. His arms were large as loaves, the shoulders twice as big as mine.

When we finished the joint, he took his shoes off. "You need work?"

"I'm okay."

He whispered something in my ear. Couldn't understand. He started kissing me. I squirmed away. He asked if he could give me a massage. His big warm hands started rubbing my shoulders.

"Stop."

He backed off. "What's wrong?"

"Go to hell!" I lost it.

"I wasn't hurting you." He looked scared. He looked even more scared when I laughed.

"You're full of it. You were going to try to fuck me."

"So?"

"Don't pretend it's a massage. That's creepy."

My heart was still pumping fast, but we just lay down on the bed after that. I needed him to know who was in control. I could have fucked him, but I wouldn't have been into it.

Besides, Randa's gun was under the mattress, so I wasn't worried about things getting nasty.

"Are you really from California?" he said at some point. "I want to go there." His flesh rose around me in mounds. I could imagine him a range of mountains, in the summer when they seem to exude heat, even after sundown.

"So you're Indian?"

He nodded. "What else?"

I explained how I wondered whether the past was still here, in some way, still haunting us. Curly shrugged and got up to take a pee.

I got my arrowhead from my carrybag.

When he came back, I asked if he had relatives on a reservation. "Do you think about a hundred years ago? What it must have been like being Indian?"

"Not really." He rolled another joint. "I have an uncle who makes

Indian masks and sells them. I could take you to his place and you could check it out." He nodded and clicked his tongue. "He makes casts of faces and then paints them and sticks feathers in the eyes. They're really weird." He winked. "Like you."

"Right." I stuffed my arrowhead in my pocket. I realized there was no point in showing it. He was as far away from any tepee-living Indians as I was from any log cabin–living pioneers. I don't know why I thought it would be any different.

And then Randa came in the door. And had her big slamming fit.

Hey Angus,

My last message didn't get returned so I'm guessing you are out there somewhere and still have your zzzipmail open and you will someday read this once you get done whuddeva the hell you doin.

I am kinda wigging out and need to write to someone, so fuck if you get this and I sound crazeee, well, try not to worry. I'm just real bored. I'm in this girl's bedroom, this waitress I work with, did I tell you about Pammy? She is just a kid and the only person I know out here. I have no one to talk to. If I work for maybe a month I could get enough money to get outta here. But that feels forever. And I'm going to turn 18 soon. And you know how I feel about that. So maybe you'll get this and I won't be around anymore. Check up on me, will you? I'm in a town called Presto. Everybody here knows me as Penelope Huck or just Huck. You could always call the Hash Knife Café, Presto South Dakota, if you had to get in touch with me.

So. I'm not out cutting wheat fields with Randa. That didn't work out. I really thought it would have been fun. But just when you think everything is going to work out and be what you thought, that's when you get whacked in the face. Reality.

Randa left. She found me in our motel room with a guy getting high. We weren't doing anything else. She's really a jealous type though. I don't know. It's over. She left.

I'm alone in the middle of nowhere.

So I really hope you are out there. I kinda need to know someone is cuzz I'm fucking losing my mind.

Huck

WHEN RANDA whacked my face, I was almost glad. I had a reason to say goodbye. To get rid of the strange marriage that we had made. I had just been hanging with Curly on the bed. She couldn't take it.

I waited for a couple of days, though. Going back and forth inside. Missing Randa despite myself. Writing Angus and feeling sick to my stomach. And then Randa did make one last gesture. a couple of days after she hit me and kicked in the wall, she came back. She knocked on the motel door and handed me a small, long box. I didn't know what to say and then she left without a word. After Randa roared away on her Kawasaki, I opened the box and found Randa's .45. There was a note wrapped around the barrel.

> Flower Girl:
>   I want you to have this now since I can't be there any more. You know how to use it.
>   Too bad we couldn't make it work. I always knew you were too young and I was too old—old in my head anyway.
>   There's not much more to say, except please forgive me.
>   love
>   Randa

The *love* was written real small.

Always talking about taking care of me. It was a fucking lie. I didn't need her damn .45. Randa couldn't give me anything. I felt like a fool for once thinking I could feel safe in Randa's arms, for letting Randa hold me all night. Or for believing her when she said we would follow the harvest. We were never going to be outlaws together, would never go from state to state, free and easy and tough and cutting all the wheat and making money and showing off for each other and making a life. It wasn't ever going to happen in a million zillion years.

Maybe, just maybe, if I had asked her to stay, called out after her after she handed over the box, things would have worked out. Was it a mistake to keep my mouth screwed shut? Would it mean dealing with a lot of stuff worse than being married to Randa?

WITH THE HELP OF PAMMY, I didn't get thrown out of the motel and arrested. I got a job dishwashing at the Hash Knife and a place to sleep in an outbuilding. I called it "the hut." It was small as a dollhouse and about a ten-minute walk from the restaurant. Pammy's parents, the Lindflotts, let me use the place for no rent. Her aunt owned the Hash Knife, and I was paid hardly anything for my work there, so it was a family trade-off. The hut was built on part of a former farm, now incorporated into the Lindflotts' land. It was twice the size of my motel room, six steps across instead of three, and only had electricity for a fan and one light bulb overhead. A cozy security enveloped me there among its collapsing, buckling walls. The floors slanted; the ceiling dipped; and it was mine.

There was no toilet so I had to shit in the ground behind a fence. My first day there, I dug the hole myself with a big shovel that Pammy brought over.

"Heave ho! Heave ho!" I said.

She stood and nodded.

I had never dug anything before. It made me crack up.

"What's your problem?' said Pammy. She sucked on a piece of her long brown hair. She was accustomed to digging holes for fence posts and actually getting things done.

"I'm a slave to you, baby," I sang.

The dirt was golden once I got a couple of inches down. I stepped on the shovel and tried to get it in deeper, but I almost needed a jackhammer. I was going to be there all day. Pammy said I needed at least four feet.

"You can't sing at all, you know that?" Her eyes got the big pupil look. She was so young and sheltered, but she occasionally had a way of looking at me that was merciless. Unlike the other Dakotans I'd come in contact with, she also liked to chatter on if I got too quiet. She told me her parents had used the hut the previous summer to lodge a guy from Guatemala who had helped remove the big weeds, like the musk thistle.

"Out with the dreaded musk thistle!" I threw a big shovel full of dirt over my shoulder.

"You probably want to put on gloves before you dig much more. You'll get blisters."

"Yeah, tell me more." I kept digging and hoped Pammy would keep me company for as long as it took.

WHEN I WOKE, I loved washing outside at the spigot. My own spigot. My own little rude splash bath. Used a bar of soap on my face and underarms and hair. I could be seen from the highway so I washed the rest of me at night, although at the rate any trucks or cars came along, I could have probably washed every centimeter of my X-rated areas without any voyeurs getting a look.

Soon my night baths became a ritual. I liked looking at the stars and getting naked, slippery, dripping. Feeling my body in the outdoors. Whitman had some ode to himself and his underarms that I once thought was weird, but now I longed to read it. I would have given anything to thumb through some books. It was damn strange to be stranded in Burnt County, and I needed to recite some words aloud. I knew it would help, a totem to keep the Lewis and Clark devils away.

My cleansing rites, I told myself, would make me holy and protected, get me ready to face disaster. I was especially scared of tornadoes that might blow through the hut at night when the sun wasn't around. I was so far out there. No headlights, just unbroken dark. I extended my nightly sessions to include a slow washing of my underwear and T-shirt. In the dark I had to do it by feel. I rubbed the soap into my clothes and then squeezed and rinsed and rinsed. As long as I was washing, I felt safe.

It was so hot inside during the day that when I hung the wet clothes on my iron bedpost, they were easily dried into strange stiff and crumpled shapes by the next afternoon.

I had always said I was into vagabondage. It's strange how you can have images of things but you can't quite identify where they came from. What could I possibly have seen that foretold this weird spot on the plains? My new life felt familiar—not familiar like I'd done it before, but like I'd seen Clint Eastwood do it. *High Plains Drifter.* Had I seen the movie or just the name?

After my first morning of work at the restaurant, Pammy cut off the long stripe of my mane. I was left with my fuzzy thatch of short, trashed dead-blond remains. My hair wasn't so different looking from the shorn hay fields that surrounded the hut. My shorn thatch: the only part of me that ever blended into Dakota Territory.

AFTER RANDA LEFT, I did have some practical longings to deal with. As much of a playboy as I was, I wouldn't let myself prey on the cute babygirl Pammy. And Curly never came back to visit. So there was nobody. I mean *nobody.* Unless you considered the old vulture men in the diner with the stained pants and caps; worn down by the land, the weather, and the debt, I suppose. Or the pot-bellied sixty-year-old hunters. They came through Presto on their way to the reservation. Hoping to get new stories about fighting rattlesnakes and shooting little prairie dogs. The town was happy to have their business, but I wasn't going to find any company with them. My other choice was the grandmas and their old clone daughters who planted themselves at their tables and croaked like sleepy frogs; their necks and breasts draped over the tables and they never really seemed to move at all.

The smell of close skin. The scent of a sweet neck or the taste of the back of a knee. I suppose I had always depended on that kindness of strangers thing. Now it haunted me. The plunge into a dark stink of a foreign body. The screams of somebody giving it up.

Here I was in the dry, dry Great Plains. Not a chance.

I kept saying out loud to myself, "How did I end up here again?"

Abracadabra!

Presto.

ONE WINDY MORNING I woke and felt sick. I went behind my fence and let my insides come out. It was blackberry and lemon pie. My boss, Pammy's flat-faced aunt, wouldn't talk to me, but she did let me eat leftovers. I'd overdone it. One too many pie orgies.

At the horizon the southern brooding clouds had a dark edge, the color of gun metal. Usually in the morning I liked the feel of sky circling me from one side to the other, fingertip to fingertip. I stretched my arms out as I walked to work and tried to become as big as the land. But on the morning I got sick, molten clouds weighed down the sky.

The whole day I was shaky doing my Hash Knife dishwashing slave gig. Pammy had told me I would see a sickening green in the sky if a tornado was coming, so I went out and checked several times. It was still windy, but it didn't look like rain anymore. By the end of my shift, the light did look strange, but it didn't look green. It had more of a yellow-gray cast to it.

I was scared to leave the restaurant, but didn't want to tell anybody. They had said they didn't think a tornado was coming.

There weren't any cars on the highway as I walked home. The wind stopped for a moment and it was quiet. The sky seemed to swallow even the bird calls. There weren't many birds flying around by August anyway, I reminded myself; they had left to go some other place.

As I walked the quarter mile to the hut, I thought of the sad military bugle call, the sunset flag-folding song. I got paranoid about the ghosts of the Plains settlers, maybe even my ancestors' ghosts.

Dead folks were in the ground under me—armies of invading pioneers that staked a claim and died of thirst. And all the Indians that got in their way. The big ole Heartland, fertilized by violence and blood. It hadn't quite occurred to me before, because nothing showed. Just like everywhere, the past was so perfectly gone.

What kind of Ghost Dance could I do? I stopped on the road and waved my hands over my head, spread my fingers, and howled.

The wind started again and I could hear it a long ways away. I looked three-sixty for signs of a tornado. What I saw, south of the highway a couple of miles, was the pouring upward of dirt lifted from the ground. Billowing plumes rose and came toward me. The wind sucked the loose earth. I ran the rest of the way home.

I hid under my bed with my blanket wrapped around my ears. Dust blew in under the door. The hair on my arms felt charged from static electricity. The wind howled and I wanted to look, but I was afraid that I'd be blown away. The winds blew louder. "There's no place like hell!" I shouted. Clicked my boots three times. Next I tried to recite anything I could remember. "Nobody knows my name. Cassiopeia. What a piece of work is man. Corona borealis. Arcturus. Spica."

Finally I yelled. "Help me!" Over and over, until at last the wind got softer.

When I asked about it the next morning, I found out it was just a little dust storm. Most storms were made of dirt here, just dirt, because there was nothing else to blow.

THE FEW KIDS that do have the real obnoxious lovebunny moms—the moms who hug and kiss them to death and feed them bacon breakfasts—well, it's always those kids that get abducted. You always see how it's their moms who are all upset on the Eleven O'Clock EyeWitness News. It's those mothers who go calling around all the intersections and ditches in the neighborhood for their missing kids. All these mamas crying out and making big floods of tears.

Sometimes I imagine my mom, looking down from up there, kicking away the passing clouds, trying to get a clear air hole to yell down to me. I know it's stupid, but it's a yearn of a dream that doesn't go away.

PUT ONE DISH DOWN. Pick up another. Hang the sprayer over head. Squirt. Stand in sopping fountain of relief.

I washed dishes with a big snake that spat water when I pulled. Grease, fried egg, ketchup, burned crumbs—the scummy bits of orange and red and black disappeared down the drain. Fire and damnation. My T-shirt suffocated me; even my thatch of hair was too thick for the blasting heat. So I gave myself showers.

They kept me in the back most of the time. I only got to be in the main restaurant for three chores: to carry bags of ice, to wash the muddy floors, and to help unload the trucks. Up front I could hear the on-and-on drone, the murmur-murmur chant of wizened folks. It was almost always old people at the tables. The only real words I could make out: *Don-choo-have-sum-murr-coffee.* It softened them a little, to have to ask that, each day they had to look up and plea for something from Pammy or another waitress. Otherwise they kept to the point, never swung their eyes around. Tired, hairless vultures, but I did feel for them. They were forgotten people, I figured, hunched over their bankrupted farms, hoping to hold some piece of homeland, yet knowing it was long picked-over, going down fast. And I sure had no place in their lives. Just like in Bonesteel, they acted as if I was filthy and druggy and in their way. To prove I could be just as tough, I didn't talk to them either. Just did my work.

FORTUNATELY I LEARNED how to be a vagabond from an early age. After they took me from my granddad, I lived a lot of places because my dad was always farming me around. I was glad to leave his clutches for good, get on my own and be in the city.

You could say I'm still looking for a place to be. I've seen *nowhere*, that was the rogues in the Haight—from nowhere, living nowhere. I formed my own famileee, but it didn't last.

I wanted Bonesteel to be a somewhere, but it wasn't. Not for long anyway.

What if my real place of belonging was the same as my mom's? There was a coziness in death. It would be quiet, and no one would mess with me. Very peaceful. My molecules would be recycled just like the corn. There's harmony that way. As simple as: *the end.* When I thought this way, it felt more right than anything. I wanted to die more than I wanted any other big american dream pageant—a movie-star lover, a big pot of money, fame and glory.

I imagined resting in a warm field of night that would never let me go.

ONE LONELY DAY, I called Irma collect. To my surprise, she accepted. I asked her about the corn harvest.

"Crossing our fingers."

"Well, I'm still alive."

"Is that right?"

"I don't suppose Randa would be hanging about your house this evening?"

"You're outta luck there. She's looking at some hogs over at the Shulls."

"I appreciate your taking my call. It's nice of you, Irma."

"What you expect?"

"Tell Dottie hi from Girl."

"Will do."

GIRLY,

You twerp! You disappeared and I never heard from U. Just checked my old mailbox and got yr message from a couple weeeeeeks ago. Guess what this boy gone done? Yep. After Viva Las Vegas we made it all the way to Memphis, Tennesseeeeeeee.

Don't chu never say never to thiz boy now. I got it good and don't try to scratch my belly, cuzz my Jim, my handsome fun-daddy duz it for me.

Where are you now, anyways? Some place called Presto? Maybe you could still go on the road and cut the wheat like you wanted. Maybe you should get the hell out of where ever you are. Or go to New York or something. Go to a city.

You sound kinda DEEPressed, as in pressed under a load of something deep and big. Are you?

Hope you get this.

Angus

OVER THE NEXT COUPLE DAYS we wrote back and forth a lot. Angus said Memphis was small, a hundred and twenty degrees and sticky. There were a lot of black people, and blacks and whites sat with one another, unlike in a big city. Kids squatted out near the Mississippi River, but he said that he hadn't gone there much. He and his rich boyfriend Jim were a real sappy, happy couple he said. Jim liked to watch videos after dinner and Angus had started painting, but on real canvas, not on jean jackets like he used to.

I kept hoping he would ask me to come and live with them.

TO BIDE MY TIME, I started hanging out more and more at Pammy's house. They had lots of barbecue potato chips and some nice cats and a collie. Her mom talked with me and fed me snacks; it was like having an afterschool friend.

One late afternoon, I lay on Pammy's bedroom rug while she sat on the bed and brushed her hair.

"Come on, tell me more about your granddad and peace and love."

"Yeah, sure." I closed my eyes and pretended to sleep.

Pammy finished brushing her hair and went back to AOL and her pagan chat room.

One of the Lindflott cats, Toto, nuzzled me with his warm nose. I petted his sleek black fur and butted him with my head. I thought about my granddad and whether he had anything to do with peace and love. I'd never thought much about that—wasn't too sharp on it, as my granddad would say.

I know that in the early pictures, when my granddad still lived in Oregon, he had long blond hippie-boy hair waving over his shoulder. But even then, his eyebrows furrowed together, and he looked like he had to figure out the whole meaning of atomic energy on his own.

My favorite memories were when we would sit on his couch while he did number theory stuff on his little handheld computer and we would watch old Clint Eastwood movies. I would make tomato soup with milk and put out a box of crackers. Or sometimes he would let me color in big sketchpads. With one blue and one red crayon, I loved to draw the Golden Gate Bridge stretching over the bay. He would grin really big when I showed him.

There was the time he helped veterans from the Gulf War and they would come back to the Winfield house. I remember the guy with the blond crew cut, sharp like a mowed lawn. I was around eight or so. I was really jealous that the guy had been in the army. I wanted to join up myself, despite what my granddad said about war. The soldier and I got stoned together, had a water fight. He showed me his scars. I hid under the table when he threw Hawaiian Punch. It made marks, little splashes over my jeans. I pretended it was blood from a battle.

One of my clearest memories was the second or third time I got arrested. Granddad had picked me up from the wonderful "Youth Guidance Center."

We sat in his kitchen. He had moved from the Winfield house to O'Farrell Street in the Tenderloin. A big building with all kinds of creeps. "Gretchen," he kept saying, as if my name was a sad thing. He shook his head and looked at my new dragon tattoo. Later he got really mad and started shaking me. Jail was something you did for a purpose, he said. He got so mad that he called to remind my dad that he better come down to get me and start acting like he had custody.

I TICKLED TOTO under his upturned neck and couldn't help but start talking with Pammy again.

"My granddad used to go be a protester and go to jail and all."

"Wow. Really?"

"Yeah. I guess you could say he used to be a hippie. I mean he did drugs and he kept his hair long and he wanted to change the world. He didn't talk about peace and love a lot, though. More about science and evolution, and things like nuclear power. He had lots of theories and could talk forever. You'll meet him when we go to San Francisco."

"What kind of drugs does he like?"

"All of them, I guess." It was funny to be talking about my grand-dad while facing Pammy's My Little Pony collection on the shelf. The pink, yellow, and blue horses with their shiny manes. "I don't know. He only speaks about drugs when he's clean, and when he's clean he doesn't like to be around me."

THE EARLIEST MEMORY. I must have been three or four. I toddled around a sandstone beach cliff and found my granddad with his arm tied and a needle up his vein. His eyes were rolled back and they were fluttering. I saw his big muscled forearm and thought the syringe was his magic, and it made him pumped up and strong.

I've never much liked getting shizzed or drugging myself. I mean, look at my granddad. Where did he go when he used? To some untouchable heebie-jeebie place.

HI FREAKHEAD,

Jim's asleep and I'm wired on ezprezzzo. I'm on the phone with my sister and she's talking about her wedding as I'm writing this. She moved back to Texas, did I tell you? I like writing you CUZZ you know how kooky cookie kooky speedy I am, and you even know my visions. I have been painting these REALLY WEIRD visions. You have to see them. Jim says I could get a job designing science fiction stuff for George Lucas. He wants me to have a show here first. A show. Can you imagine, Angus, the show boy?

I can see myself in a green paisley scarf and white bell bottoms and a long cigarette holder and a big orange clown wig. It will be so fun and you would have to come then.

Hey, I'm not famousss yet but I did go to Graceland. Jim wouldn't take me so I had to go alone. No one here goes there. I kissed Elvis's grave.

In answer to your question, yes, I do want you here so—baby, baby freakhead—but Bullet came out here (remember him? he got a truck and has been going all over) and he messed up the whole house and trashed some stuff. I'm afraid Jim's going to kick me out if I ask anybody else over. So maybe we could meet somewhere like New York. You ever want to go? I've been thinking about it lately. I don't know why. Or maybe New Orleans. Wadda ya think?

Tomorrow I'm going to Dallas with him for my sister's wedding (my outfit will be so much better than hers. Ha!) So I won't be able to write for a while. If the cowboys beat me up, it may be a long time. But Jim says he'll take care of the brutes. Pray for me, dah-lin.

Stay free.

Angus

PRETTY SOON I WONDERED if I'd ever hear from Angus again. It was only two weeks before my birthday—maybe I would just die of boredom. The easy way out. One day I sprayed my head with warm water and felt the trickles evaporate from my scalp and arms and back. I imagined my entire body evaporating. What would it be like to not be here? To not have a body anymore. Gone. I didn't want my body to be burned; I wanted to be buried. Either way, though, a person eventually disappears into the matter of the world.

On my right was a window that showed the straight line of the highway, some ready-to-plant fields, and a bright shock of a cloud. The canopy of air, the brave overhang, even with the sun, what was it to me now? What was anything when you stood in it alone. Untouched? Yeah, don't you know it; I was getting wiggy as Hamlet.

I kept washing the plates. I was thankful for them. Each one. All I knew was, I was no longer Girl. Being a rogue was for real. Thought of myself as Huck now, although I knew I didn't really want a name at all. Girl seemed best for my gravestone. Just Girl. I would write a note saying that. My granddad had to respect that.

Sweat dripped down my back, hot water poured over my yellow rubber gloves. A truck roared down the highway, and I had not the slightest desire to follow it.

More days passed, more days of looking out the window at the low clouds moving along and disappearing from the flat horizon, and I started planning exactly how to go about dying.

EIGHT THINGS ABOUT MY DAD'S PLACE OF BELONGING

My dad definitely belonged on a list. He loved lists.

My dad couldn't feel right without money. That's why he went to law school, to make sure he'd have it.

My dad belonged where things were clean, not clean as in ocean-whipped air; no, *clean as in Clorox.* Bleached, antiseptic, ordered, no fuss, no muss. Mistah White Socks.

My dad belonged in a world of thought, ideas, and words. Words that were stringy, legal, and ponderous. For example, how he spoke to me the day before I ran away: "Marianne and I believe you would be best served living in a facility that could help you. A place with other bright teenagers that need structure and have trouble with authorities." Blah, blah. He formed words into statements and closed absolutes. I wouldn't say he believed in theories, because even theories involved inspiration. My dad never got inspired. He repeated givens.

Ultimately my dad's place of belonging was right where he was. In a large nerdy cardboard cutout house with an obedient family.

Although…maybe all this was wrong. His truest place of belonging might have been with my mom. I saw it in the pictures. In a photo album of their one year together, thrown in a box and forgotten by my dad, pictures of a camping trip they took. He looked loose and relaxed in a way that I'd never seen. In one picture my mother was naked by a creek, and she must have been looking at my dad while he was taking the picture. She looked at him in a way I can't imagine anyone looking me. She would have done anything for him. I could see that. He must have loved her. (Why did she choose my *dad*? That I don't know, but people can fall for anybody if they are desperate enough.) So maybe for a short while my dad found a place of being loved. But that all came undone once my mom shot herself in the head at the Winfield house. When she messed up his back deck with so much blood, I think he pretty much decided he was ashamed he had ever known her.

I do not belong on this list. The truth is that I will never go back to my father's house. It was stupid that I went back to Redding after Cara died. I needed money, but I could have gotten it some other way. It was stupid that I was glad when he came to get me from YGC. It was stupid that I once memorized Shakespeare to impress him, even studied the constellations. He felt happier without me or anything that reminded him of the past. That's all.

THE LINDFLOTTS INVITED me over to celebrate my eighteenth birthday. Their house: The All-American Home. The long sighs of the refrigerator. The glow of the lamp over the kitchen table. I imagined Mr. Lindflott taking one of his hogs and skinning it right on that table; it looked so much like an operating room. The absence of color, the medicinal smell of Pine Sol. The spotless cool of the living room. That's where I would celebrate. Weird.

I had thought so much about turning eighteen. But when the day came, I didn't want to think about it at all. I felt sick at work even before I drank the bottles of Budweiser. A whole six-pack I hid in a box of old rags. I drank four, even though they were warm.

When I came over to the Lindflotts, I told everybody I was feeling kinda poorly. Mr. Lindflott nodded hello and then said he had to get back to work. He was so thin I had trouble imagining him working so much.

Mrs. Lindflott's slipcover face looked disappointed that I was sick on my birthday, but I asked anyway if I could go lie down on Pammy's bed.

"Sure." Pammy shrugged and finished setting the table.

"Let me get you an aspirin," said Mrs. Lindflott.

I collapsed on Pammy's blue-flower bedspread and waited for things to stop spinning.

Mrs. Lindflott wheeled her chair in to look at me and made me take her white pills and water. Her face, with its constant cover of white powder, scared me. Especially that night. It was like a ghost.

"Go ahead and eat without me." I closed my eyes.

"We are having the fried beef cubes, with the Wishbone dressing you like," said Mrs. Lindflott. "Your favorite."

"Maybe later. I think I need to sleep. I'm sick," I whispered. I pretended I was her daughter.

She put her hand on my forehead. She had to lean way over to do it. I closed my eyes again. "Oh, what a shame."

When she left, I went to the bathroom and threw up.

When I stopped feeling so dizzy, I got even weirder. I crept around on my hands and knees on Pammy's bedroom carpet. I lay on the clean blue middle of it for a while. I put my cheeks against the cool of the fresh-painted wall. I rubbed the bristles on the brush on her bureau and then scraped them against the dragon on my arm. I fingered each toy on Pam's shelf, the museum to her childhood. The Smurfs and the Care Bears. The Little Ponies with the candy-sick sheen of each colored mane. The synthetic yellow and aquamarine. I took the aqua one and put it in my carrybag. Which made me see the gun. I took it out.

Placed it on the bed pillow. Lay down and curled up. The gun with its hole faced me. Ever-ready evil. I lifted it with one hand and it felt even heavier than before. I held it with both hands. I placed the gun on my chest. A zillion pounds. I didn't want to miss. I felt sick again. I had to do it right. I raised it and gazed into the barrel.

Randa's fucking gift. A gun.

I pointed it at my chest and looked at the bumpy white ceiling. I didn't want it to hurt. I might feel it in my chest.

I would wait for Independence and do it there like I'd planned. But I needed to practice. I put the gun in my mouth, pointed it toward my brain. I had seen it done that way in a movie. It felt weird doing it lying down, so I sat up and tried it. The gun tasted cold and oily and made me gag.

I could hear Pammy's high babygirl voice say that she was going to check on me. The sound of her heavy pants dragged on the carpet in the hallway.

I stuck the gun under the pillow.

She shuffled over to me on the bed, her thighs bound in her stiff jeans, wrapped up like a mummy.

"We finished dinner. You want anything?"

"Eternal life."

"What?" She touched my forehead with her long-stretched palm, and it felt cool. I closed my eyes to feel her smooth flesh. I was still alive. It was a relief.

When I opened my eyes, Pammy was smiling her private smile.

"My parents said you are even more cracked than I am." She wrinkled her nose.

"That's good." I took her hand. "Don't go, okay?"

Pammy's other hand leaned on the pillow. "What?" She pulled the pillow up. "That's a gun." She froze.

I had trouble talking. "It's okay."

"Are you going to shoot us?" Pammy's eyes shifted back and forth to the door. "What are you going to do?"

"No. No. That's not it. No."

Pammy looked at the gun. "I think I should get my dad."

"I was thinking of something else."

She went behind the closet door and hid. "What are you doing? Huck? What are you doing?" She paused. "I'm going to call for my dad."

"I was thinking of doing myself."

"What?" Pammy peeked from the closet.

I picked up the gun. "Please. It's okay now." I thought maybe I should just go ahead with it.

"You are going to shoot us." Pammy looked from behind the door. "Why are you pointing it at yourself?"

"I'm not going to shoot you or your parents." I stood up. "Could you cut that out. I'm not a murderer."

Pammy walked from the closet. She seemed so disappointed. "Fuck."

"I can do it if you want."

Pammy choked out a laugh. "You are so weird. Why do you have a gun?"

I pointed it at my head. I felt like pulling the trigger. "Why do ya think?"

"Stop. I'm going to call my dad."

"Don't tell anybody. Please."

"Give me the gun. You shouldn't have it."

"I won't do it." I took the cartridges from the chamber. "Okay?"

Pammy put her long fingers together at her chin and her eyes got even bigger. "I thought you were a serial murderer. You were going to tie us up. And then shoot up everybody at the Hash Knife and everybody around here."

"Pammy. I am *so* sorry to disappoint you."

We heard Mrs. Lindflott roll down the hall.

"Put it away." Pammy waved her hands. "Come on. Put it under the pillow."

"I'll put it back." I reached for my carrybag and put the gun inside.

Mrs. Lindflott came in. "What is going on in here?"

"What did you hear?" Pammy squeaked out her baby voice.

"Are you better, Penelope?"

I was up and standing now. "Do you have pie for dessert? I'm feeling hungry, I think."

"Oh, dear. I'm so glad. We have a special birthday cake. It's a carrot cake like they have in California."

Pammy and I both broke out laughing.

"A special cake," repeated Pammy.

This was going to be weird. I couldn't remember ever having a birthday cake. I guess my dad never liked celebrating it cause it reminded him of my mom's death.

Mrs. Lindflott's powdery white face made a big smile. Like a circus clown, lips spread from ear to ear. "We wanted to sing for you."

"We want to sing for you," Pammy repeated again, making fun of her mom.

I laughed harder.

Pammy opened her mouth as big as her mom's smile, "Si-i-ing for you."

We followed Mrs. Lindflott and her wheelchair back to the kitchen. Pammy whispered, "Serial murderer."

I sat down at the table and planted my boots firmly into the floor. The room looked large and expansive. The hum of the refrigerator sounded comforting as ocean surf. I looked around for the fluffballs.

"Where are the cats?"

"In the living room, probably," said Pammy.

"Can you get Toto?" I asked. "Or maybe you could let Spot come in?"

Pammy left the room just as Mrs. Lindflott wheeled herself in with one hand, the other hand holding the cake. She stopped in the doorway between the kitchen and dining room. "Where is Pammy now?"

There was a constellation of candles on the cake. They flickered around and lit Mrs. Lindflott's face.

"Aren't you going to sing for me?"

"I'm just waiting for her."

The yellow birthday candles dripped their wax, and it was quiet. I didn't want to blow the candles out, just watch them. Like miniature stars: my tiny, stupid candles of hope. I laughed at myself. Was that all it took to make me feel better? A fucking birthday cake? Pammy and Toto and Spot, Mrs. Lindflott, and a California carrot cake. That's all, and it was enough.

MY GIRL HUCKSTER,

I'm back from our trip at last and I'm soooooooooo full. We haven't stopped eating since we got back to Memphis. We eat so much CORN. And Bar B Q Pork Shoulder. I won't eat the butt or baby backs though. Can you imagine BABY backs? Memphis people eat BBQ like it was a daily vitamin. But I don't see any cows. My sister and everybody in Texas was always complaining about the herds and the lack of rain. It was so boring back there that I can't even begin to tell you.

I'm thinking about a long time ago. Missing, missing, missing U. Remember the time they played Econochrist all night at Dollhouse? And you and me and sistah Cara, we jumped up and down and hollered at the big cruel world?

So whaz up? Lez be lezzies and dance
and dance
and dance.
Your Angus

BURNT COUNTY, SOUTH DAKOTA DIRT. I grabbed a handful and shook it in my hand. Would it be that different four hours away in Independence?

Still cool in the morning dawn. The slightest color at the horizon, lemon and mauve like a seashell. I longed for the ocean, but it was eons gone. Today was the day Pammy's trucker friend would take me to Independence.

My mother had not found what she wanted in San Francisco. Would she have found it in Independence? I don't know. I somehow think it could have helped her stay alive, a place of belonging. It's stupid, but I knew I was going back for her somehow. Going back to a place that my mother's people had made a home. They left everything they knew to come to Independence; maybe it was another cracked, nowhere dream, the whole pioneer thing, but it meant something to me.

The earth in my hand was dark as a boot sole. Prickly. I brought it to my nose and smelled it. Smelled like old leather, smelled like grain and shit and early morning. I rubbed the dirt into my thick cut-off pants. I walked behind the hut so I could take my shirt off. Feel the air, the morning on my shoulders. It was quiet, with no one on the highway, so I went back to my spigot, half naked, turned it on. Scooped some water in my hand, drank it. Took some more. Raised my hand and let the water drip onto the top of my head. Threw more water on my underarms and breasts. I dipped my third finger in the trickle of water and made an X on my chest. I wet my finger again and plunged it down. I dug my finger into the prickly dirt, took some back to my chest. My own mark. I kept doing it until I had painted an X from the top of each shoulder to the bottom of each side of my rib cage. I thought of Cara and her handmade stars. I stood in the first sunlight of day until it dried.

It was time to get to work and then meet up with my ride. I put my shirt back on, crossed over to the hut. Opened the door and stood for a moment right at the broken piece of threshold. Walked to my bed. Reached under the foot of the mattress. Retrieved my .45. It was mine now. Truly no longer Randa's gun. I held it flat in my palm. Not scared of it. Able, with calm, to see the gaping black hole at its tip. Able to feel the weight of it and not be scared.

I placed it back safely under the mattress.

I knew one thing: I wasn't going to use it on *myself.*

ON MY WALK over to the Hash Knife, a truck whizzed by and gave the air a jolt, pushed at my back. It felt shaky-weird to be alive. Much lighter than I expected. Eighteen years old and one full week. Older than my mother had ever lived. Yes! All I had on me was my pouch, my money, my fake ID, my arrowhead. A near empty-pocket rogue. I started to run.

Once at work, I was so excited that I forgot to put on my gloves. I burned my fingers red from the hose water. I blew on my skin and walked over to the window.

One bright beyouteefull puffcloud.

LONG AGO, MY GRANDDAD and I lived in the Winfield house, just us two. Foggy afternoons, gusts wailing and knocking against our windows. I remember one day bicycling to the beach, trying to catch up. My granddad's stocky legs charged along, pedaling hard even when going downhill. We wore our Thrift Town wool coats with the long, draggy sleeves and the thigh-deep pockets ready for broken sand dollars, crab shells, tiny jade pebbles.

We ordered chili burgers with extra pickles at Carousel. Then devoured our burgers right near the surf. Sometimes a warm mist sheltered us, but usually the ocean fog whirled around like some kind of celestial attack. My granddad talked, chili gushing from the corner of his mouth. He ranted about the world, how we could fight to make it better, the legacy of human evolution. And then he'd lick his lips, go wild, and bark poetry. "Hold fast," he said. "Hold fas-s-st to dreams...." He raised his elbows, dangled his rock-hard forearms, dropped his head to one side. Pretended to be the broken-winged bird of my favorite Langston poem. I waited till near the end, then joined his booming voice and yelled as loud as I could: "For if dreams die, life is a broken-winged bird that can not fly-y-y-y."

I FOUND INDEPENDENCE on a tiny side road that paralleled the small main highway. It had taken about four hours from Presto. The trucker had a big furry mustache and was quiet on the ride. Quiet and clean and that was good. Angus had told me stories of smelly Texan truckers and I hadn't wanted any of that. We went north and then east a long way until at last I saw the sign.

We were actually there.

"I'll be back this way tomorrow." The trucker winked at me, then bounced his elbow against his side.

I stood on the rung on the side of the truck. "You think no one else will offer? I'll have to curl up on the roadside all night and wait for you?"

"Could be, Penelope. I won't mind if you're still here."

"Well, I'm not worried. Somebody's sure to give me a ride. I'll stick out my thumb."

"See you at the Hash Knife then. Always there on Wednesdays. April through October."

"Gotcha." I saluted. "Thanks."

My great-grandmother's long-ago town looked to be about as large as the parking lot for a shopping mall. There were some houses visible, a main road and a bit of an outlying area. I wasn't ready for knocking on any doors, so I started at the outskirts.

I sprinted up the road and found an abandoned high school. Behind the empty school were broken bleachers in a chewed-up football field. The middle of the bleachers had collapsed, so that the wood planks fell toward the ground. Weathered for so long, they looked like old bones, the planks curved into a sunken bowl. A huge crushed skull.

Lightning flashed in the west. I hadn't planned on rain. The dawn had been so mild in Presto, but here it was getting dark and gray. My tornado phobia was pretty much at bay, though. I felt giddy even. A feeling of lightness in my whole body. Eighteen years old and one week. Older than my mother ever lived, I repeated to myself.

After crossing the muddy field, I mounted the far edge of the bleachers, using the handrail to keep me from sliding on the slanted boards. Thunder growled as I climbed the boards, as if my steps on the planks made the roar happen in the distance. I felt like an archeologist climbing the remains of a dinosaur.

At the top, there was a view of the small hills near a river. Ripples of green followed the road. The land of my mother's people. Ooh-wee. I laughed. Where were they all? The town was so empty and quiet.

"Hello," I yelled. "Allee, allee oxen free."

I looked down, afraid for a second of the wood giving way under my feet, and saw the faint remains of words carved into the wood. On closer inspection I saw it said FUCK. *Thanks,* I thought. *Thanks for the little godgift.* Come all this way and that's the message! I took my arrowhead and made the f into an H. "Huck." What else?

I wrote my mother's name, MARY ELLEN.

Huck, Mary Ellen. What else? I wanted to write a whole poem but it was taking forever and if it was going to rain I better get into town. I wanted to write some great stuff...*quintessence of dust, or brave o'erhanging firmament, fretted with golden fire.* I started with *dust.* I now had HUCK, MARY ELLEN, DUST. What else? I added SKY. Then for some reason, I added ALL HERE.

I ran down the edge of the wobbling bleachers and invaded the tiny main street of town. The businesses had been shut down for a long time and there was nothing alive. Most of the windows on the red-bricked buildings were broken or gone. Some had plywood boarded across; one even had a painting nailed to it; others, garbage bags stretched across. Old carved stone circled the doorways. If it started to rain bad, I could break inside one of the abandoned buildings. One place was a former auto shop with a spark plug ad painted on the brick; next to it was a barbershop pole with vines growing around it. An old Feed Store sign hung from a frayed black wire. What had happened here? It was like Greek ruins.

Another building looked blackened, but it was hard to tell whether it had been fire or time that had frayed the edges of the door frame. Sheet metal, plywood, and other scraps were nailed over the doorways and windows. At the peak of the ashen building's roof edge were carved stone letters, 1909.

I looked real close at some faded paint and made out the word BRIDAL. Of course. A bridal store. Marriage makes the world go round.

At the end of the main road through town teetered three hous-es. All of them shifting away from their cement foundations. Pieces of broken windows reflected clouds. As I got closer, I saw a few dirty trailer homes hiding behind the row of houses.

I stood for a while hoping somebody would come out and I wouldn't have to knock. I put on my cap. Then I took it off again. I cleaned my underarms with alcohol. I wanted to smell good if I met somebody who was actually related to my mother.

I walked around, waiting, hoping still that somebody would see me. Then I realized maybe they'd think I was casing them for a rob-bery and they would come out and shoot me. For a second I want-ed my gun, just in case.

When I couldn't take waiting anymore, I walked up to a trailer behind one of the rotting houses.

I knocked.

No one came for a couple of minutes, but I heard noises inside.

At last an old man opened the door. His ribs showed under his hairless chest. He looked like those pictures of starving men during the Depression.

My words stumbled, but I managed to tell him I once had rela-tives here. When he was quiet, I kept talking.

"Thought I'd ask around about the town's history. You live here long?"

"Been here a few years. Maybe ten."

"So you probably never heard of any of my relatives."

He chewed on his lip. The trailer smelled of urine. "Yeah? What's the name?"

"Oh, boy." I laughed. "God, I don't know. I guess that doesn't help much, does it?" Now that was lame. I couldn't believe I didn't remember.

The man was still quiet. I guess it didn't matter whether I knew a name or not.

"Anyone else you know live here any longer?"

"Nope. Doubt that."

I could see a few photos on the wall, but what I couldn't stop looking at was a stuffed Batman doll with a blue felt cape sitting on the table, propped against piles of pipes, its long legs stuck straight out like a toddler. "That's a nice Batman. Is that really old?"

He nodded. "Old enough."

The computer was on over in the corner.

"Are you able to get online out here?"

He hacked a little like he was going to spit. I stepped back in case he was going to do it at my feet, but he went away and coughed for a long time. I yelled inside, just to make sure he wasn't getting a gun. "You gonna stay living here?" The guy was probably harmless. Then again, who knew? Maybe he was a survivalist, a Nazi fascist, or kept stockpiles of Confederate weapon memorabilia in the next room.

The man appeared again. "Maybe."

"Do you need anything?" I didn't know if this guy had a car to get food, or how the hell he lived. "I have a friend coming to pick me up soon. We could—"

"I got what I need. What about you?" He grinned, slow and wet, his lip with spittle on it.

I looked down at my boots. "I guess I wanted to meet a relative, but that's kind of weird. I'm from California."

"I have a sister who lives there. Last I heard anyway."

"Well, it's a pretty good place. But you can get tired of anything."

He nodded. A funny wheeze came from his throat as he took his next breath.

"Sorry to bother you."

For the hell of it, I tried to shake his hand.

When I touched him, he tugged my hand and tried to pull me inside.

"Don't," I said.

He laughed and rocked back a second on his feet, delighted with his prank.

I went down the three stairs. He stood at his door and smiled at me. "Stronger than I look, huh?"

"Yeah, sure."

I walked down a block. He didn't follow. I turned around, and he was waving.

I whistled the Batman song and crooked him a snook, raising my thumb to my nose, a gesture my granddad had taught me.

I crossed the highway. Then I turned around to go back to the school. I wanted to leave something behind in Independence. Something besides a few scrawled words. I had an empty Pepsi can in my carrybag that I used as a cup. I stamped on it a few times till it crushed into a disk. Near the bleachers I dug a hole. I placed the Pepsi remains there and covered them with dirt. My offering to the ancestors.

WHEN I FINALLY got a ride back to Presto that night I called my granddad collect from the phone booth outside the Hash Knife.

"I went to Independence."

"What was it like?"

"Empty. Desolate. Like your voice on the other side of this wire. Not very real."

"Wow." He laughed. "I think I'm starting to miss you. All those pleas for more money, Gretchen, I'm a wreck without them."

"I think I miss San Francisco. How's Mrs. Jam?"

"She's cool. Hasn't evicted me yet. Nobody much is left though. I mean no one that I know. And what about you?"

"I'm getting older. Nobody can arrest me for being Beyond Parental Control anymore."

"So you going to come back and get your GED?"

"I can't believe you."

"What? You finally passed the high school equivalency thing? Oh, yeah. That's right." He paused. "I'm sorry it's the people I care about that I seem to forget about the most."

"Yeah, sure."

"So you're eighteen. I guess you can't call me from the Youth Guidance rathole anymore."

"Nah. But you still have a lawyer? If I needed help some day?"

"Are you in trouble? You want me to call somebody?"

"No, not now."

"What about Attorney Warbucks?" He said this with relish.

"Yeah. Right. Dad would love to help me."

"The pleasure would be all his."

"Grandpapa?"

"Yeah, beyouteefull?"

"Do you know my great-great-grandmother's name?"

"The pioneer farm girl?" He paused and swore in German. "*Schiesse.* I don't know."

"You don't know?"

"Well. No, I guess I don't."

"Did my mom know?"

"Well, she might have. If her mother told her."

"How about my grandmother's maiden name?"

"Before I married her? She went by some stoned hippie name that you and I both would be embarrassed for me to repeat. Your grandmother left for Oregon around your age. All the kids left. Had to make a living. Farming's always been hard, I guess. Even back then."

"Yeah," I said.

"I'm sorry. I'd like to tell you more, but she never told me much of anything. Or much of anything I can remember. But you went, huh? That's something. I think that's great."

"Why?"

"That you cared, I guess. You know. I've never thought much about it."

"I know, Granddad. You never really cared about the past."

"Well, I guess not."

"So."

"So, you all came to find me, didn't you?"

"Who do you mean?"

"You and your mom. You both ended up in San Francisco."

"Yeah, sure. My mom. Then me. I don't know if we were trying to find you, though. We both must have been smarter than that."

"Yeah, you should have been!"

"Maybe we were just trying to get away from something else." This was the first time we had talked about my mom, just kind of normally.

"What are you finding?"

"I don't know." I laughed. "You let me crash with you for a while if I come back?"

"We'll see how I'm doing with my program. And you know Mrs. Jam. She swears she'll up my rent if I have anyone else live here. Think you'll get a job or something if you come back?"

"Yeah, sure."

LATE AT NIGHT I went over to Pammy's, all restless after getting back from Independence. We stayed up and did AOL chats. And I got another message back. The one I had been waiting for.

Hey Hey Good Lookin!
    Jim says he'd like for you to come out!!!!!!!!!!!!!!!!!!!!!
    He's such a small town boy and such a big fun-daddy at the same time. We'd need you to stay just for a few days...Cuzzzz of what Bullet did. But Jim likes you he said. He remembers you. He's very nice, but he has

his ways, and I'm trying so hard to be GOOOOOD. Cuzzzz he pays for everything. Even for his friends. He always buys the drinks. Maybe we could find a nice sugar princess for you? That would be the best. Would you like that? I could just see us ladies lunching together at the Peabody Hotel. Quack, quack. (Five dollazzz for a cup of tea! Diamonds on my wrist and chain links on yours.)

Summer's just about over. Get on down here, things should be cooling off.

You sound better now. You had your birthday, right? You made it!

Hey, you still wanna go live in New York with me sometime? I don't think I want to be in Memphis too long. (Don't tell Jimmmmy.) Let's BE REAL FAMOUS together.

Peace OUT,

Angusssssssssss

road to memphis

IF I COULD SAY THINGS like they really were, the words would be less stringy and have more soul and more truth.

THE LINDFLOTTS' HOUSE looked strangely small and deflated in the dark. Trying not to make any noise, I crept along the gravel drive. Lined up next to the tractor, the hopper, and the baler stood the moon-colored pickup. Ready for the taking. An enormous truck, just right for my trek away from Presto—something dented and rusted and big, something that looked at home in the cratered landscape. As usual, the Lindflotts had not locked the truck, and inside the cab dangled the silver keys.

A cat wiggled from the darkness and next to my calf.

"What are you doing?" I whispered.

Her yellow eyes pleaded. It was Spot, the one with the white puzzle-piece markings around her neck. I opened the truck door, threw her inside, and slammed the door, not thinking. Swiped the keys hanging from the ignition in the Lindflotts' other car and put them in my pocket, so Pammy's dad wouldn't be able to follow me. Then jumped in the cab of the truck and turned the ready key.

My escape route would be the reverse of the one I had used getting to town on the motorcycle. I had no map, so it felt safer to go on the roads I knew. My headlights bore down on the empty highway. Had to push to make the old truck go sixty.

In my hurry I had forgotten to stop for my stuff at the hut. I did a quick U-turn. Parked with my engine idling and hoped the darkness would keep till I left South Dakota. I ran inside to get the stuff I hadn't wanted to carry on my run down the highway to the Lindflotts'. Grabbed my carrybag, and fished under the mattress for my gun and its soft case. After zipping the case, I threw it along with my carrybag into the cab. Before I closed the truck door, Spot ran out. She scurried away, then stopped and looked back at me with scared eyes.

I got down on my knees. "Come on, Spot."

She ran to the roadside fence and hissed. I scrambled near, pulled off my T-shirt, threw it over Spot and scooped her up. I held her between my breasts for a second to let her know she'd be okay. One paw escaped and she clawed my arm, along my dragon. I wondered if I should let her go, but instead I threw her back in the truck. I drove in the dark for a few minutes, still shirtless, sucking the blood from my forearm. Spot hid under the seat.

Once in Nebraska, I took a county road to avoid the direct route into Bonesteel, hoping to avoid meeting the skunkcop who had gotten me before. As I approached town, it was still dark and I was glad for the cover from passing trucks. I pressed the pedal harder. What the hell was I doing? Stealing trucks and looking for company in rundown houses in the cornfields. I felt desperate as I made the turn down her gravel drive. I hadn't wanted to do this.

The house looked as lonesome as the Lindflotts', a spooky house surrounded by nothing but dark fields. In the city there are streetlights, a bus, some sounds, a light or two on in a window. Houses here looked deserted as shacks.

I slowly opened the front door. The place still smelled moldy. I crept through the house to the bedroom. At the doorway I felt sure she would hear me and reach for a gun.

I poked the top of my head around. Moonlight fell from the curtainless window. Only one covered body. I heard a snore and knew it was Bill. On the night table, no gun case, only beer bottles. Randa's boots weren't on the carpet.

To make absolutely sure, I looked in the bathroom. A single toothbrush. Randa's hand lotion was not by the sink. So much for company on the road to Memphis.

Randa had ditched him, too.

AS IT GOT LIGHT, I veered off the main highway to avoid the police. No maps and no idea where the hell I was going. I didn't try to get Jessika. Couldn't risk it. I sped right through Sioux City and then followed the eastern glint of sunrise onto a county road. The pickup's struts were so shot that it felt like riding a horse. Slowed down from sixty to forty to ride the buckled asphalt without getting sick to my stomach.

To my left, gentle swells of hills came into view. It was the first land that I'd seen in a long time that had any rise to it. I stopped the truck and idled for a moment. A sign marked a tiny creek crossing. The undulating earth was near water, and the air smelled lush.

The smell reminded me of the banks of Lewiston Creek. My favorite spot to camp had always been a ways past the Lewiston Bridge, down from the parking area and away from the fishermen in a nook where I could be hidden. It was there that I had found my arrowhead. I used to put my hands in the water, close my eyes, and feel the water rushing. Something about light changing at the beginning of day next to a river. The privacy of the fish, the comforting smell of dank mud.

A warm wind pushed against the tall prairie grasses and made the swells look like waves in the ocean. What if I turned the truck around and rode it back to California? Maybe it was time.

Something caught my attention on the other side of the road. At the crest over the drainage ditch bobbed the head of a tall bird circling a carcass. Blood glistened on a skeleton, maybe the rib bones of a small dog. The bird looked at me in the dawn light—I swear it told me to go away, this kill is not your business. I shivered and drew my gun case closer, unzipped it and felt the gun inside the soft sheepskin. The handle had rough etchings and when I squeezed it, the texture felt just right against my palm.

AS THE TRUCK heated with morning sun, the floor and seats smelled of fertilizer and farm remains. a couple of hours must have passed. I didn't have to stop for gas since I had made sure to make my escape right after the Lindflotts filled the truck. I sang along to country music on the radio—"Champagne in a Dixie cup." Spot peeked at me from the floorboards, and I beckoned for her to sing along.

Soon it was glaring and hot. If I left the truck, my body would cook. The cracks of my body—inner elbows, backs of my knees, between my thighs—would start to melt; my solid flesh would turn into a sticky dew. Mixed-up fragments came back to me, things I'd memorized when I was a kid trying to impress my dad. Words that could wind the stinking ugly into the beyouteefull and make it whole. This *overhanging firmament* and its *golden fire* of sun—this bad joke! This stinking *congregation of vapors!* The raunchy, hurting, foul and golden, all wrapped up in one another. Maybe Angus was right. I could be famousss someday. As a big, screaming wacko poet! Why not? I could see myself, manic and boondagger crazed, an in-your-face sort of bucking bronco, skinning the highways, a pickup-driving bard.

At that moment I knew I could do anything. There were no destinations. Call it a theory.

Anywhere and anything.

People always think of the West as the final, hippie-dippie frontier of freedom, but it wasn't. There was no more frontier; there was no more final. I wanted to yell as loud as I could to the rest of the country: Get over it! Get over this San Francisco fascination, this California obsession. We aren't your answer, we aren't your edge of the world. There is no more edge. The edge is you. You are the edge and you brought it to us. You are the empty ones who said we had to be the answer. Listen—California has no fucking answers, so stop all your dreaming about us!

I decided there was only one place to go. That was to jump further inside. To keep going till I found some place where I belonged, a place that felt solid and right. The home of the free and the land of the brave. The ballpark anthem that Randa liked. Home of the free. Or was it land of the free? I howled at the top of my lungs everything I could remember and made up the other words. "Home of the free!" I wailed. "Make my home in your free, your free, your free! Make me, land of the brave! Take me, you big ole brave land! Take me now. Make my day, motherfucking ameri-c-a-a-ah!"

THE TOWNS BECAME AS CLOSE as thirty minutes apart and the land became more populated in eastern Iowa. Spot meowed, a dreadful hungry howl. I figured it was time we needed a fill-up: the truck, Spot, and me. I wished Pammy had been willing to come with us, but she had chickened out the evening before. It would have been fun. I hoped she would forgive me for taking her barn cat instead. I would e-mail her, explain things, and maybe she could still meet me in Memphis.

At the next Food and Fuel, I pulled in. I was still in farm country, but the gas station was modern and florescent. I found my arrowhead in my carrybag, but couldn't find my wallet. I rubbed the arrowhead for good luck and looked some more. My wallet wasn't in my shorts pocket or gun case or in the zippered front part of my pack. I had saved thirteen twenties from my slave-gig at the Hash Knife. Couldn't find a penny.

My brain was filled with holes. Finally I remembered that I had put it under the mattress with the gun. I had left my wallet in the hut! Sometimes the most important things just fall out. Was I becoming more and more brainwhacked? I didn't even have false ID. Gretchen and Girl were far behind me, and now I'd even lost Penelope Huck Crow.

I fucking panicked.

In the gas market was an older woman with a tight, curly cap of white hair and a wrinkled, saggy frog neck. I told her I'd lost my wallet.

"Yeah? Okay, then. You just get." She gave a shoo of her flabby wrist.

"You have anything to eat?"

The old lady's slash of mouth was as wide as her froggy neck. "This isn't a charity store." She pushed a bag of potato chips across the counter.

"I won't bite." I picked up the chips. "How about some gas?"

"No. I can't do that. The owner wouldn't like that."

I tore open the bag and started eating the chips. "So, how's your day so far?"

Her lips disappeared into a frog frown.

The highway by the gas station was very, very quiet. No one drove by for a long time, and those that did didn't stop. The clouds hung low and jagged, molded with shadow. I stood in a foot of shade from a dumpster and it was so hot my eyeballs sweated, but it was even hotter in the truck. When I foraged in the dumpster for something more to eat, all I found was cardboard and oil cans. Maybe this was finally it. I was stuck.

The fields on the other side of the highway were just planted, and between the new crops, the earth was yellow-dung colored. Frog Woman eyed me, but even if she called the police it would take them forever to get out here. I went in the bathroom at the side of the building and drank water from the faucet, cupped my hand and carried some water for Spot to lick. She even let me hold her for a little afterwards.

A light pink car pulled up and a large woman in tight leggings got out. I waited till she had finished pumping her gas. "Can you help me out with a few dollars?"

"Now look at that." She let her mouth drop.

When she came back from paying, she stood and stared, no self-consciousness to her. The woman reminded me of Irma, more hips than breasts.

"My cat's hungry, too."

"I'm sure he is." The woman shook her head, got in her pink car, and drove away.

"What's wrong with you?" I yelled after her.

To hell with it. I got the gas nozzle and shoved it in my truck. The gas started for a second, but then clicked off.

Frog Woman came out and raised her index finger. "I don't think you have money to pay for that."

I kept trying to pump. "Don't worry. I'll mail it to you later."

She walked directly over. "You've got to stop that now." She glared at me again, like every person I'd met out here. Like every person who had ever made me mad. She put her key in the pump and turned it off.

I opened the door to my truck and reached into my sheepskin case. The gun was hot from being in the truck and it burned both my hands as I held its heavy weight. I kicked the truck door closed. "Don't tell me what to do." I pointed the gun straight at her forehead. Cocked and locked, ready for action.

"God help me." She fell down on her knees.

I fired the gun in the air. It kicked back hard. Sounded like thunder. "Keep down. I want to talk to you."

Frog Woman croaked a weird sound, her body was bent over. "Don't."

I grabbed her mop of hair and yanked her whole head.

"Look at me!" I had to see her eyes, had to have her see me. "Let's have a little conversation. Real honest-to-god talk." I was in some kind of horrible shoot-em-up movie. I kept asking her questions. "Where were you born?"

Her eyes. My eyes.

She sat up. "You are going to kill me."

"No! No! No! Give me the key. I need gas for my truck. *Can you hear me?*"

Without looking up, she raised her hand with the key.

"Make my day. Tell me about yourself." I pointed the gun at her. It felt heavy, but everything else was light. My left hand floated over to take the key.

"Don't talk to me." She lowered her head, making her neck fold in five hundred lines, and started to pray again.

I turned the pump on with the key and the gas gushed out the nozzle again. "So, I guess you're not feeling much like talking today."

"Please, Jesus." Frog Woman moan-croaked again.

The gas pump clicked off and I yanked out the hose. I tried to screw the gas cap on but it dropped.

"I'm not going to kill you. Just get me some food." I felt dizzy and leaned against my truck door.

The woman opened her eyes and blinked a few times. "Food?"

"Fill a basket with pies and beef jerky. Don't go near the counter. Don't call anybody. And get some Fancy Feast for my cat. And lots of water bottles, you know the plain kind, lots of them."

She scurried inside.

I picked up the gas cap and screwed it on. I went to the outside of the market and pointed the gun at her as she loaded my basket. I didn't know if there was a camera so I didn't go inside. If she called somebody, it would still be a while before they arrived.

She was pulling beef jerky off the rack.

"Hurry up," I yelled. "I don't want your money. I just want food and gas. My cat and I are taking a trip."

A truck was coming down the highway. I moved the gun behind my back. "That's enough. Come on."

She brought the food over in the plastic shopping basket.

I motioned for her to put it on top of the truck hood. She did and then got down on her knees and started praying.

The truck slowed down. A teenage boy looked at us and then kept going.

She was still praying.

I opened the truck door and put my gun back in the case. I put the whole basket on the seat.

I turned back to Frog Woman. "Would you cut it out? I'm not doing anything to you. Just gave you a story to tell, okay?"

Her face and neck were very red now. Her lips had disappeared inside her head so there was a large crease from ear to ear where her mouth should have been. She was sweating along the edge of her white mop of curls. "You aren't going to shoot me?"

"No." I kicked my truck tire. "But god might have let me."

"Please go. This isn't the place for you."

"I know that."

CARA USED TO call it *The Hate Connection*. When some kid went off, did something really nasty to somebody, she'd say he found his hate connection. She made this up one day when we were hanging at the drop-in center on Polk watching a drooly dating show called *Love Connection*.

I didn't used to feel that hate was dangerous—just your everyday occurrence. It seemed to me we were all mashed together in hate and need at the same time. When I was a kid I always tried to remember that if I hated somebody it was because I needed something from them that they weren't willing to give. And maybe that's all that happened at the gas station.

When I was younger I used to get all serious; that's why I read so much, trying to understand things. I read about molecules, the solar system, history. Curling up with books, writing long lists, getting out by myself at night and figuring the constellations—it all helped me be less furious and burned inside. Then at some point I stopped trusting the heavy coldness of thoughts and books. One day I wanted to be Girl, no baggage, nothing else. No shmancy pretenses about who I was and why I was and what life was. I stopped worrying about being clean and smart like my dad. I wanted to *live*.

Figuring everything from then on would be about simple survival; I promised to make lists only when I was desperate for distraction, when I couldn't sleep or was panging with hunger.

But what now? If I was going to go around killing people, or almost killing people, I damn well better understand why. The Great Plains of Dakota and Nebraska had never let me close. They weren't going to let me in. It was true, like the Frog Woman said, I didn't belong here. I wanted to get to Memphis as fast as I could, before I killed a whole town.

AS I DROVE SOUTH, the setting sun made a rancid glare over the road. It painted my hands a rotten melon color and reflected off the hood of the truck.

I longed to be with Angus. Soon, soon, soon. I hoped he could get my head calmed down in one of our late-night talks. I needed his slim hips and goofy bird's-nest hair and the babeee, babeee, sweet darling Texas talk.

The sun burned away into dusk. I was finally putting the plains behind me. All that possibiliteee, the bare-boned architecture of the country. The vast prairie space made me think of a person who stripped naked, only to never let you touch them. The hard exposed farmland felt like that. It didn't let anyone close and pretended not to need anyone.

What had I found? The carcasses of grain elevators, the old

bricks and boards of Independence, the splayed out crumbling ruins.

All I knew was to keep going and look for the next thing. Someday I'd feel connected to something. Or was it all about crashing through?

When it got dark I pulled over. I took my pocketknife and made a neat cut at the bottom seam of the truck seat. I took out some foam stuffing and shoved my gun inside the springs. If I did get pulled over and searched, they might not see the cut.

I ran into a big Interstate highway that could take me south to Kansas City—only two hundred eighty-two miles. Spot and I would spend the night there, spare change in the morning, and see if we could get to Memphis by the next evening.

I turned the radio knob and sampled everything, more country music, eighties stud-rock and the assault of radio gospel. The engine roared as the pistons rose and fell inside their valves, hot as hell, but going and going. An engine with no regrets.

THE SEELBACH HOTEL in Louisville, Kentucky, was a fancy show-off with high ceilings, an enormous chandelier, and vertigo balconies painted with gold. Like all old buildings, it was a way to fend off the desolation of empty space.

I had called Angus from Kansas City and we had decided to meet at the Seelbach, because Jim had a bowling tournament in Louisville, and they would be there in a couple of days. He said the hotel would be crawling with gay men from all over the South, coming together to drink martinis and bowl.

A bellboy gave me a smile as he passed by, a white guy with apple cheeks. He directed me to the bar that was down a few steps, a big cave to my right.

The long bar sparkled with hundreds and hundreds of bottles next to an old ornate mirror. I asked for a complimentary bourbon, told the bartender I was broke and waiting for a friend that hadn't got there yet. He gave me some Uncle Pappy's. When I told him it was my first time in the South, he welcomed me and told me stories. Yes! I decided I was going to love the South.

MY OWN PLACE

I would build something from stones. Gray craggy rocks, huge smooth pebbles, or maybe mountain granite. The place would have a round floor plan based on a spiral and you would never quite know where you were, more and more rooms, one leading to the next. It would be quiet and medieval, a stone palace. The rooms on the outside would be large, meant for music and friends and parties. As you walked toward the center, the rooms would be more private and lovely and colorful. Always enough beds. Enough for anyone and everyone. Maroon velvet bedspreads. Tall silver goblets on old wooden night tables. Ceilings that could push apart in the summer to reveal the sky. Some rooms would even have trees growing in them, silver-dollar eucalyptus and redwoods. The ground would be dirt. The house would blend the outside and inside.

And best, it could take off like a flying saucer. It could take off and land outside any town in america—in the open spaces between places. I could land it, check things out, and then invite all the bored people back to my spinning, open-ceiling fort. Yes!

FOR SOMETHING TO DO as I waited for the gay bowlers to arrive, I headed in the direction of the old section of Louisville. I hoped I could find the skid marks of a few other souls like me.

Spot jumped from the car the moment I opened the door. She sniffed a little and ran under a nearby car. I sat on the curb till she came out and rubbed my calf. As she stretched her neck and gave me big hungry meows, I stroked her fur and kneaded the puzzle-piece spots on her neck. I leaned next to her twitchy ear and whispered, "Thanks. I'm not really a homicidal maniac."

Behind us were long avenues of crumbling mansions. Since the hotel clerk's computer said that Jim and Angus weren't coming till Saturday, the next day, I wondered what to do. I had spent two nights in my truck already, the first in Kansas City like I'd planned, but the second night I'd been stuck in St. Louis because I couldn't get enough spange money to fill my tank.

The houses were brick-colored and their porches sank. Many were abandoned and I could probably break into one to sleep. A trash can overflowed next to a nearby porch. I searched inside the green garbage sack and found newspapers, coffee grounds, a burned piece of toast. The toast had mixed in with the coffee grounds and smelled almost sweet. It was soggy in my mouth. I sucked the flavor of the coffee, and the charcoal taste reminded me of meat.

A student-type with a backpack and big black glasses gave me a worried look as he passed me on the sidewalk.

"Hey, I have a hungry cat." I smiled. "Think you could help me out?"

He squinted. "A cat?"

"Her name is Spot." I stuffed the last bite of toast in my mouth and pointed to Spot sniffing the gutter. "See?"

He walked away, and I heard a door slam.

The student still had on his backpack and stared at me from inside the window of his old house. After a couple of minutes he appeared with an orange-plastic bowl filled with sloshing milk.

He reached down to pet Spot, and Spot didn't even flinch because she was so busy lapping the milk. "I like your cat."

I nodded. "She's a good traveler."

After another couple minutes the student went inside and came back with a tiny opened can of tuna. I waited till he left, then dug my hand into the can and drank some of the milk from the orange bowl.

When Spot looked at me with her questioning eyes, I told her that I was sorry she had to share. My stomach cramped as the food went down. I had eaten the last of my Frog-Woman food in St. Louis, so I was pretty caved-in. Spot finished every morsel after I put down the can, eating as fast as I had. I put my head near her furry face and told her I knew what it was like to beg people for food.

Jail was one way to get food. Some girls were crazed on the streets and I swore they looked to YGC to get their meals. They would be fed. They would get their television. They would be ordered around by other girls, no choice but to follow the routine. I could have had that kind of life, but it wasn't for me. Staring at a closed door with no handle on it: my definition of a force-fed life of dunderfunk.

After putting Spot back in the truck, I found a pen in the glove box.

I left a note in the rusted mailbox next to the student's door. "Always talk to strangers. Thanks."

AFTER I SAW the junkie-heads start to prowl the twilight streets of old Louisville, I went to a big mall parking lot to sleep for the

night. I parked behind a trash container so you couldn't see me
from the main road. I slept in the truck, or kind of slept. To keep
us from dehydrating, I poured some of my Frog-Woman water on
my head and squirted it in Spot's mouth every once in a while.
One time I thought I heard someone outside the pickup, but it was
only a raccoon pawing around the dumpster. Spot stayed nestled
against my thighs.

The next morning I stood by my truck and looked around.
The parking spaces were filling up. So far no security guard had
bothered me out there in the clean and squared-off fantasy of
monotone normality. Smack in the sprawl. The older part of
Louisville, where Spot and I had gotten our tuna dinner, had
much more character, but if I'd slept there I would have been
dead by morning.

For breakfast I went to the big bookstore café and sat at a table.
When people got up, I ate the food they left. I scored a bit of cran-
berry muffin, some cream for Spot, and half a cup of cold coffee.
After I told the girl behind the counter I was from San Francisco,
she gave me two biscuits.

Then I wanted some pie real bad. So I went in the supermarket.
I lifted a small wrapped berry pie and put it inside my shirt. On my
way out, a woman stopped me.

"Have you forgotten something?" She had a surgically cut bob of
red hair and a smug color of coral lipstick.

I paused and wondered whether to run. "What, ma'am?"

She brought me to a room at the back of the store and called the
skunkers. They arrived almost immediately and threw me in their car.

We drove through the parking lot and passed near my truck. I
got the shivers. I wanted to say something. Ask them to stop and let
me take Spot. Or let her out. Instead I kept my mouth shut, realiz-
ing if I said anything they might trace the car. Maybe find the gun.
I didn't even look back.

THE POLICE STATION BOOKING AREA fit in a small alcove. Floors waxed and beaming. The glass protecting the woman who asked my name was clean. In San Francisco, it had a zillion finger marks and greasy smudges. Here everything was almost unused. There was some kind of pounding going next door. Hammers. A sheet of plastic hung over the hallway door, a temporary place. They must have been remodeling. No one else was around but me.

The woman behind the glass window had long hair and a beak nose. She asked me more questions and I didn't answer. The bow-legged cop who had picked me up from the store stood to my left. They talked about somebody who had just got killed over drugs. They were excited by the action and seemed to connect me with it somehow. I was afraid to say my name.

I closed my eyes. Mixed up with the drywall dust were the undercurrents of a sick hospital smell. Dead bodies and Xeroxes and formaldehyde. Words flying and lights blaring. Fickle flat fowl falling. Insaniteee. "Name?" Long Hair looked over my shoulder and growled to the wall directly behind me. I was trapped in the alcove.

Sharp, old edges to her face. So different from my round moon. I get amazed when a face has nothing left to hide. Like Bill. He was so bony, tight. With the mean, bruise-colored circles under her eyes, Long Hair reminded me of Bill's evil twin, one left in an institution, with no sun or exercise, only violence and cigarettes. She had Bill's chiseled forearms, tendons pulsing on the hand holding the pen, waiting for my name. I could imagine her in cowboy boots and young. I wished Bill could show up. Somebody. But it wasn't going to happen. It was like the time they called my dad and he didn't come. I wasn't getting out.

I kicked at the cement under her window. My granddad had taught me that you don't have to tell them everything they ask.

The skunkcop at my side grabbed me. He wheezed.

Long Hair screeched. "You take her. If it is a her. Is it a girl?"

He was a lot bigger, maybe a foot above me. He sounded choked up. "We can make you say anything," he said.

I laughed because it was like he thought he was in some action movie and could pull some secret code from me. "Come on," I said.

"We have your personal effects." Long Hair growled. "We can find out who you are. What stinking place you come from."

They were both really worked up. I had come on the wrong day. They were building a scene, some S/M drama.

The big, bowlegged, wheezing skunk had me by both shoulders now. I wouldn't look. Saw only his shoes, and they were funny. He couldn't stand right. They were all worn out on the sides. And he couldn't breathe right either. His nose whistled.

"Don't." My blood was pumping into my fists.

He shoved me against to the wall. "We can make you sorry."

"Yeah, sure."

"We can make it so you never get out of here."

It happened fast. I fell on the floor and my cheek was pressed into the waxy gleam. His boot was on my back. The muffin I ate that morning came gushing out of me.

I should have said my name. Told them my dad was an attorney. Played the right game. "I know my rights. Don't."

"She think she's a lawyer." It was the woman again, her voice in time with the heavy breathing of the cop.

He prodded his wood baton against my cheek. He mashed the baton against me, getting vomit in my hair.

Thought of Spot, alone in the hot truck, no way out, both of us trapped.

Wrenched a hand free to push the stick away. That's when it came down hard on my back. Two. I counted. Six. Seven.

"Tell us your name."

"I don't know," I said. Curled into a ball. Wriggled next to the wall.

A TERRIBLY BRIGHT ROOM with a bed. Outside, the building had been sculpted with angles and peaked roofs and lots of glass. An optimistic seventies-style jail. The inside was buffed and waxed and grinning. Different than the trash-box Juvy in SF. Sunbeams even came through my high window. I stood on my bed and got a sharp pain in my side. The window was just high enough to prevent people from looking out.

The door was painted gray metal and absolutely flat. One slit of a meshed window. No knob. Of course.

The bed was a crate with metal bars sticking up like handles at the ends. I lay down and shoved my boots against the end of the bed frame. Thank god they had let me keep my boots on; this was only a holding cell. I pushed both my feet against the bars. Then I kicked. My chest hurt. I didn't care. I spread my legs more and scooted down so I could really charge against either side of the metal frame. Someone in the next room started kicking the wall. I got it going more. Right, left, right, left. A drum rhythm. Both of us. From the gut. I yelled and my ribs felt like they were ready to crack open.

A black woman with a shiny face brought in some food and placed it on the bed.

"Our computers are down. They want me to get your address and info."

I wiped the snot off my nose. On the plate were chicken bits in a creamy yellow sauce with a biscuit. I sniffed at it while lying down because I was afraid to sit, felt sharp pains every time I breathed. Chicken bits, pink and smooth, like tiny parts of organs. I stared at the bits of choke meat for a long time. The insides of some mutilated beast.

"So, Penelope. Can you tell me your address?"

The woman was still there. Dark, coffee-bean skin, processed curly hair, and a gold necklace. Everything gave off an oily gleam. I knew if I talked I would be theirs. How did she know I was Penelope? Or did I just think she said that?

The metal bars on the bed started pulsing.

I closed my eyes.

She kept sitting there all close to me and wouldn't leave.

Eventually I asked if she could call the Seelbach Hotel, tell the bowlers where I was. I hoped like hell they had gotten into town. When I was fifteen I had spent weeks in the pen. That time I hadn't even done anything.

She said she would call for me.

I put the napkin over the food and shoved it away. "Tell them, Hi from Girl."

"Yes, honey."

"Tell them to get me out of here."

"That sounds like a plan." She put her hand on the bed and patted it.

I glared at her. Her face blinked on and off.

There's nothing worse then someone trying to be nice to you when you're stranded in hate. I felt low, meaner than the Ku Klux Klan.

WHEN I WOKE, it was dark outside, but the ceiling light blared down.

I felt something seep out of me and figured I'd started my period. Television and voices mingled outside. I stared at the ceiling. Someone had managed to write some words up there. In scratches, it said NO JUSTICE NO PEACE. Hearing the Southern accents around me made me think of the fact that I was now on land where there had once been slavery. Great. Just great. Land of the chains.

Since there was no toilet paper, I took my bandanna from around my neck and put it in my underwear to soak up what was coming out. My head felt huge, my hair matted, and I could feel the bed cutting into the backs of my ribs. I heard more sounds around me, the sounds of kids watching TV, kids teasing one another, all easygoing. They didn't even mind being locked up. I knew those domesticated sounds.

No Justice. No Peace. The words pulsed on the ceiling. Came closer and further. Bubbling. I needed to pee.

"Man, you crazeee. Man, you crazeee." Somebody was talking near my pen.

And I had thought everything was going to be okay once I left the Great Plains.

I closed my eyes. Opened them. Did it again. Kept hoping I'd see something else besides the toilet, the ceiling, the walls, the door with the slit. But it was real.

I think this is when something inside me started wanting to pray.

I stood on my mattress.

"Man, you come here. She sick." A white girl was staring in the meshed-window in the metal door. "You don't know about this one. You got to see."

"Hey," I called.

She pressed her cheek into the window. "Sick girl standing up. Come here. She gonna hurl."

Several girls were outside my pen.

I needed to pee and I didn't want them looking. "Hey."

"Wow, you see her?"

I went up to the door and pounded it. "Shut up."

Someone's eye kept looking at me. Everybody was taking turns looking. I couldn't hear them now. My ears went deaf. I pulled down my jeans and sat on the toilet. Bloody, cramped, hungry.

I knew they couldn't lock me up forever. That's what they said, though. The skunk had said that. When he threw my carrybag against the wall. He said, "We can lock you up forever and you'll never get out." God, he needed a new script.

I took some of my leaking blood and wrote on the wall under the bed.

DUST

SKY

If I got out I would never let them trap me again. And then I remembered what Joey the Muddafucca said about there always being something there. Always no matter what. And I decided to believe him. It was better than the alternative, even if it wasn't true. I rolled from under the bed and looked to the high window. A far, night-falling darkness. I saw my granddad's face and I knew I had to be with him again. I didn't want to die; I learned that in Burnt County. I tried to believe that it all could make sense somehow. That something was all around me that would never go away.

I wanted to feel something close. I thought of Randa's strong hands and Jessika's electric hair. Phantoms. I wanted to laugh with Cara like we did the time in the skunk car after we had gotten arrested on Polk Street. I talked aloud and asked Cara to help me figure out what to do. I felt different from back then with her on the street. Older.

Even though they were far away and long ago, I thought of the stars and then I thought of the sun. I put my hands together. I didn't want the girls looking at me so I moved back under the bed.

"Help me." I wanted to believe. Something out there must still exist. I think I was yelling. I said everything I could to try to get god's attention.

I had to get out somehow. Then everything would be okay.

I pushed really hard, first with my hands and then with my feet. I would push the walls away.

JIM'S BIG HEAD freaked me out. It was as if he had been carved from a boulder. He smelled of aftershave and had smooth pecs and wore clean shirts and had a plump leather wallet. The opposite of blow-in-the wind, hip-twirling, whore-boy Angus. Yet they had a similar kind of fabulicious style, a spirit that made them a matched pair, salt and pepper.

Jim had seen the bruises on my back and said I should sue, but I said forget it. I didn't want to do anything ever again but sleep, drink beer, and watch TV, and that didn't take a lawyer's help. Curled up in the backseat of his Sedan DeVille on the way to Memphis, I felt like road kill. It didn't help that my ribs stabbed like daggers when I laughed. Or that after they got me out, we had gone over to the truck in the mall and found Spot dead in my truck. Jim got a plastic bag from the drugstore and we put Spot in it and took her to the pound to burn. Spot was stiff and her hair was flat and funny, looking as if the life had been lifted from every molecule of her body, even her fluff. She had died in that hot truck, thirsty and begging to get out. I kissed her little head.

At the pound, I handed the plastic bag across the counter like it was a delivery. They made me sign something. Dogs howled and whined. All kinds of animals were smelling up the air with longing. I wanted so to get a kitten or a puppy or at least a bird, but I was scared now that I knew I had murdered a defenseless cat. I tried not to look at any of the cages. The only thing I'd been able to rescue from the Lindflotts' truck had been my gun from where I'd hidden it inside the seat. I had to make sure that when they found the truck the police didn't also find the gun and trace it back to Randa.

Hearing the chorus of animals, alive and needing and ready to be taken home, guilt overtook me. It wasn't my gun that had killed Spot, but somehow the two became linked. Once we got to Memphis, I decided, I would bury Randa's black metal death machine in the banks of the Mississippi River. Enough already.

BACK ON THE ROAD, we put the top down and Angus wailed along with Jim's disco-purgatory CD.

"Love to love you baby." Angus made his long baby moans and rocked from one side of the seat to the other. Then he turned around, pretending to hand me a mike in the backseat. When I wouldn't take it, he just sang louder.

His hair was slicked back, he had broken out a little on his chin, and with the new pencil thin mustache he'd grown, Angus looked like a miniature huckster. He got away with anything no matter what. I had always loved the unfinished look about him, his messed-up hair and small willowy chest. I'd always thought of Angus as tough and frail at the same time, and I'd always needed him around in my life, although I don't know why. But now I wondered if this new look fit him. His baggy pants and weird Hollywood mustache made him look phony in a way he never had before.

I was wearing goof-ass surfer trunks and a white T-shirt I had borrowed from Angus after throwing away my bloody jeans and my MAKE MY DAY T-shirt. Tried to feel fresh and make a new start, but my mood stayed foul and hurting, stinky and rotten even after two nights' sleep and showers at the hotel. I stretched out in the back-seat. Placed my arrowhead smack on my chest and held it there with the palm of my hand. My stomach was in knots and I wasn't even sure whether I could keep any food down. The fried chicken from room service had come up in the middle of the night.

We drove through miles of rolling green Kentucky lands with horses grazing. I hadn't hardly talked at the hotel and still didn't feel much like conversation, but occasionally I felt moved to say something.

"Is this the same planet as South Dakota?" I asked.

"Somewhere, over the rainbow..." sang Angus. He wiggled his long, skinny torso. "And are you a good witch or a bad witch?"

I shrugged, shut up again and tried to sleep. Finally they turned off the lame music. Instead Jim cooed nonstop hundred-proof Southern chatter. He was nice, but I felt at his mercy. Here he had done so much for me already, calling his lawyer and getting the charges dropped, paying for my meals in the hotel.

Jim turned his big head around and winked at me in the back-seat. "This thing needs some more freshening up, but she could be a winner."

"Go to hell." I wanted to spit over the side of the convertible but was afraid it would fly back in my face. "Is everybody so nice in the South?"

"Oh, we are so very, very nice, you'll get addicted. You'll never go home again."

"Shush, Mary. You're frightening the lamb," said Angus. He petted his mustache.

"You go to hell, too." I felt like I was dying and they were my faggot torturers.

Once in Tennessee, we took an offshoot road to get to a roadside restaurant that Jim liked. We passed a small neighborhood with some makeshift houses, all held together by boards of different kinds. The windows were covered with sheets. It reminded me of the abandoned houses in Independence, except these houses were still lived in. Trash surrounded them. In front of one was an old vanity, some boxes, and what seemed to be the car dump for the town. Farther along were trailers perched on cinder blocks, and a fleshy black girl on a trampoline bounded up and down in green sneakers. In the very next block the houses got nicer and cleaner and smug. It was strange that poor folks lived right next door to rich folks, as if they needed each other to know who they were.

AFTER OUR LUNCH of barbecue (well, for me beer and peach pie), we got back on the road. Angus asked if I was ready to tell him what I'd done all summer. "Tell me everything." He pushed down the visor and looked at himself in the vanity mirror.

I told him a little about Randa and Pammy and Bo and Curly and Irma. And then described my picnics with Dottie. Somehow I thought he'd like the weirdness of it all.

"I want to feel like everything around me makes sense," I said. "I want to be happy."

"That shouldn't be hard to find, should it?" Angus looked around the car as if he had misplaced something. He opened up the glove box and screeched. "Here it is. Happiness."

"Give it up," I said.

LATER JIM TOLD HIS STORY. "Well, I take care of my grandparents now. That's what I do."

As he drove and drove and talked, I got it: Jim sounded like a deep-voiced, big-headed Scarlett O'Hara. He purred and cooed about how his parents had sold the family farm a few years back and made lots of money. Jim said he'd been in the air force, danced as a go-go boy, and grown cotton. I believed him about the go-go thing cause I'd seen him dance the night before, to the radio in the room at the Seelbach. Jim and Angus had come to the room after their tournament party in the downstairs bar and were fooling around while I was trying to sleep on the couch. Angus pranced about with a scarf. Jim closed his eyes, grabbed his thighs, and stuck out his butt, shimmying in absolute soul-sister ecstasy.

"Can you imagine that before I gained this weight I used to shake this for a living?" Jim said to me.

His parents hadn't wanted him to be a farmer at first, so for a while he'd done some mean go-go dancing.

I asked which job he liked best.

"Growing cotton. You know what I liked best about it?"

"Tell."

"I didn't have to shave! You should have seen me. Barefoot. I was a fright. An absolute fright. But you see, I love to make things grow. We all do. Everybody in my family."

I told him about Randa.

"She probably is going right into hard times. You can't hope to start a farm now. They have to be big, a few hundred acres is nothing."

"Maybe she'll do it by sheer will power."

"Oh, you never know what's possible. That's tru-u-ue." He sighed. "Now tell me about your dreams and future plans."

The warm early September sky beat down, but the air kept moving. If you had to be stuck in a car, it was good to have it be the size of a limo and half open. I closed my eyes. "You tell him, Angus."

"She wants to be a rock-and-roll star."

"He's talking about himself, don't you think?" I moaned as my ribs stabbed when I sat up again. "Angus's always been my role model."

"Let me say this about my sweet thing." Jim looked at me in the rear-view mirror. "No one loves anybody more than I love Angus. Just wait till you see us at home. We spent the summer like two peas in a pod. I grow my roses and he paints his pictures, and we could live like that forever."

I closed my eyes and wished I had the money and the home and all the things that Jim had to woo somebody. Maybe that's what it took.

The South got hotter and stickier, but they boogied along, blasting the air conditioner even with the top down. From my prone position in the backseat, as we tore through Tennessee, all I could see was blue sky streaming overhead. I tried to convince myself, as I had in jail, that I could make a new life. Without getting into trouble. I had to believe it. Maybe I could be like a brave ex-slave following the North Star and underground railroad toward freedom.

Maybe that was what, if anything, life was about. Escaping and going onward.

When we passed through Jonesboro, Jim bought us drinks at a Stop and Shop. In the parking lot, the three of us took long sips and leaned against the shiny chrome bumper of the big white caddy. The tail lights were like sharp long tears, and I was grateful that it was a cool old car that I hadn't had to steal.

Jim fanned his face and promised to take to me to see his old Mississippi Delta land, the land he used to farm.

"He'd rather be back there in the dirt than doing anything else," said Angus. I remembered the last time I saw him was the day that he had told me Cara died; how fragile he had looked with his mashed lip and bird's-nest hair. He looked like a whole different species now. I knew whatever tidy role he was playing for Jim wasn't going to last. Too wife-like. I wished Angus could be happy-for-real, and not putting on a slick act.

"Hmm, darlin," said Jim. "When I showed Angus his first combine I just thought he'd die of shock. You know, for the longest time I didn't admit to him what I used to do for a living."

Angus combed his hair back behind his ears, as if it would make a difference when we got back in the open rush of air. "I thought he was a former drug dealer. You know, here's this guy who says he used to have seasonal work and drives a Cadillac. I thought he was taking care of half of Memphis."

Jim batted his Mizz Scarlet lashes. "Can you believe we are together? What is this girl from Mississippi doing with a pretty angel like Angus?"

Angus turned around and rolled his eyes for my benefit.

A couple of guys passing by in a car waved at us.

I'd used to think of Angus as an angel, especially when he held me with his skinny arms and swayed me back and forth. But the truth was now it was Jim who seemed like the winged blessing. He'd gotten me out of jail, was feeding me, and was going to put me up in a place he called home. A place he would invite me to live for real. At least for a few days.

Jim sucked down the last of his sweet tea and beckoned for us to get back in the car. "You got to see it. The water snakes in the delta like ribbons. And they got the gambling now in Tunaca, so people are making a decent living. Used to be that people were so poor they'd be eating dirt! I don't live there now, you know. I like my house in town, but I do miss the old days."

We piled inside again and took off in the DeVille. Jim started humming. One of his hands danced along, making figure-eights in the sultry heat of late afternoon.

"You are too much. You're my man." I laughed. Then, because I was tired of them teasing me, I decided to get Jim back. Angus had told me how much Jim wanted to be a father. "I just realized something. I want to have your baby!"

"Darlin! You are tweaking!" He slapped his thigh. "You want a baby? You can have a baby, honey. I can fill a turkey baster as well as anybody. Or come to think of it, I can still do the nasty. Oh, mama! What do you want to name it? I tell you: hold a baby in the air and it's like the sky opened up above and you saw the little Jesus."

I reached over the car seat and tapped his shoulder. "Okay. Let's do it. Just one thing, Mr. Jim. If you say anything else close to religious I will have to kill you." Then I thought about what I had just said. "No kidding. The last person who did, I almost shot their brains out."

"Why do you like Girl? She's so-o-o freaky mean," Angus said to Jim. Angus turned from the front seat and punched my arm. "You better watch out because Jim loves kids. He'll make a real killer mommy."

Despite myself, I started thinking about it for real. Somehow I couldn't quite imagine all of us raising a kid together, but it was a nice thought. You never know either. Maybe some day I'd have my own whiney kid. One thing for sure, I'd keep it close.

I curled back into the big blue leather seat and closed my eyes. My brain wouldn't shut down. The humid air sunk into my aching ribs. Hallucinations from my trip wouldn't stop. Behind my closed eyes I watched a parade of all the faces I had seen.

BY EARLY EVENING, we got to the outskirts of Memphis. It didn't look like too big a town. I hung my hands over the front seat and watched the parade of Wendy's burgers and Texaco gas. Blocks of shiny used cars with their blue and red Mylar flags passed by, and windows painted with CHECKS CASHED HERE. Up ahead the streetlights began to turn, rocks skipping against the muddy sea of twilight.

We stopped at a light, its red lamp hanging from a wire, cherry red against the navy sky. Down the road were more stoplights—beaming, purring, jewel-like bombs. Billboards loomed in rows on either side of us; ads for Schlitz beer and Jesus Saves and Doc Holliday's Pawn Shop. Bright black letters against yellow backgrounds with big staring faces. Lit by tiny searchlights at their bottom rims, the billboards were not quite bright, some daylight mixed in, a strange hit and miss glow. I blurred my eyes to make it dance.

Jim drove on after the light turned. The roadside places, the hamburger joints, the pawnshops, the storage hangers…one place after the next. I had never wanted to join the mainstream, and now I knew I never would. Back in Burnt County, I knew being a nameless rogue was for real. Now it haunted me again, but it was more than that. I mean, how do you know what you want till you can't find it?

Then it came to me…not like a lightning bolt, more like a wash; a soft bleed of deep-down knowing. I slowly formed my own little patch of outlaw truth. It was the justice of my life, the thing I could-n't fight but had to live. I knew one forever thing: *My loneliness was a legitimate place of familiar.* I could not be like anyone else, or die like anyone else, or do it any other way. It was up to me. I was on my own and had to find my own way of living. That's all.

home

I PUT MY FEET on native ground and walked west on Market from the Seventh Street bus station. It was Sunday and the worker-bees were gone, leaving the bums and the wounded. The buildings seemed taller. I walked way down to the Castro and the chirping gay clones were still there. I hadn't seen them for so many months, especially not in broad daylight. It was funny. All these people had escaped from the places I had just been, the flat places. All these people in their new sunglasses and bright shields of clothes. I knew more about their insides now.

Climbed all the way to the top of Twin Peaks, stepped past the T-shirt trucks and the camera crowds to the other side of the hill. The Pacific spread before me. The teasing golden light, the broken sky that fell so close. This open sea, this view of the west was *mine*.

I called my granddad.

He was real happy to hear from me. Said I could stay for a week, but he wasn't going to give me any money. And if I stole anything I'd be out in a second.

"It's a deal, Grandpapah-h-h," I said.

I WALKED DOWN the long way to Market, where I got the street car, and then the Mission bus that takes forever. I got off at Precita and walked up to Coso, and turned to face the Winfield house.

People were arriving with balloons and packages. I watched for a long time. Some kind of party.

At last I realized this was my day to ring the bell.

A man with a big belly and pink face answered the door. "It isn't her. Come on out."

People flooded the room. It was some kind of surprise party because everybody had been hiding. A huge cake box tied with string sat on the coffee table. I stepped inside.

The big belly man wiped his hands on his apron. "You the daughter?"

"I guess."

"You going to stand there, honey?'

He had been cooking. It smelled of sausage and garlic. A few people sat at a low couch near the window. Everyone was pretty old.

"Are you Celia?" someone asked me.

I shrugged. They seemed to think I was somebody's kid.

A woman with short brown hair and a scar on her chin was blowing up balloons using a helium tank.

"I was born here," I said.

"What?"

A man came up to me. "Are you Celia? I always wanted to meet Natalie's daughter." The man poured me a glass of wine. "You like red?"

The view was even better than I'd imagined. I stood by the window. A late daylight fell on Mission Street and the Safeway parking lot, but Twin Peaks was already in violet silhouette. The sky's edge was turning a mixture of green and orange. The balloon woman followed me to the deck.

"I love it out here," she said. She held five helium balloons. The wind came and made the balloons knock against one another. We stood near old barrels filled with jade plants, a weathered box of scraggly geraniums, some dry asparagus ferns. A Mission Street bus screeched to a halt.

"Your mom should be here soon."

"I'll wait out here," I said.

The wind pounded us. Felt dizzy, paranoid that I would fall over the wooden deck rail.

She gave me a yellow balloon. I waited till she left to let it go. It hit my cheek, then surged up like a flame.

I looked at the deck itself, the cracks between boards, the hose in the corner.

I wanted to lie down on the boards like I imagined my mother had.

Then I heard a big "Surprise!"

People inside laughed and jumped up and down. A small woman with short blond hair like mine stood with her neck stretched up like a gopher. Looked at everyone with big eyes.

She could have been my mother. I mean, what's the difference?

BACK ON THE COZY PURPLE FUTON. I never thought I'd be here again. Dr. Bronner's peppermint soap from my granddad's shower. Espresso brewing. The familiar smells wafted around me, everything I'd thought the Great Plains would take away forever. Hard to believe. Even the car fumes coming through the barred window smelled good. I looked over the books on the crammed, towering shelves. Math textbooks on number theory, wacky science fiction, political diatribes, and endless Shakespeare. I curled my body into a nest and settled with I-am-only-an-egg Heinlein.

ON SATURDAY MORNING we took a walk around the radio tower, through the dry grasses of empty lots and along the small streets cramped with cars. Then we came down on the east side of Bernal Hill and passed the old men drinking on the corner, the bragging dealers on the playground. As cars rolled by, rap songs from their radios shook the sidewalk under our feet. When we came home we watched TV on his mattress and ate hamburgers from Burger King. By the afternoon, sun came through the barred window to saturate one corner of his bed.

For the rest of the weekend my granddad and I watched *Dirty Harry* movies, cartoons, and *The Streets of San Francisco*. The same pretty girls I remembered, long hair and big smiles, always the bad men's targets.

My granddad said, "Did you notice that all killers have shaggy haircuts? And they've always just got out of the pen?" The commercial came on and he muted the sound. His stocky forearm quivered as he grabbed a corner of my sweatshirt. "Don't you fuck up again, Gretchen."

After I'd walk back into the room he would hug me like the old days, when all I'd done was leave for the bathroom or to get milk from the store. During meals he wouldn't let up. He'd talk fast all the way through a burger, dripping mustard on his shirt.

"I love you, Gretchen," he said on Sunday morning. "I'm sorry about all the shit I did to you as a kid."

"What shit?"

"I don't remember."

I shrugged. "You want to go to the beach?" I asked.

"No. Let's get another reactionary movie and more junk food from Burger King."

What about the ocean? I wanted to bike to the beach with him like the old days, and sit around and wait for the sun with its chime of color to break through the banks of fog.

I CALLED JIM. His voice was such warm Southern goo that I could feel the heat rise from the receiver.

"Oh, honey, we're sitting here drinking sweet tea on the porch."

"Sounds good."

"We're waiting for you, Mizz Heavenly Thing." Jim had Whitney Houston playing in the background. "We can make the baby when you come back! I'm planning everything. I'm so excited. You settling things up with your granddad? You tell me when, and I'll get you another plane ticket. You know I will."

"Yeah, soon."

"I'll take care of you, honey."

"Yeah, sure."

PRETENDED TO LISTEN to my granddad as we sat on his mattress for the rest of the evening. But really, I listened to the streets of San Francisco, the real streets down below, as the kids rolled their skateboards and the cars gunned their engines and the neighbors laughed.

It occurred to me that I had no less right than anybody to be on the planet. I was alive and going to stay alive.

And as my granddad talked further, I knew that he couldn't tell me anything anymore. His stories, even the ones about my mother, weren't mine.

I CALLED ANGUS in the morning, and he said he was leaving Jim. Someone had offered him another modeling contract in Atlanta and he would make a lot more money this time. I wasn't sure what this meant for me. I couldn't see living with Jim without Angus; I wasn't sure he'd want me anymore. I had been dreaming up a fantasy of going back to Memphis, of seeing if Jim would let Jessika live with us, too. Or Bo, or even Pammy. Get all my friends out there in Memphis.

Instead I'd have to crash in San Francisco for a while. The ole familiar. A place where no one really knew anything, but at least that's honest.

Maybe eventually I'd find someone I could keep.

IT MADE SENSE that it was familiar to me. Loneliness was everywhere. I saw it in the disconnected, frantic glances of people on the street. I used to think they were scared to look at me, but now I wondered if they were scared to look at anyone.

I walked back down Market Street and its big parade of noise, and I remembered my cornfields. I could find something to do here, too. It wouldn't be corn detasseling, but I could find some way not to hover at the edges, a way to somehow dive right in. Randa did teach me that. I could work with the knowledge that I was part of things; I *needed* this. And maybe my need was a place to start.

DEAR DOTTIE,

Hi. This letter is from Girl. Do you remember me?

I'm writing this at the ocean. The ocean is similar to the Great Plains. Big and stretched out. I can see your face looking at the ocean and I can see you feeling at home. The need for the ocean shows in your eyes (I hope you don't mind me saying).

I do feel strange writing after all this time. I've promised myself I will mail this and not just keep it a fantasy like all the others.

I have a job at a take-out cookie place. I work in the kitchen and clean and sometimes get to wait on a customer (Whoopeee!) I'd prefer to do something outside, more active.

We have a street, Cesar Chavez, where the immigrants from Central America line up for day-labor. People come by in pickups and the guys jump in. If I joined them, I'd end up cutting hedges, doing roof demolition, and things like that. It wouldn't be too different from corn detasseling. I love demolishing things.

Please think about coming out here. My granddad says he'd like to meet you.

That's it for now.

Still,

Gretchen

BY THE TIME Angus called next, it was an evening in October, and he was living in Bay Ridge, Brooklyn. An Italian guy named Joe let Angus crash in his paper-piled office in the basement. I told Angus about my daily gig working at CookieMonster. And how I'd gotten a couple of demolition jobs, too. It was something, at least, and enough to supplement my granddad's rent and keep Mrs. Jam happy.

"I'm making some money," I told Angus. "Things are okay."

"Sweet," he said.

He told me he had almost got chosen for a Calvin Klein ad but had ended up working at a porn palace instead. Then he talked about the rich men he met at his club and the parties they took him to. "Joe says you can measure the hostility at a party by how many heads turn to look when you enter. I think people hate me here."

"Yeah?"

"Yeah. New York feels over," said Angus. "Where should I go next?"

"How about Chicago?"

"New Orleans?"

"Why not."

"You know, it's funny," said Angus. "It would be bizarre to look down from the clouds and see people crisscrossing around the country all the time."

"Trying to find a way inside."

"Wonder what it looks like."

"A big traffic jam."

It was probably good we couldn't see ourselves from above, the crazeee view that the stars must have. As I listened to Angus's chirpy voice, I could feel the country stretch between us, all coming undone, embers sparking into the autumn night. I knew the size of it now, the whole bright and shining mess, so hurting and half brave. Land of the crashing free.

FOR WEEKS I SPENT my evenings at home with my granddad. I listened to the sound of his booming voice, the sound of the wind rattling the windows, the sound of the buses on Mission.

In the early morning, when I'd walk to work, I'd hear a few birds, and for a quiet moment, stop and look up. Remembered the sound of red-winged blackbirds flying into the ache of the Nebraska sky. The birds calling and not hearing a reply. Remembered the places of belonging and the places of dying. The sound of the past disappearing.

One morning I woke before dawn from my granddad's raging-mammal snores. Couldn't take it anymore. Went outside to the sidewalk to get some air. Above me hung the seven tiny stars of the Pleiades. A quiet night wind pierced through my shirt and stung my skin. When I lifted my arms, I could touch the sky.

Acknowledgments

This book rests in your hands through the faith and kindness of many: JJ Feryus, Tiffany Watson, Paul Calandrino, Elizabeth Stark, Guillaume Shearin, Beth Bly, Mark Pritchard, Frances Badgett, Douglas Fenn Wilson, Lynn Freed, Thaisa Frank, Mari Coates, LYRIC, Denise Daniels, Laura Abada, Annie Gage, Glenn, Matthew McKay, Anne Hughes, Chris Lippert, Judith Serin, Sumire Ishii, Andrew Harkins, Keith Hennessy, Michael Cunningham, Dorothy Allison, Christopher Beck, Frankie and F. Jasmine, Wolf, Mrs. C.J.R. Wilson, Beth, Brian, Alan, Ellen, David, Grace, Mary and Pierre Noyes, the Crones, Bobby and friends, the kids at the pit, and the farm wives who wish to remain anonymous. Thank heaven and earth for all of you.